D.

From the Edito

"About thirty-   the planet of Darkover, and have been writing about it, girl and woman, ever since. In the last few years, I have had the singular pleasure of seeing my world taken up by other writers——a sure sign that it has taken on its own reality, and, like the London of Sherlock Holmes, the bridge of the Enterprise, and Middle Earth, Darkover now exists as a real place in that region of the mind which John Myers Myers, in his splendid fantasy *Silverlock*, called 'the Commonwealth'——the land of literature. Or, to put it another way, Darkover exists on another plane of reality . . . and there the characters I have created continue to work out their destinies, even after I have ceased to write about them, because they live for other writers than myself.

"I do not think that anyone needs to make allowances for any story in this collection just because, with a few exceptions, these stories are by still-unpublished authors. These are simply the first, or second, stories by budding professionals who happen to have graced me by beginning their work in my universe——I am proud to say to my readers, '*You met them first on Darkover.*' "

Sword of Chaos

And Other Stories

by
MARION ZIMMER BRADLEY
and the
FRIENDS OF DARKOVER

Edited by
Marion Zimmer Bradley

DAW BOOKS, INC.
DONALD A. WOLLHEIM, PUBLISHER
1633 Broadway, New York, NY 10019

FIRST PRINTING, APRIL 1982

1 2 3 4 5 6 7 8 9

DAW TRADEMARK REGISTERED
U.S. PAT. OFF. MARCA
REGISTRADA. HECHO EN U.S.A.

PRINTED IN U.S.A.

Contents

IN THE DAYS OF THE COMYN

THE EMPIRE AND BEYOND

Introduction

About thirty-five years ago I invented the planet of Darkover, and have been writing about it, girl and woman, ever since. In the last few years, I have had the singular pleasure of seeing my world taken up by other writers—a sure sign that it has taken on its own reality, and, like the London of Sherlock Holmes, the bridge of the *Enterprise*, and Middle Earth, Darkover now exists as a real place in that region of the mind which John Myers Myers, in his splendid fantasy *Silverlock* called "the Commonwealth"—the land of literature. Or, to put it another way, Darkover exists on another plane of reality and meta-reality; on the astral, perhaps; and there the characters I have created continue to work out their destinies, even after I have ceased to write about them, because they live for other writers than myself.

Don Wollheim, who over the years has been the first friend of Darkover, and most helpful of editors, has helped this phenomenon to emerge, not only by urging me to continue with the Darkover series when I felt hesitant to do so, but also by publishing the first volume of stories by me and other writers, *The Keeper's Price*; and then by giving me the go-ahead for a second volume. When I made this known, through the mechanism of the Friends of Darkover, I was promptly deluged with stories. Quality ranged from the entirely professional to the frankly amateurish; contributors ranged in age from twelve to senior citizens. I read over sixty stories for this volume, and I could have bought twice as many as I did. Some of the decisions were really painful. For instance, I wished very much to bring to the readers a story by Patricia Floss, entitled "The Other Side of the Mirror." This story, published in amateur format, seemed to some writers so true to the "original" Darkover that several fans said that if it had been published under my name, no one would have detected the difference. I, too, regarded Patty's story as so much "official"

Darkover that when I came to write *Sharra's Exile* I found that I was taking it for granted that the events in "Mirror" had actually happened between *Heritage of Hastur* and *Sharra's Exile*.

Unfortunately, Patty's story was a novella, 30,000 words long; and because of the well-known inelasticity of typeface, Mr. Wollheim had given me an upper limit of 90,000 words for this anthology. I could not possibly justify allotting one-third of the available space to any one writer—not even to myself!

Because there were so many stories submitted, I was able to be very exacting about quality. I do not think that anyone needs to make allowances for any story in this collection just because, with few exceptions, these stories are by still-unpublished authors. These are simply the first, or second, stories by budding professionals, who happen to have graced me by beginning their work in my universe—after which I have no doubt they will go on to their own. Two of the contributors to *The Keeper's Price* have already done so; and I am sure the authors in this volume will do the same. Diana Paxson, Millea Kenin, Patricia Mathews and Phillip Wayne have written novels; Susan Shwartz has edited an anthology. I am proud to say to my readers, you met them first on Darkover.

After Landfall

Darkover, the planet of the bloody red sun, was colonized by a "Lost" Terran ship and, over countless ages, evolved into its own alien society. Instrumental in this great change were the indigenous chieri, *six-fingered, dually sexed, and gifted with curious psychic powers . . . and yet human enough to interbreed with the newcomers, reinforcing the erratic psychic powers of the human race.*

In a growing society where the technology of the Terrans had to be scrapped to assure survival on the fragile ecology of Darkover, where mankind had to learn how to trust and use his new powers, many of the ingrained cultural patterns of the Terran colonists had to be relentlessly put aside in favor of new social patterns which would be pro-survival. From a society where an over-populated people looked down on reproductive facilities, the colonists developed a new set of values where children were genuinely indispensable to society and to the individual.

Diana Paxson, in her first contribution to the original volume, attacked head-on the question of how an egalitarian society became feudal when it developed that certain people were more highly gifted for survival than others. Now she has chosen to study a facet of society which later became uniquely Darkovan.

A GIFT OF LOVE

by Diana L. Paxson

I cannot bear it . . . thought Lionora. *What kind of woman would bear such a thing?* She reached out to the rough stones of the hearth that dominated the great hall of El Haleine as if seeking their support. *My own hearth! Am I to stand by smiling while Darriel brings another woman to be mistress here?*

Lionora pulled her shawl across her full breasts, shivering though she stood by the fire. The Darkovan winter was loosing its grip at last, but the cold was still bitter once the red sun slipped behind the hills. She did not need to go outside to visualize the tracery of treetops on the western horizon and the gap where the road to Macrae's pierced the hills. She had watched that road only too often, waiting for her husband to return from hunting with Robard Macrae, or from more dangerous expeditions against the human wanderers who were replacing the dwindling Ya-men as the chief danger in the land.

In the four generations since the crash of their starship had forced humans to begin a new civilization on the world they were now calling Darkover, men had settled widely. But now the worsening climate made farming difficult, and too many found it easier to live by attacking their neighbors than by learning to adjust to the cold. And the landowners, reacting to this danger, had begun to band themselves around powerful men like Darriel Di Asturien, who with the help of Robard Macrae had become lord of the Valeron in fact if not in name.

And I was so proud of him—thought Lionora. *I have applauded every innovation, and encouraged him even when others were afraid. Until now. . . .*

This time, the party from Macrae's would come slowly, torches glittering on puddles as the stag-ponies trod away the last of the snow, escorting the litter that bore Robard's daughter to be Darriel's new bride.

And Margalys will be his wife, whatever title they give her to salve my pride. . . . Lionora's hand closed on the copper bracelet that clasped her left wrist—the bracelet Darriel had given her when he took her from her father's house in New Skye. Then, the bracelet had represented a good part of Darriel's wealth, a fitting symbol of his contract with the daughter of one of the greatest trading families on Darkover. Now he had wealth enough. Now he needed something that Lionora, with all her family connections and twenty years of love for him, could not provide.

Lionora had borne two children alive to the house of Di Asturien, and one that died, but the men who followed Darriel demanded of him an heir who would possess the strange powers that were the basis of his leadership. She thought of her son Dawyd, now happily learning his grandfather's business in New Skye, and her daughter Joanna. She had rejoiced when they grew up to be "normal," like herself, without sign of the episodes of pain and confusion through which she had nursed Darriel so many times. Though his sickness sometimes gave Darriel the power to see the future, or to know men's minds, it had always seemed to her that the price was too high.

But now men were calling that sickness *laran*, and requiring it in those who led them. Like Darriel, Margalys Macrae was descended from Lori Lovat, and the unhuman blood of Lori's father had given her strange and sometimes useful powers. The proposal to bring Margalys here had seemed simple enough when Darriel first explained it. Lionora was his wife, but she would have no more children. Robard had offered to send his daughter to live with Darriel and if possible to bear his *laran*-gifted child. After all, in the early days marital fidelity had been frowned upon—each woman must bear children to several men if the race was to survive. Why should she mind now?

I mind because he is bringing her here—*because she will take the place that is mine!* Lionora thought bitterly.

"Mistress—the tables are ready. Shall we begin heating the wine?"

With an effort Lionora focused on Sarena's seamed face and made herself nod. The old woman sniffed, and turned away. Sarena had been with Lionora since her marriage and, like the other members of the household, disapproved of Darriel's decision to bring Margalys here. But Lionora found no comfort in the thought that with a word she could have stripped El Haleine of people and let Darriel return to an empty hall. She did not want the love of servants, she wanted Darriel.

Men and women scurried around her, adjusting the woven hangings that covered the hewn planks of the walls, making last-minute additions to the food that already weighed down the long tables. Darriel had asked them to set a feast for Robard's daughter, as if that could compensate for the sacrifice of Macrae pride in letting her come to him unwed.

Robard's pride is the price of the Di Asturien heir, Robard's pride, and mine . . . thought Lionora, *and however reluctant Darriel professes to be, only he comes out of this with gain.*

She remembered that Margalys had been growing beautiful, and images of the girl tormented her, though she had not seen Robard's daughter since she had gone to live with her mother's people in Dellerey some years before.

I should have gone away when Darriel told me what he would do, but he said ne needed me! She could have joined her children in New Skye, told her father to cut off the trade upon which the valley of the Valeron depended. Better still, she could have called upon her family to avenge this insult with men and arms. *I would have opened the gate to let them in and laughed!*

There was noise at the gate now—a long rumbling as the heavy bar was drawn away, and shouts of greeting and ribald commentary. Lionora stiffened and turned to face the door, knowing that the firelight would pick out the silver threads in her dark hair and shadow the lines these weeks had drawn in her face, but in that moment afraid only lest she faint and disgrace herself before them all.

Tomorrow! she thought wildly. *If only I can survive tonight, tomorrow I will go away.*

Then the door swung open and torchlight flared across the worn boards of the floor to meet the steadier light of the fire. Darriel was standing in the doorway, his slight frame braced against the weight of the girl in his arms. All Lionora could see of her was hair the color of the copper brooches that clasped her cloak. Darriel's gray eyes fixed on hers, wide with appeal.

Automatically, Lionora stepped forward in response to his need. Then Margalys lifted her head, and the older woman's resentment was replaced by the realization that the girl's white face held not triumph, not even anticipation—only stark fear.

Lionora did not leave El Haleine the following day, nor in the weeks that came after. At first she was held by Darriel's panic at the prospect of dealing with a girl who was too ill to leave her own bed, much less share his. It was two weeks before he was able to sleep with Margalys, and as far as Lionora could tell, the experience brought neither of them much joy. She noted this with a dim wonder, for in the brightness of the younger woman's hair and the clarity of her eyes Lionora recognized the kind of beauty that she, black-haired and olive-skinned, had always most desired.

By that time, Lionora was coming to care for Margalys as well as to admire her, aware now that the younger woman had been given as little choice in this arrangement as she. *But I can leave* . . . Lionora would reflect as she watched Margalys struggle to swing the great bronze kettle over the hearth. *We could leave together!* She grinned unpleasantly, wondering how Darriel would fare if he were left with no woman at all.

That was before Margalys found herself pregnant. Darriel seemed scarcely to care, except that it freed him from the obligation of sharing her bed on the rare occasions that he was home. A band of wolves' heads had taken to raiding caravans on the road to New Skye, and it took the men of the Valeron most of the summer to catch them.

But for Margalys, the summer was a time of pain and weakness that continued until Lionora wondered how she could continue to carry the child. Now Margalys was trapped, and Lionora, sitting by her bed when she could not sleep, or brewing new infusions in hopes of finding something the girl would be able to keep down, knew that she could not leave her. She could not go away until the child was born and Margalys had her health again. For now, Lionora was trapped as well.

And so she remained while the brief summer passed and the cold gripped Darkover once more, and it came time for Margalys's child to be born.

"My lady, I am afraid—" The midwife's plump face creased with concern as she looked at Margalys. "The girl is too narrow to give birth easily, and she has not the strength to endure labor for long."

Lionora followed her gaze to the figure on the bed, now tensing to meet the next contraction, then shook her head. Doria was the valley's most experienced midwife, and she herself had assisted at many births. Surely they could bring Margalys through this one. . . .

"I labored longer than this with my second babe, and I survived," she said aloud.

"You were stronger," answered Doria, "and you wanted the child."

Margalys whimpered and her fingers clenched on the sheet. "Again . . . again . . . Lionora, where are you?"

Lionora moved quickly to the bed and took Margalys's hand. Doria was right, her grip was weaker now. She looked down at the girl and gently soothed the matted hair back from her brow. Even if Darriel had loved her, he would not have thought her beautiful now. Lionora's breast ached with a kind of protective longing and her body tensed as if to echo Margalys's pain. She reached out to her with an uprush of emotion for which she knew no name.

"Could we give her some of that tincture you make from the *kireseth* flowers? I don't care what it does to the child!"

"Without your lord's permission?" Doria frowned. "In any case, it would not help her. It detaches mind from body, and her only chance is to stay with it—to will the body to fight on."

My lord's permission! Would he care what happens to Margalys, would any of them care, if only she delivers this wretched child! Her mind flinched from memory of the small mound outside the stockade where the cold earth had received the body of her own last-born ten years before. *This is a hard land for children.* Anger at Darriel melted her fear.

Abruptly she gestured to Doria. "Stay with her and do what you can. I will return." In the aftermath of the contraction Margalys's fingers were limp, and gently Lionora detached her hand.

She found Darriel standing by the great hearth in the hall, smiling uneasily at the jesting of the other men. They had been drinking, but the horn in Darriel's hand was still full. He turned and his eyes lit as Lionora entered the room, but the hope there faded as he read the expression in hers. He seemed slight, next to his brothers and the other men. Even Robard Macrae loomed above him, seeming younger, though he and Darriel were of an age.

"No, the child has not come," Lionora said curtly. "By your leave, masters, I would speak with my husband now."

"Lionora—is Margalys . . . how is she?" Robard had taken a swift step forward, his voice gone harsh.

Lionora saw fear in his weathered face and knew how he would blame himself if his daughter died. "She is alive," she said more gently, "but she is weak. Can you believe me, Robard, when I tell you that I care for her? I will do my best."

Robard stared at her for a moment, then swallowed and turned away. Darriel still stood where she had found him, his body braced against her words like a man expecting a blow.

"If Margalys dies, I will have killed her," he said quietly after a moment had passed.

Lionora glared at him, feeling the remains of her anger. She had never been able to quarrel with him when they were together, and even without *laran* she could feel his pain. And yet what he had said was true.

"I want you to go to her . . ." she said suddenly.

"Into the birthing chamber? But they would not let me . . . the custom. . . ." His words trailed off. Lionora understood. A part of her stood astonished at her own words, as if she had proposed some sacrilege.

"I am still Mistress in this Hall," she said aloud, "and I will make the custom here. I want you to see what you have done!"

His head sank on his breast and she saw how thin his auburn hair had become. "Lionora . . . don't you understand?" he said in a low voice. "Seeing is the least of it! I will not be able to barrier her pain—even now I feel it as I feel the winter chill that leaks around the door. How can I face Margalys with no memory of joy to balance it?"

"You have led men into battle and seen them die!"

He shuddered, nodding. "That is why I know what this will do to me. Yet they followed me willingly, to protect their homes. Margalys . . ." he faltered. "Lionora, I swear to you that I did not take her lustfully! In weakness, perhaps, because they pressured me. Or maybe it was pride and a desire to breed a son with *laran* who could be to those men what they have made me become."

"*Laran!* Is it only a weapon then? But Margalys has it too. . . . Darriel, I want you to go to her and use whatever powers you have. Strengthen her as if she were one of your precious men. For if it is only something to be used in warfare, better that the *laran*-gift should die with you!"

Lionora's heart was pounding. She realized that she was facing him with clenched fists, though she had kept her voice low.

Darriel looked at her bleakly. "*Domna* . . ." His voice was dull with defeat, or perhaps with dread, but when Lionora turned to go back to Margalys, he followed her.

Darriel stopped short just inside Margalys's chamber, pressing his hands against his ears. Lionora stared, thinking that surely the shocked whispers of the other women could not be troubling him. Then Margalys cried out, and she realized that he must now be receiving the full force of the girl's pain. She put her arms around him. His face seemed years older, and Lionora felt suddenly taller, solider, than he. *Oh my beloved,* her arms tightened around him, *what have I done to you?*

After a few moments, Margalys's contraction eased and Darriel let his hands fall. He was pale, and though the fire in the little fireplace had been built up until the room was very warm, Lionora knew that was not the reason why sweat beaded his brow.

Margalys's eyes were open now, dilated by pain until they seemed black as windows into night. Darriel met her gaze and straightened, then eased from Lionora's grasp and held out his hands to her in a swift, sure movement like a warrior coming to grips with his foe. All indecision had left him—his complete focusing on the woman before him had given his thin frame grace and his features certainty, and Lionora understood why his men followed him so cheerfully.

Darriel settled into the chair beside the bed, still holding Margalys's hands. His voice was harsh when he spoke at last.

"I will not ask you to forgive me . . . but I must ask you to trust me. I have done this, a little, for wounded men, but a woman's mind is different. . . . I can try to absorb some of the pain for you, and to give you some of my own energy."

Margalys swallowed. Already her belly was beginning to change shape beneath the sheet as the next contraction came on. Her answer was a gasp—"What must I do?"

"You must open yourself to me."

There was pain in his voice, and Margalys's eyes widened in fear. Was this what had spoiled their lovemaking, wondered Lionora—Margalys's doubled shrinking from Darriel's penetration of both her body and her mind? Lionora had been angered by the idea that Darriel had taken the girl without kindness, but perhaps she had misjudged him.

"Margalys—" Darriel pleaded, "please let me come in. . . ."

Already tensing against the convulsing of her body, Margalys could only nod and close her eyes against her agony.

Lionora cleared her throat to ask if she could help him, but Darriel had leaned back in the chair, still holding Margalys's hand, and now his eyes were shut too. There was an inward turning in his face, as if he had closed his consciousness, and she knew that if she spoke he would not hear her now. And yet there was something. . . . Lionora tensed as though to see in darkness, or to hear a sound too soft for human ears.

Watching them, she had to force herself to breathe. For a long moment she saw only that frown of concentration on Darriel's face. Then his features twisted with astonished agony, and there was an easing in Margalys. Lionora bit her lip in anguish. Since the beginning of time husbands had wished that they could share their women's birth pangs, she thought, and now at last one was doing so. She held back the impulse to hold him as if she could protect him from the pain. Women were brought up to expect this—their bodies tuned to withstand the long agony—but men were bred for the sharp consummations of battle. How could Darriel endure?

And yet he did endure, and it seemed to Lionora that she had never loved him as she did now.

As the hours went on, she read the progress of Margalys's labor in Darriel's face. Once he had barriered her pain, the contractions came faster, as if her own resistance had slowed them before. Darriel's body twitched, reflecting the muscular upheavals that shook the woman who was bearing his child.

After her first flurry of disapproval, Doria had returned to the bedside, throwing back the covers and checking Margalys's progress with gentle expertise. Lionora went to the head of the bed and held Margalys's shoulders as if, with Darriel guiding the girl's spirit, her body was in danger of losing contact with earth as well.

And then Doria looked up from one of her examinations smiling, and Lionora felt her own heart leap.

"I can feel the child's head!" said the midwife. Her fingers rested lightly on Margalys's belly as she assessed the progress of the powerful muscles toward their goal. She turned to Darriel. *"Now!"* she cried. "My lord, you must make her push the child outward now!"

Lionora supported Margalys half-sitting against her breast. She was aware of the girl's body straining as if it were a part of her own, and wondered if this was what Darriel must feel. Then she forgot the thought as Margalys heaved again and she fought to hold her. After so many hours of waiting, things were going very quickly now. Darriel leaned forward, face contorted. Margalys's body clenched once more and released.

Then Margalys and Darriel cried out together, like warriors charging, like lovers in the climax of union, and their shout was echoed by a thin, protesting wail. Doria moved quickly, and Lionora saw her hold up something red and squirming, crowned with a wisp of flame—the child—a healthy male child.

Shaking, Lionora let Margalys sink down against the pillows once more. The other women were crowding around to sponge her and assist with the afterbirth. They knew what to do for her now. Lionora got to her feet and went around the bed to Darriel, who sat slumped in his chair. His clothing was soaked with sweat.

She touched his shoulder. "You'll need dry clothes and something hot to drink." He did not seem to hear.

Doria had finished swaddling the baby and held him out to her. He was so tiny, like a feather in her arms. Had her own children ever been so small? He butted his head against Lionora's breast and she trembled at the pang that seemed to pierce from heart to womb. She turned to Darriel.

"My lord, see here—it is your son!"

Darriel looked up, comprehension coming slowly into his face as she put the baby into his arms. Carefully he clasped it against his chest, as if he feared it would break.

"It's alive!" he whispered, in his voice a faint astonishment. He turned to Margalys, who lay cleansed and quiet at last. But her eyes were open, and as she saw him with the baby a smile grew between them, on the two faces a mirrored wonder whose radiance seemed to fill the room.

They had done it! Margalys was alive, and so was the child. But as she watched the silent communion between the two people she most loved, Lionora began to weep without knowing why.

They named the baby Rafael. Margalys did not have enough milk for him, but they found a wetnurse, and her health began to return. Lionora worked feverishly around the house, catching up on all the tasks that had suffered while she nursed Margalys, continuing with others that had waited since her own children were small. She rose early, and retired when she could no longer stand, for all too often when she did seek the great bed with its carven posts that could have held three people, she slept alone.

For surely, whatever barrier there had been between Darriel and Margalys, the catharsis of the childbirth had swept it away. They were like lovers—they *were* lovers, who did not need to touch to share delight, or to speak to communicate all they would say.

Lionora did not reproach them. How could she, when she had done all she could to bring about their present unity? But she avoided them, and as her temper grew shorter, the rest of the household learned to avoid *her*.

And when spring came to Darkover with winds as tender as the baby's skin and a sun as bright as Margalys's hair, the warmth of the awakening earth thawed the numbness that had protected Lionora's spirit, and she knew that she could no longer stay.

Lionora was already in the pass through the hills that divided the Valeron from the Plains of Arilinn when she felt the first wet kiss of snow upon her cheek. Startled, she turned in the saddle to stare down the valley, and saw behind her massed clouds moving inexorably eastward from the sea. The rich earth of the fields that stretched across the valley was veiled with green. Beyond them she glimpsed a tiny curl of smoke and the walls of El Haleine half-hidden by trees. She saw no one on the road.

Do they even know that I have gone? she thought bitterly. *Do they care?*

She had slipped away in the dawning as soon as she saw that the day would be fair, packing the stag-pony's panniers with spare garments and enough food to last her to New Skye. The sky had been clear then! Even now, the evergreens that rose before her made a sharply etched outline against a pure amethyst sky. She had been sure the weather would hold long enough for her to cross the hills. Yet it had been long since she had traveled alone—perhaps she had lost her weather-sense. *I always depended on Darriel for that. . . .*

She shut the thought away and dug her heels into the stag-pony's sides. The little bells on its horns tinkled merrily as it shook its head and broke into a trot. Lionora peered up the road. Some half-melted snowdrifts still edged it, but on the hillsides she saw a jeweled scatter of early flowers. Even if the storm overtook her it could not be too bad—it was spring!

She had seen a herdsman's hut at the top of the pass the last time she came this way. There would be firewood there and walls to shelter her and her mount from the storm. But the wind seemed colder now. She pulled her hood over her head and kicked at the pony's sides once more.

Two hours later, snow was swirling blindly around her, and the pony stumbled so often she could not be sure they were still on the road. The sting of snow against her cheeks had become a dull ache. Even through her heavy gloves her hands ached with cold, and the extra layers of clothing she had put on could no longer stop her convulsive shivering. Even the heavily furred pony was moving more slowly now. She had not believed a storm could come on so fast.

Soon, she knew, the aching would go away. Her limbs would not hurt once the cold had numbed them, and the snow would seem warm. Then, she would feel no more pain of body or of mind, and perhaps it would be better that way. Darriel and Margalys might be able to forget her and be happy if she were truly gone. She wondered if they would grieve for her.

But her body was still clinging stubbornly to the saddle. The pony stopped, she struck clumsily at its neck. It took another two steps, shuddered, and sank to its knees in the snow.

Old friend, I'm sorry—thought Lionora. *Now we will both die.* Her mind hovered somewhere above her body. She watched it fall as the pony rolled onto its side, saw it crawl free, then huddle against the dubious shelter of the animal's still-warm belly while the showering snowflakes covered what had seemed like a bundle of rags until they were only another hummock in the snow. For a moment her thoughts whirled as aimlessly as the snowflakes; then, like the snowflakes, the wind scattered them and she knew no more.

Her hands and feet were on fire. *But hell is cold . . .* Lionora thought vaguely. Someone moaned and she strove to get away from the sound, back to the place where there had been no pain.

"Get her closer to the fire. Isn't the water hot yet?"

She was in a hell of fire then, as the monks believed at . . . the name fled away. Through her closed eyelids she sensed a ruddy glow. Her body twisted and she whimpered as the needles of fire pierced her limbs.

"Lionora, you must wake up and help us! If we cannot get you warm, you will die!"

It was a woman's voice. Had Margalys followed to torment her here? "Why are you punishing me?" she whispered.

"Oh Lionora, *preciosa*—we are trying to save your life!" This was a man's voice, that broke on the last word. Lionora struggled to open her eyes. She felt something warm and wet on her forehead and saw dimly above her Margalys's face, shining with tears, and Darriel's face, contorted in an attempt to smile.

For the moment it was too much to wonder how she could be alive, and what they were doing here. She closed her eyes again, but now she could feel hot cloths being wrapped around her limbs, hear the crackling of the fire and above it the howl of wind against thin wooden walls. They must be in the herdsman's hut. Darriel and Margalys must have brought her here.

"How did you find me?" she whispered at last.

Darriel's face eased a little as he looked down at her. "Margalys joined her mind to mine. We could sense the flickering of your life even beneath the snow."

"You could have died. . . . You should not have followed me," Lionora said.

"*You* nearly did die! Lionora, how could you do it?" Darriel gripped her shoulders. She could see clearly the reddened patches on his cheeks where the cold had bit deep. Margalys had drawn a little away.

Lionora shook her head slightly, flinching from the pain in Darriel's face. "I was trying to reach New Skye, but the snow came. . . . I would not have wanted my death to stain your happiness. . . ." She closed her eyes, trying to shut away the tears. She was too weak for self-control, and there were things in her heart she must not say aloud.

"How are her feet?" asked Darriel curtly.

"Better—the circulation has returned. We were in time."

Darriel set his hand on Lionora's brow, lifted her wrist to feel her pulse. Lionora shivered and his grip tightened on her hand.

"We may have beaten the frostbite, but shock and exposure are the danger now. . . ." He broke off. "Somehow we must get her warm."

"It's all right," Lionora said tiredly. "It's not your fault. Just let me go. . . ."

"If it isn't my fault why did you run away?" cried Margalys. She cast herself down on the piled cloaks beside Lionora, clasping her as if to force warmth from her own body to hers.

Words flooded from Lionora's lips as if Margalys's touch had set them free. "You don't need me—you have the child and you have each other now. You have each other! Don't you understand? You can share each other's every thought, but I can neither speak to you nor hear what you say. You have found that your curse is a gift after all, Darriel, but it is one I cannot share. . . ." She gasped for breath. "Margalys is one of your kind and I am not . . . and I am old, and she is beautiful!"

"But I thought . . . I thought you loved me, Lionora . . ." whimpered Margalys.

"I do love you, *breda*. That is why I had to go away."

"Breda!" Margalys's voice held wonder. "I never had a sister, and my mother . . . thought I was only trying to get attention when the *laran*-sickness came, and sent me to Dellerey because she said I was no use to her. I was no use to anyone until they thought of breeding me to Darriel!"

Lionora stretched out a hand to her, thinking that if she had only known years ago she might have been able to ease the child's life somehow. But that was long ago. . . .

"But now you have Darriel, and he loves you," she said aloud.

"Yes, and that is a wonder that astonishes me each day," said Margalys, coloring. "But I know it is partly because he is different too. He is able to love me because he values himself, and he learned to value himself because of you!"

Lionora stared from her to Darriel in astonishment. Her husband smiled at her a little crookedly and raised her hand to his lips.

"And it seemed to me this summer that you loved me, too!" Margalys shook back her fiery hair. "Can you imagine how much that meant to me? When I was bearing Rafael I felt the strength of Darriel's mind. But I felt strength coming from your body, Lionora, to mine as well. I *need* you!"

"She's right, Lionora. You must know how I need you, after so many years," Darriel said softly. "You understand me, and when the minds of others are clamoring so that I can scarcely tell their thoughts from my own, you have the gift to wrap yourself in silence. In all these years of warfare, I thought of you when I wondered what we were fighting for. The only reason I would ever wish my gift on you, beloved, would be to convince you how much you mean to me."

Lionora felt easy tears slipping from her eyes. She fought for control, but there was nothing in her left to hide behind. She saw by their faces that whatever barrier had kept her thoughts from them before was gone. She shivered again and closed her eyes.

"She is still too cold . . . I think our clothing keeps our warmth from reaching her," said Margalys.

Lionora heard garments rustling, felt her own being pulled off, and looked up, startled, as Margalys slipped beneath the fur cloak and clasped her in her arms.

"I have fulfilled my purpose at El Haleine—and at least I have known love for a little while. I must not steal your happiness. I will be the one to go away."

"No. . . ." Lionora shook her head but could say no more.

"Lionora—" now Darriel was holding her too. "When I was gone this summer, weren't you happy to have Margalys there?"

"Happy?" Lionora tried to smile. "It was the first time I didn't miss you, Darriel. I suppose . . . that after living with you, my own kind of people don't seem very interesting. But you want me to be strong for both of you, and I cannot do that, not all of the time. . . ."

"Oh Lionora!" Margalys's tears were wet on her neck. "When Darriel and I are apart, we need you to survive, but when we are together, we will cherish you!"

Darriel kissed Lionora then, and something that had been frozen within her began to melt at last. He curled himself around her as he had done so often in the great bed at El Haleine. Margalys chafed her hands and set them at last in the warm fold beneath her arm. Crying a little, Lionora held the girl against her breast.

Lionora scarcely knew when she began to be warm again, and the touch of other hands upon her body became a caress. At first she was sharply aware of the difference between the familiar wiry strength of Darriel's body hard against her own, and the wonder of Margalys's smooth skin and silken flame of hair. But as the moment extended, Darriel's experience taught Margalys, while her understanding of a woman's body educated him, and Lionora no longer knew who was touching her.

It seemed to her that this gift was more than she could bear—even in her ecstasy she was briefly grateful that she could not live on such heights for long. It was enough to share her love with Darriel and Margalys without losing her own identity.

But in the end, perhaps the intensity of the moment allowed her barriers to open, for she never knew if the final fulfillment belonged to Darriel, or Margalys, or was her own.

The Cycles of Legend

Between the colony of the "lost ship" from Terra, and the time when the Comyn and the great Towers of Darkover created their laran-based culture, a great gulf lies, bridged only by legends. The great legend cycle of Darkover is of Hastur and Cassilda, how Hastur, son of Aldones, Lord of Light, met with the daughter of a human woman and a chieri, Cassilda by name, and from their son came a whole line of Hastur kinfolk, descended from the Gods. Darkovan religion acknowledges four great Gods: Aldones, Lord of Light; Evanda, Goddess of life, and spring and growing things; Avarra, Dark Mother of birth and death; and Zandru, Lord of Fire, of the knowledge of good and evil, and of choice.

The origin of all these things is lost somewhere in the gulf of time between the colonists and the time when they emerged into what we now know as the Ages of Chaos; somewhere in that time lies a remote Golden Age, the time of the heyday of the Towers. Terry Tafoya, in "Legend of the Hellers," and Jane Brae-Bedell, in "Dark Lady," have chosen to write of that legendary time in the history of Darkover.

DARK LADY

by Jane Brae-Bedell

Legend has it that Avarra, Dark Mistress of night and death, is served by a mortal woman, Eadar, the Lady of Solace, whose name means "Between". . . . How she came to be handmaiden to the Goddess is also legend. . . .

The Keep of Buchan stood for generations in the Caol, or Firth, of Altyre in the Aillard Domain. Strongly built of stone and a few well-seasoned and massive timbers, it clung to the steep hillside as if it had always grown there. Its vaulted halls were hung with thick tapestries woven from the fine wools of Buchan sheep, and pelts from the same animals cushioned the granite floors. The seaward side of the Keep plunged straight down, a sheer wall broken by but few windows, tightly shuttered against the ravages of the often angry sea. The landward side climbed up the north slope of the firth in a series of wide, stonewalled terraces which lay sheltered from the salt spray by the bulk of the building. In summer, these terraces would bloom with all manner of vegetables and flowers, for the southerly current of the sea tempered the climate here, and summers were gentle and peaceful, the air clear and the sea calm.

No one then living could remember the Keep of Buchan without a Torcall of Buchan in residence. Passed from father to son in a long, seldom broken line, the name was synonymous with the Keep, and both were a symbol of the quiet good order that the household and allied land owners took as the natural state of things in Caol Altyre.

One late summer's day, as the season began to wane into autumn, and the leaves were starting their change to gold and red and royal copper colors, the Torcall of Buchan, a tall, well built young man of twenty-eight seasons, lay in his tower room, dying. The healers had been summoned, had come, consulted, examined, and had gone without leaving a cure for the malaise that was wasting the young body. Night and day

someone sat with him, holding his fevered hand, urging him
to eat and drink. His mother, Roualeyn, who had come long
ago from the high mountains to gaze upon the sea and had
stayed as wife to the Torcall of Buchan, was there; his nurse,
old and wrinkled Ailean, who had nursed the boy's father
with her own son as babes, now kept vigil on her favorite fos-
terling; and, in her turn, came Eadar, Torcall's youngest sister. She was just fifteen, a tall, slight maid with eyes green as
the summer sea and hair black as the soft summer nights. Torcall, of all her brothers and sisters, was her favorite.

"Come, child, I'll sit awhile. You go to your lady mother
for a bit." Ailean drew Eadar gently to her feet. "Go, now."
She settled herself in the chair by Torcall's bedside.

Dutifully, the girl went to her mother's chamber.

"Oh, come in, Eadar. I was just looking over the woolen
skirts Shonnag wore last winter. I should think they'll do you
this year. Shonnag is too tall now." Roualeyn held a tartan
skirt up to Eadar's waist. "As I thought. A good fit for this
year, until you grow too tall." She began to take garments
from a stout, wooden summer chest, tightly jointed and
lidded against the depredations of insects. Eadar helped shake
out of them the sweet, resin-scented chips of wood, inspected
each garment and folded it again on the bed.

Once, mother's and daughter's hands touched over a beau-
tifully knitted jacket, trimmed in fur. Their eyes met and
locked in tight embrace, but when Eadar opened her mouth
to give words to the comfort and solace welling up within
her, Roualeyn shook her head faintly. Too near to tears, too
close to despair, a word would have broken the fragile, momentary peace. Roualeyn smiled, and continued folding
clothes.

Days passed and Torcall grew no better. As his reservoirs
of strength drained, he slipped now into coma, now into fevered delirium.

Eadar was with him one late grey-yellow afternoon, as
the red sun sank balefully into the glassy sea. She had been
sponging his face and neck with cool water, as this seemed to
ease his torment somewhat, and left for a moment to change
the warm water in her basin for cool.

When she returned, she was startled to find a strange
woman sitting by Torcall's bed.

"Oh! I beg your pardon!" Eadar stopped in the doorway. "Are you one of the healers?"

The woman looked up at her from beneath the cowl of her dark blue cloak. Her face was thin and pale, the fine planes of bones nearly visible beneath the translucent skin. Silvery-white hair was drawn back from a high, smooth forehead and the arch of cheekbone curved down to finely carved nostrils, with a full but bloodless mouth beneath. Then Eadar looked into her eyes.

They were colorless, like pools of water which reflect both sun and moons impartially, and seemed to shine faintly with their own inner luminescence. They were too large for the delicate face, and seemed to grow even greater as Eadar stared down into the immense liquid depths. For several heartbeats the two women remained thus, joined by the sight of their eyes; then the fair lady slowly blinked, and destroyed the spell.

Released, Eadar, too, blinked, but in confusion, and advanced hesitantly across the room.

The lady gestured to the bowl Eadar held forgotten between her hands. "What do you, child?"

Stupidly, Eadar looked down, then back up. "Water. I . . . I lave Torcall's face with cool water. He quiets then, and is not so restless."

She placed the basin on the table beside the bed.

"You must be Eadar, the youngest." The lady's voice was deep for a woman's, rich with undertones and harmonies, yet somehow, for all the warmth, heartrendingly sad.

"Yes, *domna*, I am." Curiosity made Eadar suddenly bold. "Please, and who are you? Are you one of the healers?"

The lady smiled gently, her eyes seeking a distant horizon, before she answered, very softly. "Yes, I suppose you could say I am a healer." Then her head turned to look again upon Eadar. "You may call me . . . Akhal, if you like."

Eadar smiled shyly, taking a sudden inexplicable liking to this strange lady.

"*Domna* Akhal."

"Eadar," and Akhal smiled back.

Then Torcall turned on his bed and softly sighed. Instantly Eadar knelt beside him, soothing him with her voice and a cool hand on his sweated brow.

Beseechingly, she turned to Akhal.

"He is no better. Nothing we do seems to help. Can you

help him, lady, please?" She looked at her brother's face, wasted to skin over bones by the illness, and the tears gathered afresh in her eyes. "I would do anything, give anything, anything at all, to give him back his life."

"Anything, Eadar?" Akhal asked softly.

Eadar looked up into the dangerously placid face, and again swam in the crystalline depths of the fathomless eyes.

"Anything!" she whispered fiercely, and the tears slid down her cheeks.

"Very well, my child, I will make you a bargain. For every day you spend with me, in my service, I will give your brother back one year of his life, in good health. But," and she held up a slender, six-fingered hand, "you must be with me every moment, without fail, no matter where I go or what I do, or the bargain is forfeit."

Eadar stared wide-eyed at her. "Who are you, that you can do such a thing?"

The lady sighed. "Do you not know me, child? My daughter presided over your birth . . . but no matter. Let us say, only, that I do have the power to make such an agreement. I need your answer, Maiden of Buchan."

There was no sound—even the ceaseless murmur of the sea was stilled—as Time held its breath for the long-awaited answer.

Eadar firmed her jaw and her eyes narrowed. With tears drying on her now proudly resolute face, she answered, "Done, *domna*. I will serve you in exchange for my brother's life."

"So like your father; you are indeed his true daughter. Go, bring your mother to me, for she must be told and we must be gone before the sun sets."

As Eadar left the room, she looked only at her brother, and so did not see that there were tears now in the lady's strange, nonhuman eyes.

"Eadar," came her ghostly whisper. "I have waited so long. . . ."

"You have never named her, *domna*?"

"No." Akhal smiled. "For no one but you can—will ever—ride her. To you, therefore, belongs the naming."

Eadar patted her mare's neck. "Well, since you are fair, but not altogether white, I will call you Bhan, which is 'fair' in the old mountain speech."

"And this is Liath, then, because she is gray."

Eadar rode behind her new mistress down the narrow but smooth road that led from the Keep through the village of Buchan-in-Altyre and thence to the hills beyond. The girl was frightened somewhat at leaving her home, for she had never journeyed farther than the village, but her fear was tempered by a rising sense of great purpose. All her life, it seemed, she had been waiting not impatiently, but none the less waiting, for her life to shape itself and now it was beginning to happen. She felt dedicated, bound by more than the bargain for her brother's life, to this strange lady riding so silently before her. The tides of Time in her soul were nearing the flood.

Eadar was lost in thought, her eyes fixed upon the dark blue cowl that covered her mistress's head and face; so gradually did the plain, smooth road turn into mist that she took no notice. The mist flowed quickly about their horses' hooves, swiftly passing them like a grey wraith in the deepening twilight. The horses' hoofbeats grew muffled, quiet, in the gloom.

As gradually as it had faded, the world grew solid again about them and off to their left a faint glow appeared in the night. Liath turned toward it, Bhan in her wake, as if guided, but Akhal's still figure did not move.

Eadar sat up straight and looked about her. They were passing through the outskirts of a rather large town, with dwellings closely lining each side of the roadway. The houses appeared normal, usual, without anything remarkable about them, but somehow they were all unreal. They lacked substance; the white boulders up the mountainside showed ghostlike through them.

Eadar looked around in amazement.

"Mistress!" she cried, but softly. "What is this place? Nothing is ... solid. Look there at the houses!"

"No, child, they are not real for you and me, in this time," Akhal answered. "We have only one purpose here and that lies yonder."

Eadar followed Akhal up to a structure which had just recently collapsed; ghostly motes of dust still sparkled transparently in the thin torchlight. A group of equally wraithlike people were gathered, with torches, to dig through the rubble. Akhal guided their horses to one side and slipped easily out of the saddle, Eadar following closely. They made their way through the broken masses of fallen stones, Akhal searching for something on the ground.

Suddenly she stopped and bent down. Plunging her arms through the swirling dust, through the very stones, she caught up a young child. Turning to Eadar, she said, "Here, you carry the boy. I must get his father," and laid the child tenderly in Eadar's arms.

The little one was only about six or seven, a small, limp bundle of arms and legs and tousled hair. Eadar smoothed the dark strands from his forehead, as she cradled the child against her, and made the soft crooning sounds mothers make to soothe restless babes. The boy did not move.

Akhal was returning, carrying a dark form as easily as Eadar carried the child, moving around groups of people who took no notice of her passing. As she neared, Eadar saw it was a man she carried so, with his head against her shoulder.

"Come. We must go," was all she said, and mounted her horse, still carrying her burden.

The horses turned away, moving quickly out onto the road, pale in the torchlight, and the lands dissolved beneath their silent hooves again into mist.

A great, gray plain lay stretched before them. Featureless and flat, it went endlessly in all directions beneath an equally plain sky. There was no real horizon, as both land and air were the same color, and distance could be anything from arm's reach to half a world away.

Akhal alighted, startlingly dark in her midnight cloak amid the pale grayness, and set the man down upon his feet. To Eadar's surprise, he remained erect and Akhal gently turned him away from her, with her hands on his shoulders.

Without a word, the man began to walk away into the grayness, each step carrying him a tremendous distance away. He swiftly vanished into the endless gloom, never looking back.

Akhal then came to stand at Eadar's knee and held her arms up for the child. Eadar looked a long moment into the luminous eyes, and then gently handed down the boy.

Again, in silence, the boy followed his father, dwindled quickly to a dark speck, and was gone.

Akhal mounted Liath, so nearly the color of that overworld place, and turned the mare so that she stood beside Bhan. Again the eyes met, mistress to follower, with Akhal's face unchangingly calm. No joy welled in the shining fountains of her eyes, but no despair shadowed there, either. There was only acceptance without judgment of what was, and what will be.

The battle raged furiously about them as they sat their horses on a small hillock; like the angry seas of Eadar's homeland, the tide of embattled men foamed up and back on the green shores of the mound, but without noticing the two shadows standing thereon. As silent as the enduring hills, Eadar and Akhal waited.

The clansmen from the Domain were better trained than the bandits, and far better commanded: Eadar spotted the leader's black uniform, and so knew him at once for one of the fabled Guards of the City. When the bandits finally broke and ran for the safety of their hills, the Guardsman marshalled his men, allocating some to tend to the wounded and reformed the rest into fighting order to pursue the outlaws even to their own mountain fortresses.

Now, as she had done many times before, Eadar received the dead warriors into her arms, holding their frail essences with gentle ease for the long, strange journey that ended in the gray forever of land and sky. The second man thus handed her was but a boy, with smooth cheeks untouched by razor, the blond hair shining in the morning sun as his head fell against her shoulder. Akhal lingered a moment, the colorless eyes fixed on the youth's fair face. The lady never spoke while at this, her grisly business, but Eadar thought she heard a word, or more, whisper softly in her mind. ". . . Alas, so young. . . ."

After the forest battle, Akhal led them to a small sheltered clearing, bright in the warm sun and pleasant to both sight and smell with summer's last blossoms. The horses were left to crop the grasses and Akhal sank to the sun-warmed turf with a grateful sigh.

"Ah, it feels good to have the sun on my face!" She pushed back her hood.

"Here, *domna*." Eadar handed her a cup of water. "The spring is cold but sweet."

Akhal took the cup and looked into the water for a minute, then raised her eyes to Eadar.

"My thanks, child. You are kind to me." She smiled gently and drank.

Setting aside the empty cup, Akhal leaned back against a

great boulder, smoothed by eons of persistent raindrops, and looked up at the sun. Straight into the fiery orb she stared, neither blinking nor turning aside from its fierce red light, but meeting it as an equal. Suddenly, to her surprise, she felt Eadar's head against her knee, and looked down out of the brilliant light to the girl's dark head.

"Tell me, *domna*, why when we are alone like this the world is real, as I have known it all my life, but when we are among people it becomes only a shadow?"

"Well," Akhal began, "it is because here we are not about our . . . business, but are here only for ourselves. The rocks and the sky do not belong to us, as does man, and so are whole for us here, now." Tentatively, she raised a hand and gently stroked the shining dark hair. "It is not an easy thing to explain but perhaps. . . ." Her voice trailed off and the hand became still. "Eadar," she said at last, "you have bought your brother a long and healthy life. Sixty-three days have you been with me. Now you may go home without fear."

Eadar did not even raise her head. "Yes, mistress, I will go home, but only to tell my mother that I have found my heart's desire. We will tell her I go to become a healer under your tutelage."

"Look at me, child," Akhal said, brought to speech by the girl's words. "Do you know what you say?"

"Aye, I do," Eadar replied evenly, sitting up. "I know well what I'm about."

"No, no." Akhal gently touched the pink cheek with her cold, cold hand. "You do not understand. Do you not know who I am?" Immortal sadness now flickered up in the great eyes.

"I have known all along, *domna*; I have known from when I just met you that you are the Goddess, the Lady Avarra who brings night. And death."

"So you cannot remain with me," the Goddess whispered, "and I will not hold you here. I am not cruel."

"I can indeed remain for you have need of a companion." Eadar took the cold hand between her own warm, human ones. "I was afraid of you at first, afraid I would lose Torcall's life, and my own, but that passed long ago. Do you remember the old lady in Shainsa who seemed to know you and smiled when you took her into your arms? She told her granddaughter your secret, and I have remembered it well.

She said: without death, there'd be no room in this world for children, and who would want to live forever without children? So, *domna*, I have found what I want to do." Eadar smiled, her expression beginning to mirror that of the Lady's: a timeless, gentle acceptance.

The Goddess met her smile, probing deeply into the sea-green eyes, so bright now under Darkover's sun.

At last she spoke. "Very well, daughter, but I will not bind you to me ever against your will. You may companion me as long as you wish, but you have only to ask and you shall be returned to your family the same day as you left them. Time is mine to command and I promise you this upon my name: you can go back. I swear it!"

The green eyes became luminous on their own. "You know why I stay, Mother; for love of you. And now you must lie back," and Eadar, whose touch is comfort and whose name means "between," gently held the Lady's shoulders. "For cannot even a Goddess sleep under the sun when She is weary?"

A LEGEND OF THE HELLERS

by Terry Tafoya

There is an old tale they tell in the halls of Hastur when the moon's move in a certain way and the chill night beckons like a Hellers harlot.

Long ago in the Age of Chaos the Ghostwind echoed its madness into the souls of men with small power, and because their hearts were also small the call to a greater power resounded inside them. And so it was men and women became cattle and then gateways to breed the unknown to aid the known.

Erharth, a minor king of a minor kingdom, looked out on a rocky barrenness, straining narrow gray eyes to peer into the boundaries of yet another of the factions that would one day be known as the Hundred Kingdoms.

"Another dead baby," he threw into the wind. The wind said nothing.

"Another dead son," he shouted at his advisers. "And this is the army you would raise for me? Is my seed as hopeless as the crops our fathers uselessly threw on the rocks and ice of this worthless land?"

Three men looked at each other and then their eyes sought the tips of their furred boots; their silence they wore like their thick cloaks while Erharth's eyes grew more green than gray.

"My *laran* must not die," he whispered, as he had whispered so often into the hard stones of his homeland. It was as though he hoped the persistent softness of his words would etch itself into the permanence of granite like a trickle of water. But the strength of such a trickle is time, and time for Erharth was as rare as star flowers in his crude castle.

There is a way, insinuated itself into his mind, and one adviser's eyes were not stuck to his feet.

Erharth turned to the snow-heavy doorway to seek his mind speaker.

"Would it were not the only way," Erharth said aloud. To

35

Erharth's shame, his mind heard, but was barely capable of speech. In truth, Erharth's mind could pass on feelings, but no words. And now the three advisers and the fourth one in the doorway were washed in despair as Erharth's eyes dulled to gray.

Risk or brood like a nesting Banshee, Mighty Erharth, stung into his mind, and there was a bitter brittleness to "mighty."

"Enough, Danlyn!" shouted Erharth, and all four advisers flinched at the mind touch of their king. Though his anger could cripple, they knew it could not kill.

Erharth's sigh shot its dragon plume into the air, and his decision was made. "Fetch her," he whispered, and disappeared into the coldness of his castle to stare at his still colder son.

And that night when the second moon blossomed into fullness, Danlyn and his sister Danla sang into their blue stones a dank witchery. These were the days when *Leronis* truly meant sorceress. This was the time before circles formed completion for towers yet unbuilt.

Brother and sister sang ugly harmonies into pulsing blue ribbons swirling in a shared stone seemingly the size of the moon shining through the window. The large stone's brilliance flared, blending into the lesser fires of four equal stones set at the four directions of a table.

On they sang, while a third moon lit the sky, and their words were of a language older than Casta.

Then, by the light of starstones and two moons, all metal in the room shattered. The ceremonial daggers at their waists splintered to the floor and from the table blue flame spun up and out as high as a human.

Brother and sister were flung to the ground as the light became intolerable and the room grew colder than the outside, something unheard of in the Hellers.

Frost sparkled five stones, now black as onyx, and a woman stood on the table, her eyes a blue brighter than the stones.

Her gown was of a forgotten style, and her hair was bound in yellow satin. Beautiful she was, and icy as the Hellers' night.

"Who calls me?"

Danlyn shivered, but not from cold. Danla answered, *"We of one womb call you, from your home to the Hellers to feed the dreams of a middle-aged king of an unimportant kingdom."*

"*Danla!*"

"No," murmured the woman aloud, regal on her tabletop. "Cower in your corner while your sister tells of small kings and large dreams." Her voice was soft and her words oddly accented in a pleasant way. Her eyes were ice.

"Know then, oh Queen," and to her credit, Danla bowed her head while her sharp fingers clung to the floor, "it is not our desire to call you forth, but this land is hard and its ruler harder. Five wives and three times that number of children have died while King Erharth tells his sorrow to the wind. His seed bears fruit that does not quicken."

"And are his dreams only of children?" she asked, looking down and smiling for the first time.

"What is the sport of a commoner grown king but conquest and dynasty?" muttered Danlyn.

"Yet there is more," said the woman, and the siblings did not notice that her breath alone did not leave its mark on the air.

"Do you not think we would have gone beyond stones and ice long ago to seek warmer climates rumored in the south? We are held here by his wishes to leave an heir before he ventures into battle." Danlyn stood up as he spoke.

"Yet his children die before they are born," added Danla.

"He seeks to fix his *laran* in his children, breeding into commoners and Comyn alike for the strongest power of his female partner."

"Breeding?" the woman asked, sitting down gracefully on the table.

"The strongest to the strongest," said Danlyn.

"Like breeding Syrtis Hawks," she said softly, her right hand caressing the shiny black of the large dead crystal. "Speak quickly. Why did you call me? My time here is short. Do not flatter yourself that you are the first to summon me. Your starstones' spell was dearly bought for a span of my time. I will return to my rightful place regardless of what you do now . . . but I am curious. What is it you want of me?"

"A blessing, a child, a motive for movement to turn Erharth into the warrior he once was." Danla stood up, her gray eyes level with the blue eyes of the woman sitting on the table.

"And does your king," she asked quietly, "bring love to his

bed and his brides?" And Danlyn shivered again because her tone was the same as Erharth's had been that morning as he etched stones.

"His love," answered Danla, "is for his kingdom and himself."

"Let me see this king of your unimportant kingdom."

And so they led her from the room of ice and metal splinters to a hall coarsely hung with tapestry stolen by Erharth's father.

Erharth's gray eyes widened at her beauty, and a warmth poured from his mind touch, but her eye remained ice. Erharth's warmth was not lust, for her quality was such he could never possess her, and so he admired her from his hard throne, as one admires a dawn, or the ocean, for the first time.

He stood without thinking, and his eyes could not leave her face, her beauty framed by a curious yellow satin cloth.

"Fifteen dead children," she counted, in her odd yet pleasing accent. "Five dead wives and an unyielding throne. Is your *laran* such a treasure to this snowed rock of a place?"

"Speak not to me of statecraft, my Lady . . ." began Erharth.

"Speak not to me of breeding, you of small gray eyes and of smaller, grayer heart. Your witching servants have paid for my words with their starstones and a portion of their lives, though they did not know the price. Hear then, what has been paid for. Though you lie with five times five wives, and each ruptures her womb with five children, none will live. Sit alone on your wooden throne, fool, for you who speak so knowingly of *laran* do not even recognize your own."

And though Erharth's anger rose like the forgotten moons, his lips were silent as she spoke on.

"You hug your cold corner because you fear to lead your tattered army." She drew from her bosom a starstone set in gleaming silver and, as she spoke, wove a Truth-spell, until the pale glow of the gem shone on every face present in the hall. "Though you know it not, Erharth, you use the excuse of childlessness to save yourself from the battlefield." The stone's fire never faltered. "Fifteen children, five wives have you slaughtered in birth with your *laran*."

"No!" shouted Danlyn. "His power cannot kill, it can maim, but not murder. This is not why we brought you!"

Erharth's gray eyes shifted to the color of stone as he

looked away from the yellow-clad woman to Danlyn, and the adviser began to jerk, his fists clenching and unclenching in a senseless dance. Blood fell from his lips, and he curled into death.

Erharth's stone eyes ran tears as she turned again to the woman who had begun to fade like the twin morning stars.

"Curse you," he whispered, as she disappeared. "Curse you, Cassilda!"

In the Hundred Kingdoms

Upon emerging from the lost and legendary times, Darkover was swept by the winds of change. The Towers became decadent. A breeding program to fix the laran *gifts of the great families, who had not yet quite become the Comyn, grew, like many well-meaning attempts to improve the lot of mankind, into an end in itself and into great tyranny. Warfare raged in the land, splitting the countryside into many little kingdoms; Tower warred with Tower and king with king, using weapons of* laran *and sorcery. There is an ancient Chinese curse which says: may you live in* interesting *times.*

And yet these times were interesting . . . and many of the writers about Darkover have chosen these fascinating and complex times for their own tales. During this little-known period in the history of Darkover, when the powers of laran *were being discovered and rediscovered, used and misused, almost anything could have happened . . . and probably did.*

In the first of these volumes, Susan Shwartz told the story of the burning of Arilinn Tower and the dreadful death of the Keeper, Marelie Hastur. Now she tells the story of a survivor of Arilinn, Amaury the Harper, and his attempt to escape his memories . . . and himself: "In the Throat of the Dragon."

Mary Frances Zambreno, in "Wind Music," tells a story of the days of the breeding program, with its failures and its successes; and a young boy relentlessly measured against his family's search for laran *and the power of* laran *for sur-*

vival. One of the more bizarre uses of laran appears in Leslie Williams's story of a trapped sorcerer, "Escape", and after reading it, during the makeup of this volume, Elisabeth Waters discovered that the story "Escape" gave her the creeps, so she promptly provided a sequel to it, "Rebirth". . . . "So I could sleep at night," she commented.

Many writers confuse laran with sorcery . . . perhaps because, during the Ages of Chaos, the dividing line between the technology of the starstone matrixes, and the powers of magic and wizardry, was a very fine line indeed. In The Heritage of Hastur, I wrote of a sword on whose blade was written, "Draw me never unless I may drink blood." And here, in "A Sword of Chaos," I tell the story of that sword of dreadful legend.

IN THE THROAT OF THE DRAGON

by Susan Shwartz

The man who called himself Amaury the Harper knew that only madmen or desperate ones risked traveling the Hellers near winter. Even in the foothills bordering Serrais, the gales could blow a man off the mountains into chasms far below. Amaury feared he might have been mad once, seasons ago; now he was only desperate. He spurred his chervine, and the tired beast stumbled, fell, and began to plunge about.

Amaury rolled free. "Zandru's hells," he swore. "This finishes me." He knelt to recover his gear, then dispatched the chervine with the knife that was his only blade. Though three packs of bandits followed him, he couldn't abandon the beast, which had served him to the limits of its strength, to death of hunger, pain, and cold.

Then the bandits struck. He'd been tailing one group all day and had suspected that they had known it since their last halt. Some of them must have doubled back. One moment Amaury was crouched over the dying chervine; the next, a blow thrust him sprawling in the snow, and someone's hands grappled for his throat.

Years of practice let him counter that grip, brought him to one knee, his hand flashing down automatically for the sword he no longer wore, then for his knife, for any weapon at all. But a savage kick sent it spinning out of his hand; another caught him in the ribs, throwing him onto his face in the trampled, blood-reddened snow.

"Amrek! Kill a harper, and you die howling!" he heard one bandit warn his attacker.

Would he owe his life to a superstition? He hoped so.

The quotation from Ezra Pound, *Personae*, "The House of Splendor," copyright 1926 by Ezra Pound, reprinted by permission of New Directions.

"This is the spy who tailed us from Carthon! Are you saying I've got to let him live?" His attacker paused while Amaury felt himself go hot with fear and scalding shame. *Coward! I thought you wanted to die.* After Marelie Hastur had died at Arilinn, Amaury had broken his sword, had left Arilinn to wander, abandoning hearth and lord-right to sing love songs and laments until one night, pacing sleepless outside a serai in Carthon (his food, pallet, and harsh wine paid for by enthusiastic listeners), he'd heard a whisper, pressed closer, been discovered, and forced to flee until he could hide out. Bandits were riding toward Serrais.

For the first time since Marelie Hastur's death, Amaury woke concerned with something besides his own heartbreak. Serrais was where he'd been fostered; south of it, near Temora, was his own estate, a small holding in Domain El-halyn which he suddenly remembered he loved.

Amaury lay in the snow, waiting for the Drytowner's blow and thought of his home, burning, his people dying. Once again he couldn't save what he most loved.

"Quiet, you!" The man standing over him kicked him again, lower than before. If he'd groaned before, this time he retched with pain. The irony of it made him almost as sick as the kick to his groin: to think he'd die failing to save the home he'd abandoned . . . just when he'd learned to care for it!

"He's swordless, Amrek. What *kihar* do you get from butchering a swordless man? Plus the curse. Knock him out and let the storms take him, and the harper's curse too. Get his pack."

Something thudded down beside Amaury's head in the snow. "Your harp, harper," Amrek growled in a Drytown dialect so thick that he could barely make out the words. "Sing to the gods that Alar's wolves, not I, killed you."

"Are you coming with us? Or are you an *ombredin* to take your pleasure with him there in the snow?" the leader shouted.

"*Ombredin*, am I," Anger roughened the man's voice still further. Pain exploded in a storm of lights—*like the fire in a starstone, a backflow . . . NO!*—at the base of Amaury's skull. In the fires burned a face, beautiful, beloved, but burning, being consumed . . . and he was burning too. . . .

Then there were hands lifting him, wrapping him against a

jolting ride which drew moaned protests from him as he lay across a well-worn saddle, to a ruin that blankets and dead branches made into a lean-to: roadside shelter of a sort. There were hands then, too, lifting him down, examining his skull with agonizing care. Then, after a time of increasing comfort, even warmth, there was blessed water bathing his head and washing the sickness from his mouth.

"This time you won't die, harper." It was a woman's voice. Did Drytowners bring their women along on mountain forays? Amaury didn't think so. So it was safe to open his eyes. The woman was thin and wiry, her clothes battered and dark, her hair chopped short; what sort of woman was she, who traveled the mountain ways alone?

"That's right, sit up now," the woman said. Now Amaury could place her. She must be one of the Amazons that Varzil the Good had chartered, permitting them to live apart from men, work as men, free from men's rule. In all his life as fighter, *laranzu*, and now, self-exiled harper, Amaury had never before met one.

"Renunciate," the woman corrected him sharply. He must have spoken the word aloud. "I am one of the *Com'hi Letzii*."

Amaury ran his tongue over his lips. "There is a life between us, *domna*."

She laughed, a sound even more harsh than her correction had been. "No need to call *me domna*."

"You saved my life, *mestra*, and I thank you. I owe you a debt."

"Save your fine words! All those *gre'zuin* left you was your harp. When your head stops ringing so you can hear the music, you can play for me. Use those words then."

Amaury blinked. Never before had he heard a woman use that epithet.

Again, she laughed, this time a sound of wry amusement. Her face crinkled with her laughter, and Amaury saw that she was young, with dark eyes wary in a pale face, half-hidden by that preposterous tangle of hair.

"I shall have my own harper like a Comyn lady! Now, before you say another word, drink this."

Amaury sipped at hot soup, hoping that, after that last knock on the head, he could keep it down. It stayed with him, warming him, and he half-sat, half-reclined, blinking at the tiny fire the Amazon . . . *no, the Renunciate* . . . had

kindled, cradling the wonderful warm mug in his harp-cal-
lused hands.

"May I," his voice was stronger now, though still a wisp of
the hall-filling resonance it had had, "know my rescuer's
name?"

"You may. I'm Chimene n'ha Gwennis." She watched him
as if expecting a comment on the form of her name she used;
Chimene, daughter of Gwennis. "Why so glum, harper? The
name may be a bit plain, but then, so am I—not some lyric
performer whose charm and voice must earn my bread for
me. What's your name?"

"Amaury," he said, and closed chapped lips before the rest
of it came out. Only Comyn bore more names than one.

"Amaury. You never got that name, I'll wager, in a byre
. . . nor that red hair. Some lord's bastard cast out, with a
headful of songs and not much sense, is that it?"

A headful of songs and not much sense! That described
him pretty well these days. Strange, strange that he didn't
resent her jibes. He glanced away from Chimene around the
tiny shelter. Her saddlebags lay beside her; he was propped
up, he discovered, against a second pair. But he'd been
robbed of the little he possessed. That would be it: her partner would be outside, tending their chervines. Not even
Renunciates would travel alone in these hills.

"Not much sense, indeed, *mestra*, being captured by rob-
bers." He smiled, trying to use the charm and voice she'd rel-
egated to lyric performers. Whatever else he was—Comyn
lord, fugitive, coward—he was a harper, and harpers didn't
like disgruntled hearers.

"They're Drytowners, Amaury. As I think you know. Not
just bandits, but invaders trying to weaken the Domains so
they can settle in them, just like the Ridenow did at Serrais
so long ago. Where've you been, harper, not to have heard
that all over the Domains these past three seasons, bandits
have . . . why even at Arilinn . . ."

Then Marelie's death fit into a larger plan. Pray Aldones
he could help stop it.

"I knew they were on the move, yes. I tracked them from
Carthon, in fact. Home . . . I've got to warn them . . . then
get to Elhalyn itself. . . ."

Amaury struggled to rise, and Chimene pushed him down.

"You couldn't get to the next bend in the track," Chimene
said. "Rafaella and I were on our way to Temora Guildhouse

when we heard the news. Little love we . . . I . . . bear toward Comyn, but as for Drytowners! Gods, I hate them, I wish I could blast the filthy lot of them, Zandru strike them with scorpion whips!"

Rage quivered in her voice. Amaury, remembering the blow to his head, flinched slightly, shutting his eyes to block off his awareness of her anger. Amazons *would* hate Drytowners, who kept women in chains. But the rage in Chimene's voice told of a deeper, a more personal hatred.

"Rafaella, *mestra*? I noticed another pack and thought that perhaps your partner had stayed outside."

"Rafi . . . my poor Rafi . . . she's dead. A few days ago, we were separated on the road. I . . . I have kin around here and wished to see them. So I turned aside. By the time I caught up to her, there she was, dead, an honor guard of Drytowners about her. She'd put up such a fight they hadn't been able to rape her and . . . they'd left her her equipment."

Amaury glanced tactfully aside from the taut face, thin cheeks under dark eyes hollowed further by memory and grief. "A wolfpack of men—" her tone made the word an evil oath—"the only animal that rapes as well as slays. But she died before they could rape her."

"I am sorry, *mestra*," Amaury began. Marelie had been raped, but she'd made it back to Arilinn, and he hadn't known, hadn't been able to comfort her, share the burden of Arilinn's defense, and she'd died.

"Sorry? Why? I honor her memory." She bent over the fire, stirring it emphatically to new life. But something hissed on the embers, and Amaury knew that she wept.

"You must have cared greatly for this Rafaella," he began delicately.

"We were freemates!" she said. "The only woman, the only *person* I've ever really loved! You, does that shock you, with your Comyn hair and harper's hands?"

Malicious tongues clattered that all the Renunciates were lovers of women. Amaury had shrugged off such stories. Some of them, he might have guessed, would be; just as some men, in all groups, loved men—except perhaps among the monks at St. Valentine-of-the-Snows. Comyn lord that he'd been, he'd been raised to be outraged that a woman would turn to another woman when any man would tell you how important it was that he have heirs, male heirs, and many of them. But Chimene and her freemate had loved one another, had one another for at least awhile. He hadn't been so lucky.

Chimene was waiting for an answer, her hands gripping and twisting what Amaury recognized as the carrying strap of his *rryl*.

"Let me take that," he said. "How do I feel? Love is . . . love. If you found love, were happy with Rafaella, what can I say but that I regret her death for your sake? I . . . I too—"

"That's why you travel so recklessly in the Hellers, isn't it? Someone you loved died too, and now you don't feel like you have that much to live for."

She might have been Ridenow herself to read him that well. Amaury shrugged, trying to block the pain her words reawakened.

"And you feel, Evanda and Avarra, you blame yourself. The times I've counted the hours, wondered if I couldn't have cut my visit shorter, traveled faster, not stopped . . . at least have been there to fight at her side. Surely something I might have done. . . ." Chimene's words came softly, and Amaury knew she'd forgotten his presence. Then, as if recalling it, she shook her head, the dark crop falling over her forehead.

"The one you mourn, Amaury, tell me—"

He reached out to unwrap his harp. She'd put a hand on its case, but he avoided touching it with as much care as if she were Keeper within a circle. Gently he worked off the leather casing—fine leather, a princely instrument—and ran fingers caressingly over the harpstrings. One had been jarred loose, and he tightened it. Chimene raised eyebrows at the fineness of the instrument and its deep, rich tone as he swept fingers in a windsoft arpeggio over the strings again.

"You want to know of my lady? Her name was Marelie, and never was she love of mine, but Aldones—how I dreamt of her." In the firelit darkness, it seemed easy to talk, even to this sardonic, grieving Amazon, of the woman who was dead: Keeper, comynara, so very different from anything Chimene or her lost freemate could ever have been. He hummed, his lips together, trying the sound. Yes, he'd be able to sing in key.

"I have seen my Lady in the sun,
Her hair was spread about, a sheaf of wings,
And red the sunlight was, behind it all.

And I have seen her there within her house,
With six great sapphires hung along the wall,
Low, panel-shaped, a-level with her knees . . ."

His voice broke shamefully, and he fumbled the last words
and notes of the song.

"You speak of her as if she were the daughter of Gods.
Unless, of course . . . your hands, and that red hair! Amaury
isn't your only name, is it?"

She had saved his life; she had earned the right to know
his full name. "Elhalyn-Ridenow. A younger son, but quite
legitimate. I've an estate near Temora. And I used to be at
Arilinn. I left . . . after the Keeper there . . . died."

"Marelie Hastur," Chimene said, in the tone of one finally
solving a puzzle. "Raped by bandits and abandoned for dead.
But she came back, she came back, and she fought the bandits. I've heard songs. . . ."

"She died, and I couldn't help her!" Amaury flung the harp
down, a shimmering, discordant crash painful to hear after
the music. "So they sing of her, so I do, but dead is dead. I
don't think, after what they did to her, that she wanted to live,
that she could bear what men might . . . that a Hastur of
Hasturs had been so abased."

"We of the Renunciates, none of us regard rape as a
woman's sin. Hastur your lady was, and Hastur she would
have been, no matter what. Would what happened, what they
did to her, have made her less in your eyes?"

"Oh Gods!" Amaury said, then fought to choke down sobs.
Words worked themselves from his lips like blood from a dying man's. "If only she'd confided in me—I was her technician, I could have stopped her. Do you know what that was
like, being her technician, loving her every minute but
concealing it so well that she, who was a Keeper who knew
her circle to their souls, never guessed? You can't possibly!
But I did it. And if I could do that, maybe I could have
spared her some of the . . . but it's done. She died, so I
stayed only long enough to see the monument they built for
her at Arilinn, and then—"

"And then?" He dared look up at Chimene, and almost
gasped. There was no condemnation in her eyes.

"I left. Wandered to Nevarsin, and beyond, past the Kad-
arin, singing my songs."

"In our Guildhouses we teach women that they need not regard rape as worse than death, that neither they nor their kinsmen should punish them for being victims. If only your Marelie . . . Lady Hastur, had been one of *us*, she never—"

The idea of Marelie, radiant, imperial, slouching across the Domains in breeches and tunic, a cropped-haired Amazon, made Amaury wince.

Chimene laughed briefly. "At least shock's better than self-pity, *dom*," she said. "But that's three seasons ago. Surely, since then your domain, your estate—they've lacked you, needed you—"

"I swore after *she* died—" Amaury emphasized the pronoun as if her name were too sacred for him to speak—"that never, since neither *laran* nor weapon availed me to save her, would I serve in a Tower or carry sword. After I failed her, how could I hear any man call me lord? *Vai dom!*" he laughed bitterly.

"But I'm not so lost to honor that I can stand by while Drytowners kill my people. And I have a blood debt now against these bandits—"

"Granted. But you're in no condition to travel alone and afoot. I have a spare chervine now. Rafi's. Since, as you said, there is a life between us, let us travel together."

"You lend me grace, *mestra*."

Chimene shook her head. "Save formal courtesies for your own hall, *dom*; we're not there yet. Ho! This is something like an old ballad: the harper turns out to be a Comyn lord. Of your grace, *dom* Amaury, sing to me. Rafaella . . . she loved a good tune." Her lip trembled, and she went on too quickly. "Sing me something of yourself."

"What shall I say of myself?" Amaury asked the air wryly. "Perhaps this?

'The moon's my constant mistress,
    And the lowly owl my morrow;
The flaming drake and the night-crow make
    Me music to my sorrow.'

I imagine an *owl* to be something like a small banshee," he added.

"Must you hurt yourself with your own gift? Like the man who drove thorns into his flesh to assure himself that he could still suffer . . . I think that these past seasons you've

been tormenting yourself, driving thorns into your heart just
so you know you can still hurt."

"Isn't that better than the numbness? *You* know."

In the next breath, Amaury regretted his question.
Chimene's moods flickered between sarcasm and compassion;
he didn't want to alienate her. Gladly he would have tried to
comfort her, but he had little comfort for himself.

"Never mind the numbness. Sing to me. Sing a song for
life, for Rafi, who can't hear it, but who would have loved
your music. Please."

Amaury bent his head over the *rryl*, watching its copper
insets glint in the fire. Idly he touched it, his fingers wander-
ing from one tune to the next until, of themselves, his fingers
began to play a song of dreams, of waking from the dreams
to healing and life; a song of winter, yielding to spring and to
the harvest as winters had done; he sang, for so many yester-
days, and would do in all the tomorrows circling under the
moons. He was never aware of the exact moment when the
music died in the cold air and the *rryl* fell from his hand. He
slept, dreamless, pain and guilt assuaged.

"Harper, Amaury!" Chimene's voice brought Amaury back
to wakefulness. "I let you sleep as long as I could, but we've
got to break camp now. Breakfast's ready. I noticed you
didn't have a knife. So, if you're going to eat, you're going to
have to use Rafi's little skean. Here, but . . . but . . ."

"I understand. I accept the knife, without assuming that it
means what the gift, or the loan of a knife ordinarily would
mean." So Renunciates hadn't renounced the idea of sworn
brothers—or sisters.

Chimene, Amaury noticed, was even more abrupt than
usual, as if the confidences over the fire the night before had
embarrassed her. Harper, runaway Comyn lord and Renunciate: what did they have in common beyond grief? Amaury
didn't need Ridenow empathy to sense Chimene's embarrassment. He shared it.

After a silent meal of porridge and dried meat, they went
outside. Chimene showed Amaury the one he was to ride.

"I am ashamed," he murmured. "You found me with nothing."

"We agreed yesterday that no one travels alone in the Hellers willingly. It's a fair trade. I only wish you weren't
swordless."

"But I'm not defenseless." Stung by her implied criticism of his oath, Amaury brought out his matrix, unused since that dreadful night when Marelie died. "This will enable us to see if anything like Ya-man or catmen follow us, or if they've allied with the Drytowners. You know, sometimes they fight alongside the cats."

The matrix glittered, and Chimene approached, intrigued.

"Don't look at it," he warned her.

Amaury gazed into its depths, his mind searching with the empathy of the Ridenow for the nonhuman's telepathic spoor. *Think cat, Amaury: ferocious precision, pride, swift savage violence . . . kihar . . . the cats!* His matrix stone flared, and he fought against his fear of seeing in the stone Marelie Hastur's face, as she had looked just before she died. Then he sent his mind soaring out of body. . . .

Touching a hunger, vanity, preternatural alertness . . . Cat! And catmen had some sort of *laran*. They even said that generations back, before the Ridenow had been anything but Drytowners themselves, that they had catman blood. There was a mental "wail" as this one detected his presence. Amaury withdrew hastily, feeling, as his mind returned to his body, the lunge of sharp mental "claws" at him.

"The hunt's up!" Amaury told Chimene. "The bandits are only a few leagues ahead, and one of their tame catmen sensed my probe."

He sadled Rafaella's chervine, regretting the seconds he had to waste lowering its stirrups. "I know this road," he said. "Follow me off the road."

The rider in him cried warnings at the speed they went, but Amaury forced his chervine at a near-gallop over the crudely blazed trail. Would the outlanders know of it? Or would that catman's senses detect him and lead them straight to him?

The rough ground rose sharply, and Amaury reined in, swinging down off his mount.

"We've flanked them by now, if they haven't moved yet. So now, look here. I came down from Carthon by this route—" he was kneeling in the snow, mounding snow and rocks into a crude map—"and *this* is a ridge of the Hellers. Beyond it is the boundary of Serrais."

"The Guildmother told Rafi and me to avoid the passes at this time of year," Chimene said. Gloved fingers traced a

route out of the Hellers and down, around them into the
Domains again. "This was the road we should have taken."

"Much too slow. By the time we reached the boundary of
the Domain, the Drytowners could have been there for a tenday."

Chimene looked distressed, causing Amaury to revise his
guess at her age sharply downward. Had she and her Rafi
ever been sent so far from that Guildhouse of theirs before?
He doubted it. The girl was absurdly young to have this burden suddenly fall on her.

She was afraid. Courteously, as if she'd been a woman of
his own caste—*like young Felizia, struggling now to fill
Marelie's place*—he looked aside as she blinked back tears,
tried to control her own fear. Perhaps. because of his long
service in the Tower, he could understand that a woman too
must face and master fear to survive. Wasn't this what the
women of Arilinn did every time they entered rapport? And
Marelie herself, how afraid she must have been that last
night. . . . As for him, he'd vowed to be done with fear, but
he felt it now too.

"How long will it take us to cross the passes?" she asked at
last, her voice steady.

"There's only one pass," Amaury said. He pointed toward
it. "But it's the highest one in this part of the Hellers. It's
called Dragon's Throat Pass. I've crossed it before; it's just
barely possible for chervines to make it across too. Look, I'll
show you."

In a fresh patch of snow he started shaping the Pass. In order to face fear, you had to see what you feared—and
Chimene needed to know what the Pass looked like.

"First there's a long approach. We'll have to walk, but
we've got one consolation. Since there are only two of us, we
can move a lot more quickly than our enemies. Probably
they'll split up into two parties. One group may take the low-
land route your Guildmother suggested. Probably the one
with the catman; cats don't like the high passes. I hope you
do."

Chimene shrugged. Her accent was upland; so she must
have some head for heights. But what Amaury worried about
was her endurance at the altitudes only crack mountaineers
or fools risked. If her body couldn't take the rarefied air,
she'd probably die of a heart attack, young and sturdy though
she was. Amaury started to warn her, then broke off. He'd be

lucky if his head injury didn't make him an easy prey to the vertigo which could topple him from the rocks. Vertigo, winds, and rockslides were the enemies at Dragon's Throat.

"That's no well-omened name," she said.

"It's a good name for this pass. The approach is narrow and twisting like the way to a dragon's hoard—with the dragon waiting too. Then, here one of the rockwalls we pass between drops away fast. One minute you'll be closed in by sheer rock; the next, there're several thousand meters of cold air on your right, and the wind is . . . pretty bad. That's the dragon's breath. It's an icy dragon, believe me."

"And the fangs are the rocks below? Any Banshees?"

"There weren't the last time I crossed."

"Rockslides?"

"They're worse in the spring."

"That's no answer," Chimene said.

"Chimene, Dragon's Throat Pass doesn't give answers. If there's a slide when we're in the approach or on the ledge, which is less than a meter wide, we're finished. But if the bandits are close behind, it'll get them too. At least, they'll have to go the long way, and maybe Serrais can defend itself if it has that much time."

Chimene laughed. "So we're simply bait! *Dom*, if you weren't suffering from a knock on the head already, I'd say you'd been listening to too many of your own ballads! Nevertheless, I don't see that we have any other choice . . . and they owe me a life. When do we set off?"

Amaury rose, brushing off his hands. He withdrew his matrix again, cupping it against his mouth, using breath to warm crystal and hands alike. Once again his mind quested outward to touch the catman's, to flick it with a taunt which would make the nonhuman howl with rage, impelling the bandits to follow. Mentally he dodged catman anger—claws, fangs, spitting fury—and withdrew, leaving a hint of their location to tease the creature and be passed on to his allies.

"One good yowl from that cat, and the others will be on our trail. Come on."

They mounted and rode for the rest of the morning. At noon, they stopped. Again, Amaury checked for the bandits' position. They were still on their trail, but they were close, far too close; Amaury and Chimene had almost no margin for safety or error.

He started to say so, then suddenly almost fell, the unaccustomed matrix work, the blow to his head, and the increasing altitude catching up with him. The dusky sky darkened almost to night, and violent lights began to swirl behind his eyes. From a great distance he felt Chimene tugging at his shoulders, heard her voice calling his name, urging him. . . .

"Can you ride?" she was asking. Her thin arm was around his shoulders, holding him in the saddle. When she drew it back, he reeled again. "Where—?"

"I'm here, Amaury," her voice reassured him. "I've just dismounted so I can tie you in the saddle. Let yourself fall forward if that's more comfortable. Just go to sleep. I'll take the reins."

Amaury woke with a start, tried to turn, and found himself tied up. It was a moment of pure terror.

Then he remembered he'd blacked out and entrusted his life to Chimene. Again she'd saved it.

She had heard the movements he had made in that convulsive struggle for freedom. "You're awake again. I'll untie you at our next halt."

"You put chains on men, *mestra*?" Amaury forced a laugh.

"I don't want to take the time to dismount. We've been climbing steadily for the past few hours, and our pace has slowed."

Of course she was right, Amaury thought. But while he had had to trust her lead while he was unconscious, he found now that he didn't at all enjoy this sensation of being in someone else's power, and said as much.

"It's a new experience for you," Chimene said ironically. "You are older than I, you've traveled all over the Domains, while I—this was to be Rafi's and my first major venture. We'd planned to see the port, maybe even sign on one of the boats. You've seen everything, been everything from *laranzu* to vagabond harper, but you've never felt tied down."

"Have you?" Amaury found the idea of Chimene docile, Chimene subdued, looking at her slippers like a Comyn lady, incongruous. Hawks were made to fly.

"Before I came to the Guildhouse, they—my uncle, who was my guardian, and my aunt—they wanted me to marry one of their younger sons. Oh, he and I liked each other well enough, but neither of us . . . like me, Coryn wanted to wander, and already I knew that I preferred the company of women to that of men. And there was a girl in the village. . . . This was found out, and my uncle, though he had the use of my lands, though he'd profited enough from me, locked me in my room and threatened to whip me unless I married Coryn immediately and behaved 'like a real woman.' " She spat out the phrase.

"He allowed my aunt in to see me; she spent most of her time weeping. But Coryn—well, the girl spoke to him and, to make a short story of it, they helped me escape. And I went to the Guildhouse, where I met Rafi, and I thought my life had ordered itself just as I wanted. . . ."

But, like mine, it was interrupted by tragedy. I'll shrug off your bitterness, Amaury thought. *You're younger than I, you haven't had a tradition of heroic ancestors dinned into you till you're their puppet, but you keep on fighting. If Aldones were to judge us right now, you'd win. You never fled your duties, you never wandered around singing sad songs after your Rafi died. And you might die helping me, helping me atone for my own neglect of my duties.*

When finally the slope toward the Pass became so steep that they could no longer ride, Chimene dismounted to help Amaury, stiff from his long immobility, to slide off his chervine's back. Both rummaged in the saddlebags for dried fruit, nuts, journey bread—anything that might fill them with energy for the next, and hardest, part of their journey. As he ate, Amaury forced himself to stride vigorously about. He clapped his arms back and forth, trying to restore the blood flow to his fingers and toes.

Chimene looked up at the sky. Though Liriel hung low and shining in the violet light of afternoon, they still had several hours of day left. And, praise Evanda and Avarra, the sky was clear of all but a fine hatching of high clouds. Amaury watched her stare up slope, then look at him, a clear, measuring gaze.

"Are you fit?" she asked. "Because if you are, and you know this land, you'd better lead." It was a reluctant concession of the authority he knew she enjoyed.

"But if they jump us, then you—" Amaury broke off before she would have to remind him that he was a swordless man. "I'll lead," he agreed.

The bloody sun was guttering down toward the horizon and the wind was rising when Amaury paused. "Get some-

thing to eat while you can, Chimene," he ordered. "This is
the last place we can stop. I'm going to check on our
friends."

Using the matrix might drain his energy fatally now, but
the doubt, the not knowing how far behind them their enemies were, might be even worse. They dared not lose them;
but if, in the next instant, they heard the jingle of harness,
the crunch of boots and hooves on the snow of the high,
winding approach to the Pass, they were probably finished.
After this stopping point, they no longer had an escape route;
sheer, jagged fangs of rock hemmed them in on both sides.
The stone in Amaury's hands shimmered. Almost immediately
he cried out, and thrust it back within his clothing.

"Quick!" he cried.

Dragging her beast by its reins, Chimene followed him past
hope of escape into the approach to the Dragon's Throat.
Now, on either side of them, icy rock knifed up.

"Remember," Amaury warned her, "the rock drops away
right before the ledge we cross. We'll have to make a stand
there, or maybe we can get across first—"

"And maybe Durraman's donkey has wings and
he's—Zandru wither his manhood—guzzling right now in his
Great House. But by all means, let's press on as far as we
can. At the worst, we can leap from the rocks. Rafi was right;
better dead than dishonored. That's my choice. But you, *dom.*
Will you be content to be held for ransom?"

"I've disgraced my family enough already," Amaury said.
"Come on, you!" He jerked at his beast's reins, forcing its
head up, practically dragging it up the path with him.

"If we can only make it onto the ledge, that's the Dragon's
Tongue—"

"They can knock us off at their leisure," she objected.
"We're perfect targets."

"The chervines will give us some protection." Amaury
plowed through the contents of Rafaella's saddlebags, pulling
out a blanket, food. . . . "Try to pack as you walk,
Chimene. Even if we have to sacrifice the beasts at the Pass,
we'll still need food if we make it across."

This approach was steeper and colder than Amaury
remembered. He hoped he'd remembered the pass better than
he'd done . . . other things. His glance fell on the worn
leather of a scabbard. Rafaella's sword. But he'd already disgraced his family enough, he'd told Chimene. Even if he took

that sword, sent Chimene on ahead, and died in an attempt to buy her time, he'd be breaking an oath. And he doubted she'd go.

The rock was jagged underfoot. Amaury braced himself with one hand against the barrier to his left. At the right, the fangs would drop away into a dizzying chasm. The air, already cold and thin, seemed thinner as haste, yes, and fear constricted his chest. His breath rasped and sweat scalded down his sides. Knives seemed to stab inside his lungs, and it was anguish to hurry. He had to stop, bend over, and struggle for breath.

"At least," gasped Chimene, "they'll have . . . same problem . . ."

He marveled she was even able to speak; gods, she was strong!

Years ago, long before he'd lost his nerve in a blast of blue flame from a dying Keeper's matrix, Amaury had led chervines across the Dragon's Tongue. He'd have to do it again: a misstep could destroy the woman who fought for each step behind him. Ripping his scarf out of his clothing, he used it as a blindfold. "Easy now, Surefoot, good fellow," he murmured, trying with hands, voice, and *laran* to calm the chervine. "Steady." If it plunged ahead in panic, it would probably knock him off the ledge . . . and Chimene with him.

Wind tore at him as the approach opened onto the pass itself. He pressed against the face of the cliff, willing himself not to think of the emptiness so far below, or of the savagery of the wind, sharp as the teeth of Alar's wolves, and far hungrier. Below his feet and to his right roiled clouds, mercifully hiding the rocks.

"Steady," he chanted, moving ahead, too intent on feeling out each step or handhold to spare a thought for Chimene. The chervine whickered as it felt wind on its flank, but it came along.

He edged out onto the thin ledge he'd called the Tongue. Halfway . . . careful of that loose rock . . . three-quarters. . . . *"Turn here!"* he called, hoping the wind would blow his warning back. Ahead the ledge suddenly angled down; a fool could hurry here, and it would be the last folly he'd ever commit.

Down.

Careful.

Rocks splintered from the ledge, striking glinting shards off with them, clattering, deadly if they touched him, deadly if they distracted him. And then he was through, across the Throat, tugging the chervine, slapping it past him into the track which would widen and lead down to the valley and safety . . . if only they had time to hide.

He held out a hand for Chimene's, as broken-nailed, harsh, and strong as his own, and pulled her into safety too.

"There!" she pointed. "Behind us, at the ledge. They abandoned their chervines . . . is it safe to ride?"

"The path's wider here, but we'd still break our necks," Amaury said. He felt sick. They'd crossed the pass, faced an easy descent, and safety, but they couldn't reach it. They'd have to fight. And he was a swordless man. Nevertheless, he would fight. His hand fell to the belt-knife Chimene had allowed him to borrow.

"Take Rafi's blade!" she ordered.

"Not to save my life . . . or yours!" he protested. "My oath. . . ."

"Men's games!" she raged.

"And you, do you Amazons think so little of your sworn word?"

"Damn you, you don't know a thing about the Renunciates! Take her blade. It's not a *sword!* Don't you know anything at all? When Varzil the Good chartered us, he let us bear arms, but not swords. . . . It's a long knife, different around the hilt, just enough. . . . Take it!" She drew it from its sheath, and passed it over by the blade that was not, by several inches, a swordblade. "My knife, and yours!" she gasped. "Or would you rather sing while they kill you?"

"My knife and yours," Amaury consented. The weapon was shorter than the swords he'd renounced, and lighter, but the feel of its hilt against his palm filled him with strength. No longer was he the houseless singer for whom mourning had replaced honor. Again he was himself, Amaury, Prince of Elhalyn, defending Serrais, which had fostered him. He swung the blade, hearing the whistle of the rare steel (this Rafaella had taken an expert's care of her weapon) as a long-absent sweetness. He laid a finger against the blade to draw first blood and, as he stepped up beside Chimene to fight, he laughed.

Faced with a bright blade, two blades, bare rock, and clouds swirling below him, the first bandit panicked and fell screaming. The second. . . .

"To me!" Chimene cried. Amaury turned and they guarded each other's back. She had a skean in her right hand, long knife in her left, and both were reddened. He kicked a bearded fellow in the belly, heard him grunt, then shriek as he overbalanced, knew it, and fell. Then he whirled around to help dispose of the last of the men.

"Got him!" Chimene said. She swept her blade down in a flashing arc, but the man jerked aside, and the blow fell on the rock. Her blade rang and shattered, the hilt jerking from her grasp as the bandit closed with her. As Amaury plunged toward her, she let herself fall against her attacker, taking advantage of the man's surprise to drive her skean into his throat. He collapsed heavily, dragging her down, and they rolled, closer and closer to the edge. Amaury threw himself down on the rock and grabbed her arm.

"Hold on!"

As the bandit fell, taking Chimene's dagger (and almost taking Chimene) with him down the Dragon's Throat, Amaury felt her arm strain up to clutch his. For a heart-bursting instant they both balanced teetering between rock and nothing, and then she had both arms on his, she had freed one, she was clutching the rock, and he was helping her to swing her legs over so that they both lay on the infinitely welcome safety of the ledge.

Her breath rasped against his face, and he pulled her close before he let her crawl on ahead. Half-crawling, half-rising to his knees, he followed, and found her around the bend, leaning against the rock, still straining for breath. Knifehilt and the shard remaining to it, secured by a cord, dangled from her wrist.

Amaury staggered to Chimene, flung his arms about her, half in triumph, half to help himself stand, and they clung together.

Aldones! The feel of her, live in my arms. . . .

Marelie had been a queen, a goddess, to him: serene and never-to-be-touched in her red robes. But this woman, barely out of childhood, with her short, tangled hair, the wiry arms that had supported him, the strong, rangy frame forever too thin for beauty, she was no goddess; she was Chimene who had saved his life, and he held her, unaware when his hold changed from the hug of victors to an embrace. He bent his head, his lips seeking her mouth; he was dizzy with more than altitude and the fight—

And she pulled away from him.

"To think that once I told Rafi that maybe Comyn lords had other things besides wenching on their minds!" Her sardonic words, more surely and cruelly than any struggle, broke his hold on her. In a daze of embarrassment and exhaustion, he watched her take hold of her chervine's reins. Down the track a few minutes would be a place they could stop. And then, by all Zandru's hells, he was going to have it out with her. Saved her life, hadn't he, and all she could do was hurl bitch-insults? Silent, he followed.

Chimene stood waiting for him, her animal unsaddled, and a blanket thrown over its heaving sides. She held her hands open at her sides, the swordhilt (not a sword, which was why they were both alive) dangling absurdly from its frayed cord.

"Let me speak first," she said. "I . . . not even you, Amaury . . . I do not wish the touch of men. Nor of women either now, not so soon after Rafi . . . you know what I am." She raised a hand to her face, wiping clean streaks on it.

The gesture was so absurdly vulnerable that Amaury's rage faded. And he'd thought he had no *kihar*, no pride of maleness, left to lose! He'd been wrong about that, as he had about so many things. In relief and victory, he'd turned unthinkingly to her and, having made a choice, she refused him . . . and refusal was her right.

"I had forgotten that you . . . are a lover of women," he said. "I forgot everything. I am sorry." Sorry to insult her, sorry that she grieved for Rafaella, and sorry that the blood which thickened in his veins would have to cool by itself.

"As am I . . . but there is a knife between us, *vai dom*. And a life. Mine. I thank you."

"There has been a life between us before," Amaury answered. "You saved my life. We are even. . . ." He watched her narrowly. *Shall we call it even, and quits? It might be easier than facing each other all across Serrais.* Sorrow flickered across her face.

"You gave me a blade . . . your Rafi's blade. Would you have it back?" Without thinking, he had dropped into the most formal mode of *casta*, covering the awkwardness between them with ritual courtesy.

"The gift . . . was well given," she said, using the same mode. "Rafi would have no complaints. Nor do I. Your knife and mine, *bredu*."

The inflection she chose made the word mean "beloved brother." Not lover. It would do, Amaury thought. Let them laugh in Elhalyn or Serrais, let them rebuke him in Council, but he was going to be proud—to the end of his days—to be this woman's *bredu.*

"*Breda,*" he said simply, and held out his hands. She came to him for the embrace of *bredin.* He held her briefly, carefully, then drew back before she could. That touch and his care not to offend her awoke his *laran.*

. . . If I were not what I am, menhiedris, a lover of women . . . yes and I've no quarrel with it . . . But the Guildmother told Rafi and me when we vowed . . . "the day may come when you wish children . . . when you are older . . ." how can I know now what I will wish later? . . .

Her thoughts stung him into answers. "I'd never try to tie you down, Chimene. As well try turning you into a Drytowner. But I'm Ridenow, and I sense your thoughts. A day *may* come, as your Guildmother said, when you want children. Lover of women though you are, if such a day comes . . . come to me. It would give me great joy to know that you and I shared a child."

"And would a Comyn lord give an heir, a child who perhaps had *laran*, to an Amazon?" The name, as she'd told him sharply several times, was Renunciate. Tears lashed across her cheeks though her voice was harsh and thin with sarcasm. But he knew this *breda* of his now, knew the knife-edge of wit, of hurtful words she used to defend herself against her emotions. Like him, she felt all too keenly.

"What kind of question is that for my *breda* to ask? *Bredin share,*" Amaury said. He'd be proud of a son with her courage, or a daughter Chimene would raise to be as strong and proud as her mother. Yes, he would marry and have legitimate children, heirs to his land, but if Chimene wanted a child, he would love it, welcome it, and her for as long as she wished. Or if she never wished of him more than the warmth of the hearth he was now eager to return to and defend against the coming invaders, he would accept that too. Gladly. With the tact of a Ridenow empath—or a harper—he changed the subject, knowing that whatever decision Chimene made would be good.

"If we push on now, we can be in the valley by nightfall. The borders of Serrais aren't far off then, and we might find a roadside shelter, Chimene. That would be luxury! Don't you think we deserve it? We can stay and rest the chervines, then press on for Serrais, or my estate, or a place close enough for me to send a message with my *laran*. But I do insist that you try the hospitality of the Comyn you're always so quick to disparage."

She met his eyes. "I must report to Temora Guildhouse soon."

"I know. But you need equipment for the journey—food, fresh clothes, a new blade." He gestured at what remained of her weapon. Her eyes followed his, and she laughed without bitterness for the first time since he'd known her. She let the cord fall from her wrist.

"I suppose noble houses maintain a supply of such blades?"

"Hardly. You Renunciates keep as far from us as we do from you. But there's a sword—mine when I was a boy—that's short enough not to violate your Charter. And if work needs to be done on it, the smiths on my estate will obey your instructions."

She tossed her head defiantly. "Shouldn't such a blade pass to your son?"

"Let me have a son first. You didn't begrudge me Rafaella's weapon, and I won't begrudge you this one. Carry it, and my blessings with it. Any son I ever have can wait till he grows up to carry the sword I renounced. You know, Chimene, each of us has renounced something. But won't you accept my blade?"

"With pride, *bredu*. And now if we're done trading courtesies like a pair of grandsires at Midwinter, let's *get* to Serrais before we freeze."

As the bloody sun set in the dusky sky, the path out of the Dragon's Throat widened out into a track, then into a rough-packed trail that wound easily down toward the road. The moons were out to light their way, so that it was safe for them to travel by night. The first shelter they came to was empty; wood, dry and plentiful, was stacked beside the fire-places. After they ate, Amaury piled more wood on the fire and drew out his *rryl*, tiredness and firelight lulling him into a reverie of song-crafting.

To his own surprise, his thoughts did not turn to minor-key laments for a lost lady. Instead his fingers began to pluck a martial tune. A good tune for a song of adventure, Amaury thought. It would serve for their own adventure.

"How about this song for our journey, *breda*?" he asked

Chimene. "Harper and heroine, I'll call it. You choose. Shall I write it as an epic or a ballad?"

"Make it a satire," she told him, yawning. "Even after the Drytowners are driven back, no one's ever going to believe any song you make of us!"

For once, Amaury decided, he was going to prove Chimene wrong.

WIND-MUSIC

by Mary Frances Zambreno

Corys Ridenow put down the small harp and sighed. "I can never strike that chord properly."

"And what is properly?" asked the Lady Marelie Ridenow of Serrais in some amusement. "So that it sounds right?"

"No—oh, you know. Making it sound good is easy." Small, fine hands—delicate boy's hands, hands of other promised children, rippled over the strings. "That sounds all right, but to do it properly—" He tried again, and again his fingers seemed clumsy. "I suppose you think I am foolish."

"I? No." His mother was very glad she had contained her smiles; he was astute, this youngest son of hers. "Give me your hand. There—now spread it." Wearily, he complied. "One, two, three, four, five, six—what is so terrible about having six fingers? Your hands are not yet large enough to play the chord with five."

"Nothing so terrible," he said. "It's just that—oh, I don't know. Auster and Kell have only five—and Dorata—"

And his father, Marelie added for him silently. Rannan, whom the boy so admired, yet feared—the boy who did not see what there was in him for his father to resent.

"Margatta has six," she said briskly.

"Margatta is just a baby."

And you are a man grown? Oh my son. . . .

"Six-fingered hands are not uncommon in my family," she said patiently. "It is a part of your heritage. You should be proud."

Although—her smile was secret, but Corys caught it—it would never have occurred to any of her Serrais brothers to be proud of six-fingered hands. They were the sign of *chieri* blood and occasionally of the *emmasca*. But to a son of the Ridenow, whose mother had no right to bear him, they might well be a mark of pride, indicating kinship with the blood of

64

Hastur and Cassilda—or, she corrected herself, with the sorcerer-lords of the Domains.

"Mother, what are you thinking of?"

"Of my own father."

"Do you often think of him?"

"No." Deliberately she turned her thoughts away. The younger brother to the lord of Serrais would not approve of what she did now—of her marriage, her children—but a woman can watch just so many babes die, can live just so long alone. She had been young when Rannan had chosen her, but she went with him willingly. Had not the eldest daughter of Serrais herself led the way? Even then, it was hard to believe that every child stood a strong chance at life—and none had as yet been lost at adolescence. Though old fears died hard, and where there was *laran*, there was threshold sickness. "He died long ago."

"Before you married my father?"

"Long before."

"Mother—" the boy's hands stretched harpstrings moodily, "why did you? Marry Father, I mean."

"Why, because it was my desire. You know that, my son."

She calls me that, but never Auster or Kell. Because they are older? Dorata says so, and she should know. Dorata is married herself now, and she says mother only cares for the young ones. Little Margatta is too small to know, but I can see. . . .

"Did Lady Cyrilla marry my Uncle Garris for the same reason?" he asked daringly. "Daryl says sometimes he thinks she hates his father."

"Lady Cyrilla resents being forced to the choice she made," Marelie said. "But she would not have made it had she hated Daryl's father—and she loves her children. How is Daryl? He has not come—"

"He's been ill—coughing."

"That could be bad. His mother died of the coughing sickness."

"Old Anya says it's nothing. She says he's always making a fuss over little illnesses. Mother, why does old Anya dislike Daryl so? She does not mind Lady Cyrilla's children."

"Your uncle married Cyrilla when his first wife was already old and had been supplanted once—by Daryl's mother." *Poor, frail little Damris, so pale and obviously unfit for the harsh weather of this mountain-region her husband* had brought her to. "Anya's children were all grown and established in Shainsa by that time, and she had long since ceased to start new jealousies—" Besides, against Cyrilla she could only lose, and she knew it—"but she has not forgotten old ones."

"Oh." This would take some digesting, but it was oddly unsurprising. "Shall I try the chorus again?"

"Do." She picked up her thread; the way growing children went through clothing. . . .

"What's this? Music again?" Rannan Ridenow stood in the doorway, large, blond, and overpowering. Corys seemed to shrink into himself.

"He entertains me as I mend," his mother said quickly. "Such boring work."

"Get one of the maids to do it," Rannan said gruffly. This elegant wife of his—he was never sure of her. She loved him, she said, tried to obey him, but he could not know—it did not please him to see her doing menial work. And why must she always shield the boy?

"It's a new song," Corys said calmly, staring straight ahead. "I was trying to get it right."

His mother bit her lip. *My son, my son, all redheaded pride and defiance—do you think I do not know how you dread your father's rages?*

"I ought to take that harp of yours and break it over your head!" Rannan shouted. "Music! Why, at your age—"

"Rannan." Directly. "It is no shame to be musical." *Please understand,* she pleaded. *He is my son—the first one I dared to love from birth. He is different from what you are accustomed to.*

For her sake, Rannan tried to contain himself. She seldom corrected him, even in front of the children. And unlike some Serrais wives, she held her husband's honor dear outside the immediate family. If she could learn obedience, he could learn to be gentle. It was only this one son who made matters difficult. Even with the baby it was not so bad. If Corys had been a girl, like Margatta, then he would not have sensed this divided allegiance. Why, even the boy's name—he had wanted this last son named Sheen, after his grandfather, but somehow Marelie's choice had stuck. Corys, the joyful one. . . .

"When I was your age," he said temperately, "and it was a

hunt day, I did not have time to waste my morning on music."

"A hunt?" Marelie looked up.

"I—I forgot," Corys said lamely.

"Forgot! Why, you—" Hoped I'd forget to fetch him, more like. "Get your things. I had Auster saddle a beast for you, We leave in moments. The *rryl* can stay with your mother."

Corys set the instrument at his mother's hand and hurried off, reluctance in every fast-moving line of him.

"Must he?" Marelie asked. "He hates hunting so—"

"We need meat," Rannan said shortly. "We'll be back tomorrow. Garris is of no mind to be caught out in a storm—or to be caught without meat during a storm."

"I know—but Corys. . . ." She shivered. He did not look at her. "I am afraid for him."

"Why?"

"He is different—he reminds me of my brother Edric."

"I don't know that name."

"No. He died when we were small. Rannan—take care of my son." Pleading, she looked at him, and he was moved. She so seldom asked anything, his proud mountain-lady.

"He is my son too." He bent to kiss her good-bye, knowing she would not kiss in the crowded courtyard. "But he must learn to take his part."

Corys was fuming as he ran to get his gear. He *had* forgotten—but his father would never believe that—the youngest son's dislike of hunting was well-known. Oh, if only they had gone without him. He whipped around a corner and almost fell. Too fast—

"Take it easy, boy," Kell said cheerfully. The child was snow-white; wonder what father said to him? "Over there—by the wall. Young Daryl is holding your beast."

"Daryl? Is Daryl coming too?" Corys peered up at his tall brother; absently Kell noted how much the boy had grown this past season.

"It seems so—though myself, I would not say he's well enough for a long ride. Well, he'll be company for you."

Corys slid through the crowded courtyard, trying not to attract attention. If Daryl were coming, it might not be so bad. Daryl so seldom came hunting. He was often unwell, and Uncle Garris would get so angry, he'd swear he'd no part in breeding such a weakling son, that the bitch must have played him false—as though anyone with eyes could not see that Daryl was his son!

"Rys! Here!" Daryl was holding the reins of two placid chervines, his fragility quite dwarfed by even those beasts considered suitable for young boys. No one would believe that he was two full seasons older than Corys.

"I thought you were ill," Corys said, as he took possession of his chervine.

"Oh, I was," said his friend. "But father says I'm well enough for a short easy hunt. There will not be many more before winter sets in, you know."

"I know—praise Aldones!"

"Rys!" Daryl looked around fearfully.

"Why not? Mother does."

"I meant . . . bother, there's the signal."

Hastily Corys checked saddle and supplies, waved good-bye to his mother, and followed the hunt. Marelie stood watching them go, the baby Margatta in her arms, but she who had been trained as a sorceress in her youth knew well how to hide what she wished to. No one, not even the serving-women, could tell who her eyes followed, or why. Margatta squirmed anxiously; she was cold. Sighing, Marelie turned indoors to the threads of her life.

They had bad hunting all day, and camped in the lee of a small hillock without a single kill. Garris blamed the late start loudly, and Rannan had to thin his lips to keep from excusing his youngest son, angry at the boy for having laid him open to this. But for once Corys did not care. He had felt strange all day, as if the wind whistling through the tall trees were inside his head, it ached so. Times it seemed he could not hear Daryl's low-voiced warnings, or even his father's shouted commands. Rannan would be angry if he made a spectacle of himself, he realized, but the wind howled so . . . he was heartily glad to halt for the night. Auster, who had a new wife and had hoped to get back early, was not.

"Unsaddle your beasts, Daryl, Corys," he said sharply. "Don't dawdle. Daryl, your father wants you by the fire when you have finished. Corys, there's a stream down by the big tree. Fetch water and be quick about it—time enough for nattering when we've made camp."

"Rys, are you all right?" Daryl said. "You look so strange."

Corys shook himself. "I'm fine," he said firmly. "Where did he say that stream was?"

"I'll help you."

"Go to Uncle Garris first. No sense getting him mad at you."

It might have been a respectable stream in spring or high summer, but now it was dried to a thin trickle coursing over hard ground. Corys knelt to fill the buckets: the wind came at him as the stream did, its howling muted to an intimate whisper. Entranced, he listened. It was calling his name.

His father found him there with a strange dark look in his eyes that would have frightened Marelie. Rannan saw only daydreams, and struck. He clouted the boy over one ear. To Corys, it was as if the world split in two.

"Fetch water," his father said curtly. "Now. You've delayed us enough this day."

Corys shook his head to clear it. The wind—was gone. But somehow he knew it would be back. He was trembling, and he doubted his own strength.

"Rys!" Daryl hissed. "What happened?"

"Father—father was angry that I took so long." He sat up, blinking. "I did not realize. . . ."

"Did he hit you hard?"

"Yes—I think so. I'm dizzy."

"Here—give me those."

With Daryl's help he made it back to camp, but he had no appetite for the meal. Not many did—it was journey-fare, poor stuff. His father watched unobtrusively. The boy looked pale. Good: time he faced up to a few of life's hard realities.

Corys drew first watch. It was Kell's gift; first watch got to sleep the rest of the night through. He would rather have stood a watch with Daryl, but he dared not say so, with Kell looking so pleased and generous. He likes me, Corys realized. My brother is fond of me.

That gave him something to think about at his post. Loran, Garris's son, stood with him, but Loran was at best a poor conversationalist. For some reason it was very hard to stay alert. Talking would have helped. Wearily, he tried to count shadows. There were so many. . . .

"Bandits!" On the left. "We're under—" A choked scream—who? Shocked fully aware, Corys reached for his bow and stepped back to the fire, calling his own warnings.

"Father! Auster! Kell! We're attacked by bandits!" Real

mountain-bandits, or lords from the Domains making a night-raid on the Drytowners?

"Corys, to the fire. Kell, stand with him. Auster, to me." His father was there, tall and infinitely reassuring in the suddenly noisy dark. "No, Garris, I don't think it is invaders; they would be better organized and would not bother with a hunting party. A few well-placed arrows will scare this rabble off."

Arrows? But there were *men* out there. He could see them—white eyes in the darkness, desperate, afraid, angry at an ambush gone wrong. He clutched his crossbow with both hands and tried to pray. Aldones, Lord of Light. . . . Daryl, at his side, let loose a bolt. A man screamed.

Blood, blood gurgling in his throat, awful, searing pain and fear, then darkness . . . he was crying.

"Corys, fire!" Daryl shouted urgently. "They come at us!"

No. Wavering, he tried to shoot. His hands trembled so he could not aim, could not free the arrow. A single bolt tilted up at the cool safe stars.

"If you are going to waste arrows, don't shoot," Auster said angrily, and shouldered him aside.

No. More pain, more fear, a dull heavy throbbing at his temples.

Auster took a dagger in the shoulder; neither Kell nor Rannan was scratched. Aside from the guard who'd been killed giving the warning, no one else was seriously injured. Four bandits lay dead, one with Daryl's arrow in his throat. Garris was extravagantly proud of his weakling son; he boasted to all and sundry that the boy had good blood in him, and by the gods he'd known it would come out sooner or later. Daryl smiled worriedly: his father's praise meant little to him these days. But Corys. . . .

Rannan took his son aside, ashamed. He tried to make excuses for the boy—it was his first fight, he wasn't ready, the boy's mother had coddled him—but the fact remained that Corys had disgraced father and mother both this night.

"You will stand guard the rest of this night," he said, with a quiet coldness that should have chilled Corys to the bone, "to make amends for this—behavior. It will give you time to think. Tomorrow, you will travel with your brother Auster, who was wounded, perhaps, by the man you should have killed. Do as he bids you. You will not again hunt or stand with me until you have proven yourself worthy to be called my son."

Corys scarcely heard his father. His head still rang with pain, and he was beginning to tremble again, as by the stream. Am I a coward? he wondered. Perhaps—but the fear is gone now. Everything is gone. . . .

Daryl had no chance for a private word with him. Oh, why did I call attention to him like that? he thought wretchedly. He has protected me so many times. If I had not shouted like that, maybe no one would have noticed he was not firing.

They killed twice in quick succession on the way back, which was good, for Garris would have been angry at returning home empty-handed except for a dead man. Auster lost track of Corys in the hurry, but did not speak of it. The boy was probably sulking. Well, no doubt he'd deserved whatever tongue-lashing Rannan had given him, but father could be hard sometimes. So it was not until they reached Serrais and Rannan faced a frightened, enraged Marelie that they learned Corys's chervine had come home alone, moments before the rest of the hunt. Daryl, looking for his friend, was an unbidden witness to their encounter. It shocked him. Cyrilla and Garris never shouted so—all was distant politeness in his house, except for Anya's malice. This raw emotion was new to him.

"You left him?" Marelie cried, white-faced. "Your son— and you did not even make sure he was with you?"

"I told him to stay with Auster," Rannan said impatiently. "He'll probably come sneaking in after dark, ashamed of himself. No need to worry."

"Why should he be ashamed?"

Rannan's face tightened.

"It is enough that he should be. Now let me pass. I'm tired, and Auster is wounded."

"Auster's wife can tend his wound," Marelie said. "Where is my son?"

"Your son is here, wounded, woman!" Rannan roared. "And your other son brings back meat for your table. Will that not content you?"

Marelie's anger was worse than it had ever been; for the first time since their marriage she did not heed his honor in public.

"Corys is thirteen," she said, with a calm that suddenly unnerved him. "Old enough for threshold sickness."

Rannan snorted.

"Well, if that's what it is, no doubt he will be in before dark, feeling very sorry for himself. But don't expect me to excuse his conduct easily."

"No. Oh no." Marelie smiled coldly. "If he comes back, I will not expect you to excuse him."

She swept inside. Rannan chewed his lip, staring after her, then shrugged. If the boy was ill, that explained a great deal, of course, but for now he was tired, cold, and hungry. The walk home might not be pleasant, but no storm was due for several hours and it would do the boy no harm. Auster and Kell had both had some measure of the peculiar disorienting sickness that came with the awakening of telepathic power and were none the worse for it. Corys would have a fright which might do him good. . . . Still, it made one uneasy . . . but he couldn't start a search. There was work to be done, and to fret too obviously would disgrace the boy and himself. Surely Marelie would see that. Time enough for worry if the boy had not returned by nightfall.

By nightfall, Daryl was a half-day's ride from Sarrais, urging his chervine through the gathering dusk. He had not thought it would be so far. The beast had not wanted to leave its comfortable stable—it smelled a storm coming on. But he could not leave Corys out here alone and ill, not when it was partly his fault. And Daryl had known for some time that nothing he did mattered very much any more. He would not even be missed.

Corys lay where he had fallen, in the shadow of a small hill. One six-fingered hand was cast out into the waning light. He lay on his back, listening to the wind, conscious of Daryl's cautious approach but not really caring—not really caring very much about anything anymore except the spasms that shook his body at shorter and shorter intervals until he thought he would tear apart. . . .

"Corys." Gasping, Daryl tried to lift him. "Corys, I'm so sorry." His friend's eyes frightened him. They were dark and empty, like the eyes of the dead bandit. Loran's eyes hadn't looked like that, when he'd had threshold sickness. "Rys! It's me—Daryl!" Shaking him—"Wake up!"

And suddenly Corys was there again.

"Daryl," he said wonderingly. "What happened? Did I fall off?"

"Yes, you stupid fool!" Weakly, Daryl tried not to give

way to laughter in his relief. He coughed instead. It was cold; the snow was starting. "We left you behind. Have you been here all this time?"

"I don't know. I think so." In anguish. "Oh, Daryl, I felt him—the man you killed. I felt him die!" The tremors started again, and his body began to twist in anticipatory agony.

Something hard, cold, pushed against his lips. Moaning, he tried to turn away.

"Drink it, Rys," Daryl urged. "It's what Lady Cyrilla gave Loran when he was ill—he was the sickest, she said—"

More to please Daryl than anything, he swallowed. The liquid had a pleasant, strange taste. He could feel Daryl's concern burning against him, like a fire one could warm one's hands at. . . .

"Now up, Rys! Come on, move! You have to!"

The world seemed steadier, upright. The spasms eased. Whether it was the medicine or Daryl's presence he did not know, but he was grateful.

"There is a hollow nearby," Daryl was saying. "I saw it this morning—a sort of half-cave. We can rest there."

No, the wind whispered.

"The storm," Corys choked out.

"You can't ride now—we'll wait it out if we have to!" Daryl cried "Come on!"

The storm hit in earnest shortly after the stumbling pair reached shelter. A real mountain snowstorm, the first of the season. Daryl settled the placid chervine across the entrance. The beast would give some warmth, and he could build a small fire.

Corys was ill throughout the first night. Once Daryl gave him a few drops of the medicine; he had no more and would not have dared use it in any case. Corys raved as the wind did, and calmed in the moments when the quiet snow fell. Toward dawn he woke half to himself, in Daryl's sheltering arms.

"Rys?" Daryl hardly dared breathe. Once, during the night, a fit of his own coughing had set Corys off again. But the fever seemed to be easing.

"It will be back," Corys spoke to the thought. "Is the storm bad?"

"Very. No one will search for us in this."

"No."

They lay quiet a moment.

"Rys. . . ."

"Yes?"

"Can you tell what I am thinking?"

"A little—why?"

"I didn't know *laran* worked like that. Loran can't—"

"I don't think Kell or Auster can either, much," Corys agreed. "But Mother can, sometimes."

"Oh. Did you expect, then—"

"No. And it doesn't seem to matter now." He twisted to look up at Daryl's thin face, the shock of blond hair escaping from its hood. "Do you mind?"

"Not—not really. It will take some getting used to, though."

"I suppose so."

Silence. Daryl coughed nervously.

"You shouldn't be out in this, with that cold," Rys told him. "It'll be the death of . . . a poor gift to give in return for my life."

"Oh—do you think I saved your life?"

"Do you doubt it? If the sickness hadn't killed me, the storm would have. Now it may kill both of us."

The wind returned.

By the next noon it was Daryl who twisted and murmured with fever, and Rys who held him, waiting the return of his own weakness with certain dread. The coughing was beyond the fair boy's control now; there was blood on his lips. Worriedly, Corys pressed him closer, trying to warm him. It isn't fair, he thought bleakly.

"What isn't fair?" Daryl asked, blue eyes fever-bright.

"You—came to save me," Corys said haltingly. "And you did. Now—we will both die. It doesn't matter about me—I would have died anyway, if you hadn't come. But you—"

Daryl chuckled, and the soft sound turned into a coughing fit.

"Shall I tell you a secret?" he said, when he could speak. "It doesn't matter about me either. Can't you tell? I've known for a very long time now. Oh Corys, Corys." More soft laughter, harsh coughing. "Isn't it obvious? I am not made for these hills, any more than my mother was."

Soberly, Corys regarded him. Yes, he could see it now. There was death in the calm blue eyes, the flushed, thin face—an old familiar death, like a friend of the household.

"Why doesn't your father send you back to Shainsa?" he

asked, fighting it. "The desert air is not so harsh—you might
get well."

Daryl shrugged.

"What would I do in Shainsa?" he asked reasonably. "I
was raised here, and Anya's sons have my father's place
there. No," he coughed, "I am better off as I am. Besides, it's
already too late."

Yes—too late. Illness was not long tolerated in Shainsa,
less so even than in the Domains. There was no place for
Daryl anywhere but here, in the heart of the storm—a storm
worse than anyone had imagined would come this early.
Corys's arms tightened as his friend began to cough again. It
was growing colder as the day faded; he did not think he
could call out now, even if searchers did come by.

The wind raged on.

He was in his mother's house, a face bent anxiously over
him. Lady Cyrilla! Why should she be so worried? He opened
his mouth to ask, but no sound came. *I cannot find him,
Marelie*, said the shadow-Cyrilla. *He is too far gone.* His
mother was weeping, but before he could comfort her the
wind blew it all away.

Kell, white-faced, stood at his mother's side. *I will fetch
Auster and Dorata*, he said. *Perhaps—No*, Marelie answered.
*Auster is wounded, and Dorata carries a child. There is noth-
ing we can do now. When the storm ends you must go with
your father and search* . . . and again the wind took her.

Tall, pale, gentle—Daryl? No, too tall, and the hair was
silver, not blond. *I have seen you before*, Corys told the
shadow in his mind. *Have you, little one?* the white stranger
said. *Rest now* . . . Daryl stirred and murmured . . . Strange
that he who had no mother should call for one . . . and then
Corys felt warm and safe and knew somehow that the wind
could no longer get them. He slept.

Corys woke first, in the second dawn. The storm had eased
a little—it was possible to see into the swirling whiteness. But
only a madman would attempt to travel alone now; better to
wait till the sky was clear. Anxiously, he looked at Daryl.
The blond boy was no better—worse, if anything. He was in
no condition for a hard ride, if the weakened chervine could
carry double at all.

Sighing, Daryl opened his eyes.

"I was having such a lovely dream," he said drowsily.
"Such a lovely, warm dream."

"I know," Corys said. "I dreamed too."

Daryl struggled up. "There should be a little food in my saddlebags."

Corys had already found it. He nibbled briefly; Daryl ate even less. He did drink a cup of snow melted at their small fire. Strange. . . .

"Daryl, you built the fire. Was there much wood about?"

"No, not really." Daryl regarded the fire thoughtfully. "It should have been used up by now." He started coughing. Corys caught him by the shoulders and pressed him gently back to the ground.

"I can see trees from here. It won't take long to fetch enough to last the day."

It took three trips to the small copse to gather sufficient wood, and by the third trip he was so tired that if it were not for the chervine's reins, tied together and to his belt, he would not have made it back. Halfway, he froze. That noise—oh, *damn* this snow!

"Daryl, look!" Crouching in the shadows, the boys looked down the small valley. A troop of men was passing by, riders, lords, *leroni*—more strangers than Corys had ever seen before.

"Invaders," Daryl whispered. "Look at their hair."

Corys felt his own red scalp prickle.

"They are heading for Serrais."

Daryl looked at him wordlessly.

"The storm," Corys said. "I've heard—the *leroni* can control the weather somewhat."

"Lady Cyrilla says that's nonsense," Daryl answered. "But they can take advantage of it."

An invading army, come to attack Serrais. It was not the first time such had happened; the sons of Hastur and Cassilda did not take kindly to their womenfolk marrying Drytown barbarians, even willingly. And there were some who would never believe it had been willingly.

It took forever for the army to go by. Corys, with his new awareness, knew that this was not a major strike force but only raiders, intent on crippling with surprise. And with the storm for aid, that surprise might well succeed beyond their wildest imaginings. Serrais was well defended, but the severity of the weather had taken everyone unawares.

"They must be warned," Daryl said at last.

"What?" Corys turned from his fascinated contemplation of this brother-enemy.

"*You,*" Daryl was firm, "must warn them. Take the cher-vine and go. It will not be easy."

"And leave you here to die?"

Daryl shook his head, impatient.

"You are just as likely to die as I am," he said, "playing tag in a snowstorm with enemy soldiers. But someone must go, and I—I am not strong enough for such a journey. You must be."

It was true—Daryl was not strong enough. Corys stared at him, denying.

"Rys," Daryl said gently. "Please go. Please warn them."

For a long moment, Corys held him steady. The coughing—even the wind—paused.

"I'll have to go now," he said finally. "Before I get sick again. I'll leave the wraps and food—there's wood. . . ."

"I'll be all right."

"I'll come back for you."

"Yes. Be careful, Rys. You must get through."

"Yes."

They did not speak again.

A half day later, Corys fell out of the saddle into Kell's arms, chilled, shaking, and fighting off the old dizziness.

"Daryl—out there," he gasped. "I—I had to warn . . . must go back. Must get through."

"Warn? Corys, you look like a man five days dead! Mother's been frantic. Where's Daryl? Warn about what?"

"Invaders—a big raid . . ." Then the darkness took him. Vaguely, he heard Kell's shouts of alarm—one could always rely on Kell—and never knew that Rannan himself carried him indoors and stood blankly over the limp, broken figure while Marelie prepared to fight this illness with the air of one who battles an old enemy—an old and feared enemy. None of the others had ever had threshold sickness so, and he had always smiled when the serving women offered thanks each time a child lived through it. . . . Marelie's brothers had died, but Rannan had never really considered the manner of their passing as relevant to his children. And now there was a battle to fight.

"Go," Marelie said to him directly. "You can do nothing here. Go win your war."

"Your war too," he said, suddenly angered.

"Yes." Her smile was bitter. "My war too. But today I fight on a different field. Cyrilla can play *leronis*; I stay here."

"Fight well," he whispered, and was gone before he could see the way her hands stretched out to him in sudden need.

Corys did not die, but it was a near-run thing, and left the men who had married Serrais women shaken to the heart—more shaken, really, than the little battle, some petty lordling's attempt to please his king, got up in a hurry to take advantage of the storm—though it, too, might have been unpleasant had it not been for the warning.

Three days after his return, Rannan finally received permission to see his son. He found the boy pale and thin as his own ghost, staring at the ceiling.

"Corys." The boy did not look at him. "Your mother must have told you—the battle is over. We won." Still nothing. "They were counting on surprise. . . ."

"Daryl?" He spoke without turning his head.

"Garris sent to look—we could not find him."

"It was his idea—the warning."

"A good thought."

Long silence.

"I promised to return for him."

"Yes." Rannan cleared his throat. "Well, you're ill. If you tell us where to look. . . ."

Corys turned to look at him, gray eyes burning holes in his face.

"I'll tell you," he said. "But I'll go too. I promised."

Well, a promise was a promise—nor would Garris be ill-pleased at this tribute to the son who had turned out so unexpectedly well. But—

"Lad—there isn't much hope."

"There is no hope," Corys corrected him. "He is not there. I cannot find him anywhere. But I promised."

"I see." Something, anything, to comfort that bleak, remorseless pain. "It—you had to come, Corys. Many would have died. Daryl—Daryl was a brave boy. He saw the necessity."

"He saw it better than I do," Rannan's son said to him, and turned away. The ground they stood on cracked in two. Rannan stared, shocked.

"Corys, you would not condemn your mother, your sisters—all of us—to death or enslavement. . . ."

"No." The young voice was implacable. "I condemn no one to death. Not ever."

The rift split open; Rannan saw it gaping at his feet.

"Corys. . . ."

"You made this war, between you. Daryl was content to kill and die in your war. I am not."

"We made you too, between us," his father said. "You would not be what you are were you my son alone. And were you only your mother's son you would be dead, as her brothers are dead. Too sensitive to live."

The grey eyes looked at him coldly. The rift was widening, and Corys seemed content to have it so. He made no answer.

"Well, well, you are tired—and ill," his father said, attempting to speak normally. "Foolish of me to disturb you now. You will feel better after you rest."

Corys closed his eyes. He did not listen to his father going, or to his mother coming and going. Outside, the wind was calling his name.

ESCAPE

by Leslie Williams

Dom Felix withdrew from picking the man's mind and
sighed. "This is most disturbing."

Caltus moved eagerly forward in the cell's red-washed sunlight. "Shall I have the jailers killed, my lord?"

Scowling and running a hand through scarlet locks, Felix
shook his head. "No. This deals with sorcery, not security."
Slowly he circled the seated captive. "This is odd. He is not
in his body, yet I cannot find him in the Overworld. He's a
simple commoner, a secretary—he should not be able to hide
from me!" Pausing and rubbing palms together, he asked,
"You say he was alone in his cell?"

"Yes, my lord—well, except for his hound."

Felix's sapphire gaze sought out the silent beast leashed
firmly beside another guard. Shaggy-pelted and huge, it had
followed its master submissively into capture, and now waited
patiently beside the window.

"No one else has entered or left, then?"

"None."

Railing viciously on his paxman, Felix snarled, *"Then
where in Zandru's seventh hell is he?"*

Stepping back a pace, Caltus averted his eyes. "I don't
know, my lord."

Drawing himself together and folding his arms, the Comyn
lord began pacing. "I won't know where to send the *clingfire*
until I see those maps he copied. I am tower-trained, lord of
a Domain, and the filthy *grézuin* hides from *me?* There is
something not right here!"

Silently ruminating, the master watched as the guard holding the hound unobtrusively scratched the animal's head. As
the beast ran out its tongue and licked the man's hand it
turned great gray eyes on Lord Felix and—

Rational intelligence stirred in that gaze, then veiled itself
as the head lowered to snap at a flea.

80

Felix smiled. Drawing himself erect and sauntering to the motionless body of the prisoner, he lifted an eyebrow in appraisal. "Well, Caltus. I thought this man might be of some use, but it seems not." Glancing at the hound, he smiled again as fear awoke in those gray eyes, "As for his beast— put it with my hounds and train it carefully. Take care of it and be sure it doesn't run off. It'll be with me awhile."

"And as for this man's empty shell. . . ."

Terror lanced from those watching eyes and the beast sprang, was throttled back as the guard jerked the leash.

Whipping out his glass knife, Felix slit the prisoner's throat.

REBIRTH

by Elisabeth Waters

Ann'dra whined as he woke from his nightmare and looked around the kennel, dimly lit by two of the four moons. All the other dogs were asleep around him, but they had the advantage of having been born dogs, while he, until a month ago, had been human, secretary to a neighboring lord. He had been captured by *Dom* Felix, lord of this castle, and tortured to make him reveal the information he had been copying. Rather than break under torture, he had left his body, and, knowing that *Dom* Felix would find him in the Overworld, he had hidden himself in the body of his hound. Unfortunately, *Dom* Felix had guessed what had happened, and Ann'dra still woke from nightmares, seeing *Dom* Felix's malicious smile as he ordered the dog taken to the kennels and cut the man's throat.

Ann'dra scratched at a flea and tried to find a comfortable position. Being a dog certainly had its disadvantages, but at least he could no longer be forced to reveal the locations *Dom* Felix had wanted to send *clingfire* against. Filthy stuff. There must be better uses for *laran* than making *clingfire* and sending it out to burn crops, animals, and people indiscriminately, or spying, or all of the other things that the *leroni* did in the service of their warring lords. Well, at least *laran* could get him out of this flea-bitten body for a bit.

He slipped gratefully out of the dog's body and watched it curl up and settle back to sleep, animated now only by the dog's mind, then wandered into the castle. Checking on *Dom* Felix, he found him in bed, as he had expected, but neither *Dom* Felix nor his lady was asleep. Ann'dra, being no voyeur, was about to leave, when he noticed something that stopped him in his tracks. The lady was *raiva*, and a new body was being created. Choosing his moment carefully, he merged with the embryo, taking the new body for his own and settling down to await rebirth.

82

"What do you think it will be this time, Felix?" the lady murmured sleepily.

"A son," Felix replied without hesitation. "He will be a *laranzu* and warrior and no one will be able to stand against him, and he will be known as Varzil the Great!"

No, thought Ann'dra/Varzil. *No more wars. It's time to end the fighting.*

A SWORD OF CHAOS

by Marion Zimmer Bradley

Thoughts are things. Any thought which stirs the ether leaves no atom unstirred, but the imprint of that thought leaves an eternal trace upon the very stuff of the universe. Whatever is wished for with all sincerity and with the whole heart prints itself upon time and space so strongly that it must inevitably come true. And therefore, my brethren, take ye heed for what he shall pray; for it will inescapably be given unto you, and from this there is no escaping in time or in eternity.

From The Book of Burdens
Nevarsin monastery.

Rape had always been something which happened to someone else.

Before this.

Mhari was crying. She had been crying for a long time; as long as she could remember, it seemed. She could not remember anything much on the other side of the tears; the person she had been, maybe forty days ago, seemed to have existed at the far side of a great chasm, someone safe, secure, happy, someone she had dreamed about a very long, long time ago.

It seemed that the worlds she lived in now had begun with screams and shouts and the angry clashing of swords—and all the rest. She had seen her father die, and two of her brothers. She had never known what happened to her mother, and now she was glad of that. Her sisters—the sound of their screams still rang in her head every time she stopped crying long enough to think about it, to try to remember what had happened that day. There must have been a dozen men, maybe more. She was not sure which had been worse, hearing them scream or trying not to think about what had hap-

84

pened after the screaming stopped. The same thing had happened to the best of her mother's women, and to her father's own *barragana*.

Mhari supposed that she had been lucky. The bandit chief had wanted her for himself; so there had been only one man, and since he wanted her to survive, there had not been more brutality than she could endure. She was, after all, his only passport to legitimate ownership of Sain Scarp; she was the only living Delleray of her clan, and while she lived, and sat beside him in his high seat, and slept in his bed, he could claim to have married the only survivor and speak of inheritance, not banditry.

Now it occurred to her, with the detachment born of forty days of thinking about the unthinkable, and enduring the unendurable, that perhaps what had happened to her was not much worse than what happened to any woman married for political reasons to some stranger, and unwilling. And she cut off that thought because *that* was really unendurable—to think that her father's father's father's-many-times father had won Sain Scarp by some such means as this. Through all the Hundred Kingdoms, crowns and castles had been won and lost, and who knew how or by what right lord had succeeded lord?

But there came an end even to tears; and Mhari, who had once been proud to call herself daughter of Lord Farren of Sain Scarp, sat up and flung her wet hair back from her face, sensing that she had reached a place beyond tears.

Below her on the slopes, the castle still stood, and the last crimson light of Darkover's red sun lay like blood over the old towers. Three of the four moons were hanging in the sky; as she watched, a fourth crawled slowly up over the trees. Four moons in the sky; a time of omens and of strangeness. *What is done under four moons*—so ran the old saying— *need never be remembered nor regretted.* Perhaps, at this time of portents, she might somehow learn how to face what her life must be from this day when she had at last exhausted the depths of the measureless well of her grief.

There was always a choice, so ran her thoughts. I can live as I now must live, resigned, bearing children to the bandit—her tongue refused the very name—helping a dynasty grow, Narthen of Sain Scarp where once it had been the seat of Delleray. Dispassionately, she considered it. Some women had met worse fates—her own sisters, her mother—and no mourning or grief could bring the dead back to life, restore Farren Delleray to his high seat or set her brothers in the place their father had made for them. She lived where others had died; should she accept that fate and rejoice in sun and wind and the life in her veins where so much life was stilled? Would she, some day, take pride in her sons if not in the father of her sons, and thus compromise with fate and inevitability?

No. That was to be lower than the meanest of the faithful servants who had followed father and lord and leaders into the silence of death. The faces of those who had died for Sain Scarp would reproach her forever beyond the grave if she should seek such treacherous forgetfulness. Better than that, to follow the faithful and seek them on the shores of death. She was not watched so closely now; somehow she could come by the means of death. Her small hands could not, perhaps, lift the dagger of vengeance against the usurper and ravisher, but they would serve to open a vein in her throat, and the swift death she had sought on that day, a cleaner death than that of her sisters and her mother, would evade her no longer. To die with honor when life was no longer honorable—that was worthy of a daughter of Delleray of Sain Scarp.

No. That was to abandon once and for all any thought of avenging father and kinsmen, mother and sisters. That was to do nothing, submit meekly to the fate that had somehow preserved her alive. Why had she lived when they had met with death? Surely the Gods—if there were, after all, any Gods—had saved her life for something other than this.

And yet. . . . Mhari looked down, despairing, at the busy courtyard which lay below her. From where she sat, the men and horses in the courtyard looked like toy figures from a child's paper castle. It looked much as it had looked when her father reigned there . . . save that her father would never have given house-room or service-oath to any such bunch of villains and cutthroats. Only the Gods knew where Narthen had found such a collection of brutes! Or how he reigned over them—only by being a bigger brute than the worst of them!

Escape? She was watched, night and day. Even now, a burly ruffian lounged below her on the slopes, bewhiskered, a great sword-cut on his cheek, prize rogue of all Narthen's cutthroats; watching the chieftain's woman, a sinecure given to this man for faithful service. She was alone on the hillside only because there was nowhere to run to and no one to take her in if she managed to escape. Forty *vars* of the bleakest, most desolate trails in the Hellers lay between Mhari and her kinsmen at Scaravel, and she had no horse, nor was likely to be allowed near enough one to steal it; nor food, nor even warm clothing to survive the bitter winter nights, which would soon close in between Sain Scarp and any civilized men. If she could not escape in the next few days before the snows closed down, there would be no chance until spring-thaw, and by that time, Mhari knew it well, she would be dead, or forever beaten into submission; or her mind would snap into madness and she would survive, a vacant-eyed mindless thing, placidly sharing Narthen's bed and bearing his sons without will to resist or thought to wish she could do so.

Escape seemed impossible; yet the alternative was worse. Escape, perhaps, to bring her kinsmen down upon Narthen and avenge father, mother, sisters, brothers . . . all her kin, slaughtered in one fell night by the treachery of Narthen . . . who had, after all, once been her father's sworn man and knew all the defenses of Sain Scarp.

No near kinsmen left, even for revenge . . . save for the one brother, fostered at Scaravel with their cousins, and not knowing of the death of his kin, or that Mhari survived, or *how* she survived. She let herself think of Ruyven, safe at Scaravel. *If he knew, he would come to me. He would rescue me. And with him, his sworn brother Rafael. Rafael, who at midwinter night danced with me, and whispered to me, and stole a kiss from my fingertips, and swore that with another midwinter night he would make suit to my father, so that Ruyven would be his brother-in-law and not his sworn brother alone.*

At midwinter night, if the passes were open, Ruyven and Rafael would come here . . . if they lived. But by then—she sensed it—she should be beaten forever into submission; would Rafael take Narthen's leavings? No doubt, by then, she would be pregnant with Narthen's child; even now it could be so . . . and would Narthen let even a last Delleray live, some day to recapture Sain Scarp? If indeed, he was not waylaid before he crossed the passes. . . .

If I were trained in *laran*, or if the household *leronis* had survived, they would already know, and kinsmen would already be on their way to rescue me. . . .

But no. There would be no rescue. It was unlikely she could even gain a moment's access to the messenger-birds, to loose one to Scaravel, with a brief message tied to its leg. Although perhaps, if somehow she could contrive to set fire to the stables, and in the confusion loose the birds; even without a written message, if three dozen birds were loosed, a dozen might arrive at Scaravel and they would know that something was amiss here.

Watched, night and day, to get access to the stables? She might sooner try to climb High Kimbi in her soft summer sandals!

Hopeless, then, hopeless. . . . I cannot even warn my brother and his kinsman, let alone lead them to vengeance! She beat the air in angry frustration.

Gods! Gods, if there are any Gods, where are you now? I would pawn my life and my soul for revenge! She clenched her fists, staring up at the pallid faces of the moon-disks. *Omens, portents, Gods, what good are you? Revenge, revenge, my life for revenge!* It seemed that she could *see* the intensity of her words, trembling in her heart as her hands trembled, pulsing through the empty place left behind by the dried tears and the mourning. She cried it aloud.

"Gods! Hear me! Gods or all the demons!"

Silence. She had not expected an answer. Silence dropped around her, except for the neighing of a horse somewhere, the distant barking of a dog, the rustle of some small animal in the grass. She shivered; it was cold. She felt empty, vacant, as if death had come into her where there had been mourning; a numbness worse than all the tears of the past forty days. She drew a long, shaking, weary breath. Soon, now, as the moons rose higher and the darkness thickened and drew in, her ruffianly bodyguard would approach her and escort her down to the fate that awaited, to which, she supposed, she would become resigned unless somehow she could be lucky enough to die. She could hope for no greater revenge on Narthen than to die in bearing his first child, so that he would have no son of a Delleray to back up his lying claims.

Is that how I will give my life, then, for revenge? Is this how the Gods hear my prayers?

I know nothing of Gods and prayers, said a voice in her

mind, *but if you will truly give yourself to revenge, I will help you.*

Mhari started and stared wildly about her, wondering who had come to answer her prayer. She was alone on the twilit slope. Then there was a little shimmering in the air, a pallid bluish glow, and a man—a man? —stood before her.

He was tall, with the russet hair and slender, sharp features of a *laranzu*, a sorcerer; a ring glowed on his finger and he seemed pale as frost, snow lying on his hair and his eyes holding the metallic glimmer of ice. She stared at him, then, shocked, at the lounging bodyguard who should have rushed up to interpose his own body between the chieftain's woman and any male stranger.

Then she realized that she could see rocks, trees, the very stones and grass *through* his body.

Well, he was not there; her mind had snapped at last, this was no more than a comforting dream, an illusion. . . .

Vengeance, said the stranger, and for a moment, so clear the word, she looked guiltily down the slope, fearing the bodyguard must have heard. But there was no sound save for the buzzing of some small insect in the grass.

Do you doubt your sanity, Mhari, my most distant of kinswomen? Good; for you must be quite, quite maddened for vengeance before I may help you, and you must swear to pay my price.

"Anything," she said fervently. "But how can you, who are transparent, bodiless, without substance, bring me the revenge I crave?"

That shall be revealed to you when you take my sword. Is there any price you would not pay?

"None," she whispered. "I swear it."

A sword. In her childhood, she had shared her brother's lessons in swordplay; she had hunted and killed game. Did he think she would shrink at the sight of a foe's blood?

It is that I crave, he said, and his lips did not move. *My sword will have the blood of the usurper. Swear you will feed my sword with their blood and it shall be yours.*

"I swear it on my life," she said aloud, and then looked anxiously downslope, fearing the bodyguard should hear her talking to herself.

If that is true, then go to the Chapel of the Four Winds and there repeat your oath, then take what you find there.

Madness. Mhari gathered up her skirts and fled down the

hill. Looking back, she saw that the strange youth was no longer there . . . had he ever been there at all? Certainly not. She was mad.

And yet—if he was no more than a voice in her mind—then why should she be sent to the chapel to swear? A madwoman's oath could be taken anywhere!

She had run only a few dozen steps when she became aware that the man was dogging her steps, hard at her heels. He said, his voice a strange mix of insolence and servility, "Where go you, *domna* Mhari?"

"To the chapel," she said, her voice shaking, "to pray for my dead kinsmen and kinswomen. Or do you presume to stop me?"

He stepped aside, bowing his head, and let her precede him. At the door of the chapel of the Four Winds, she stepped inperiously past him.

"Wait outside, fellow! Or I will call down the ghosts of the dead to torment you!"

"Ghosts!" he snorted, laughing all through his great beer-belly, but he shrugged, leaned against the wall. "There is no other way out of here, *domna*. Pray in peace, I shall be waiting."

She had been taught never to present herself in the Chapel except when washed, attired in her best; that was no more than respect to the Gods. Yet she knew, in her heart of hearts, that it did not matter; and if she was mad, what difference did it make? She went inside, looking around at the flickering lights—ancient luminous stones—by whose pale glow she could clearly make out the paintings hanging above the altars to the Four Winds; Avarra, dark mother of birth and death; Evanda in the springtime green of her flowers; Aldones, glowing with the sun behind his head; Zandru, with the scales of choice, good and evil weighed in balance. She knelt at the central altar, all her soul pulsing with the passion that swept her.

I will have vengeance! I swear it!

Slowly, before her eyes on the empty altar, she began to make out a frostlike glow; pale, shimmering, like the pallid glow that had surrounded the strange *laranzu*.

It was the form of a sword, where no sword had been before.

Reach out, said the stranger's voice, though she could not see him. *Take the sword.*

Her heart was pounding so hard that she felt it would burst the walls of her chest. Surely there was nothing there, it was a dream of madness. But her fingers closed over something hard on the altar, and as she drew it back the frostlike shimmer faded and there was a sword in her hand. Solid, hard, cold and real; a sword with silver hilts, wound with pale-glowing blue silk cord, a glowworm shimmer in the pale light. There was no ethereal glow around it now; it was simply a sword, encased in a leather scabbard. Clasping the hilt, she drew it forth a little way. Curling, shimmering letters glowed with a crimson light, and she strained her eyes to read them.

DRAW ME NEVER, SAVE WHEN I MAY DRINK BLOOD.

With the sword hard and real in her hand, she actually gasped aloud. The voice said in her mind:

You need no skill to wield this sword. It will drink the blood which is its due, of its free will, and the life of your enemies with it.

The ruffianly bodyguard pushed his way through the open door. He said suspiciously, "I thought I heard a voice—" and stopped, staring about him.

"Go on," she said icily. "Search behind the altar and the hangings; perhaps my dead kinsmen have risen from the grave!"

"I heard you talking, *domna.* . . ."

She said, "I was praying."

She moved so that the sword was hidden behind the altar, between the stone and her body. He came around, stared, scowled. Something in her cried out, *Kill, kill, he is the worst of them.* . . . It was almost a pain, the high singing in her mind, *Draw me never lest I may drink blood, blood. I will have blood.* . . .

No, she thought. Not now. Narthen will die first. Why kill the man while the master survives? If it were known that she had a sword, she might have no chance at Narthen. And if she killed *him,* what did she care what happened after that?

He shoved against her. It seemed that the sword leaped in her hand, and she thought, *I may have no choice.* . . .

Blood! I will have blood! Kill him!

He was staring straight at her. He said, scowling in confusion, "I thought you had something in your hand, *domna.* . . ."

She said icily, "Come and see . . ." and thought, *I may*

*have to kill him, kill him, drink his blood with this
sword. . . .*

He laid his hand on his own sword . . . then stepped back,
shaking his head.

"Must have been the light . . ." he murmured, slid his own
weapon back into the rude scabbard.

Mhari let her breath go.

He could not see the sword! Yet it was cold and firm in
her hand, the high humming like a hundred bees coming
from it. . . .

He turned his back and clumped his way out of the chapel,
muttering. "This place, damn it, it gives me the creepy-
crawlies all down my spine. . . ."

Mhari swallowed. Her throat was dry. She started to push
the sword back into the scabbard.

Pay my price! Blood. . . . The sword resisted her efforts
to thrust it into the scabbard, and finally, knowing intuitively
what she must do, Mhari laid the razor edge against her hand
and sliced, smearing the blood on the blade. Then it went
back into the scabbard meekly, as if she had dreamed the
resistance.

When I draw you again, she resolved, you shall never be
sheathed until Narthen's blood dulls your blade. . . .

No one else could see the sword . . . not Narthen himself,
Not his man. Mhari belted the scabbard around her waist;
she could feel its weight but looking down at it, she herself
could not see it, unless she gripped the hilt in her hand.

Now for Narthen—and revenge!

Narthen had arranged it so that she sat beside him, in the
High Seat at the end of the long table, and although, for the
past forty days, Mhari had never seated herself there without
tears blurring her eyes, seeing in agonized memory the pale
noble face of Farren Delleray there, her mother Liana beside
him, and on the other side his *barragana* Stelli, pale and
pretty and rather like Liana had been as a young maiden—
she was, in fact, Mhari's own cousin and close kin to Liana.
Every night, every night, tears had blurred away the faces of
the bandits seated in rowdy array down the long table, clink-
ing tankards and bawling out bawdy songs with the worst of
the household's women and the few faithless servants who
had survived; showing her burning eyes the beloved faces of
her dead.

Tonight, though, her eyes were hard, dry and tearless. It seemed that she could almost read in Narthen's eyes the grateful surprise when for once she took her seat without weeping, and when he handed her a dish of meat she put out her fork and took four collops on her plate. One hand lay in her lap, clenched around the invisible hilt of the sword, and she ate hungrily, feeling her teeth grinding and chewing on the tough seared meat as if they worried Narthen's very throat.

He thought then that she was past weeping, had decided to accept the inevitable. She followed his eyes as they strayed to her waist, and she could almost hear, too, the conjecture in them. Forty days; time enough for her to know if he had gotten her with child, so it was surely time enough to resign herself and accept what must be. He belched, patting his belly, his hands lingering on the fine fur-trimmed garment he had found somewhere in the bulging storerooms of Sain Scarp, and he positively hummed with content, like a cat who has been locked into the dairy, contemplating a life of good living here in his new home. Mhari's teeth crunched on a bone. It was the first good meal she had enjoyed since that day when the world had dissolved around her, and she did not take her eyes from the thick red neck of Narthen, except once, when she turned to stare at the bodyguard, and wonder, speculatively, if somehow she could manage to kill them both.

Sword, you will make as good a meal as I!

When they had eaten they sat long over their wine, roaring drunken songs, and a man lifted one of the women—she had been one of the dirtiest sluts of barn-wenches, now wearing draggled finery, smeared with kitchen grease—on to the table, bidding her dance for them.

"Go on, girl, kick up your legs, shake your tits now," yelled one of the soldiers, and the girl, clumsily reeling among the plates, hoisted her skirts in a gawky parody of one of the dances Mhari had danced at midsummer. She clamped her teeth on sudden queasiness. That dress, violet silk embroidered with butterflies—it had belonged to her sister Lauria, she had embroidered it herself before she was fifteen; and now Lauria was dead, dead at the hands of Avarra knows how many men, brutalizing her young body. . . .*Oh Lauria, Lauria, this I do for you too*. . . . She clamped her hands on the hilt of the sword until her knuckles ached, knowing that if she did not she would get up and tear the dress from the girl's blowsy freckled shoulders. . . . *I never saw, I sat here night after night and never saw that filthy slut Beria wearing the dresses my mother and her women made for her daughters. . . .*

Lauria and Janna and Gavriela. And I, sisters, and I . . . you died and I lived for forty days of it. But I will avenge you all. . . .

Even the bandits around the table finally began to wander off from the hall, pulling at the women and pawing at them as they went out, arms enlaced. Two of the men fell into a fight and knives were drawn; Narthen leaped down from his seat at the high table and separated them with a well-placed kick or two, wresting the knife from one hand, tossing it contemptuously into the fireplace. "Hell's fire, lads, what's the difference between one skirt and another when the lamp is out? Find another wench or take turns with this one, but no brawling at my table!"

My table. How quickly he thinks himself master. Enjoy it while you may, Narthen. She felt the sword in her hand as if it were struggling to fight its way out of the shield. Yet she must not draw it yet, not till the moment was ripe to feed it on the blood of Narthen. She forced her hand to unclasp on the hilt, promising in a whisper, "Soon, soon . . . soon you shall be fed. . . ."

"Were you speaking to me, *Domna* Mhari?" Narthen said, in that sickening parody of kindness which was more hateful to her than his worst brutality. "What will be soon?"

She wanted to scream out at him, to gloat in his face . . . but the time was not yet. She said sullenly, "I was speaking to my pet dog under the table, promising him that soon he should have a tidbit from my plate." She forced herself, with shaking fingers, to tear some tender scraps from the roast haunch in the center of the table—now nearly bare but with a few oozing scraps, blood-rare, clinging to the bone—and lean forward, letting the dog take them from her fingers. The puppy whined and drew back, refusing the offered dainty, and Mhari felt the blood darkening her fingers.

"What's wrong with the damned little beast?"

"She is afraid of you," Mhari said steadily. "I doubt not you have kicked her when I was not by."

"Zandru send me scorpion whips," he snarled. "Do you still think me such a monster? There's no pleasing women or dogs; they'll both bite you when they will! Come!" His hand clenched hard in her shoulder. "Go to your room. Get your women to undress you. I will be there soon. I want another cup of wine."

On any other night, Mhari would have heard this news with joy. Once or twice he had indeed lingered half the night, fallen asleep so that his body servant had to bear him to his bed, or reeled his way too drunk to do anything but fall into a sodden snoring sleep at her side. Now it seemed she could not bear the delay. She said, looking up at his flushed face and forcing her lips to stretch back into a ghastly parody of a smile, "Do not be too long, my lord."

His face turned red with satisfaction, and Mhari flinched at what she knew he was thinking, but her hand was tight on the sword-hilt, and she felt herself whisper, "Soon, soon." His rough hand moved over her face and breasts in a crude caress. "Oh, I won't be very long," he promised, his eyes heavy with heat, and Mhari, even as she flinched, felt a hot lust of joy, thinking of how she would strike and see his blood gush out over her, over the sword. Narthen bellowed, "Beria! Lanilla! Attend the lady Mhari!" and the women came, fawning, clustering around her all the way to her chamber.

For forty days she had shared Narthen's bed in the great chamber where her father had slept with Stelli, ever since her mother had come near to death—eight years ago—when her last child had been stillborn. Stelli had not borne a child, and although Mhari had been sorry about it—she had loved the yearly babies born in the household and would have liked a little half-sister or brother—now she was glad there had been no little ones for Narthen to kill, or turn over to his men, or bring up corrupted by *his* lordship here.

Mhari contrived to lay down the sword across the bed. She was sure that none of the women could *see* it, but it felt so hard and firm in her hand, she could not believe that one of them, as they were undressing her, could not *feel* it, tied about her waist. They washed her and put her into a silken night-dress which had belonged to the mistress of one of her father's paxmen. Narthen, she thought wryly, would never have believed that the lord's daughters slept in plain linen shifts and wooly bed-socks, with hot bricks at their feet. She hated the silken gown which left her breasts bared for his lustful gaze, hated the chill of it. But when they had put her in bed, she reached out, clutching at the invisible hilt of the sword, soothing herself with its firmness beneath her hand, and again the high humming began to pulse in her mind, *blood, blood, I will have blood, draw me that I may drink....*

When at last Narthen's flushed face appeared around the door, she could not keep back a little cry, not of fear this time but of pure joy. He misunderstood, and said in his drunken, foolish voice, "Ah, you cannot wait now, can you, my little one. I told you you would like me well enough in time—I am coming to you," and his drunken fingers fumbled with the lacings of his garments. He came toward her, naked, on drunken feet, his organ already pulsing erect, leaning over her....

Blood! Draw me that I may feed! The high shrilling was all through the room, and through the mist before her eyes she could see the frosty eyes of the spirit of the sword, the pale translucent red of his hair like a *laranzu,* and it seemed that it was his hand rather than her own which whipped out the sword. Narthen murmured, "Ah, my little Mhari...."

The sword whistled as it sang through the air, and with a strength Mhari knew was never in her own arms, sliced through Narthen's naked belly. He had a moment to howl wildly, "Help! Murder!" then he fell forward, gushing blood, across Mhari's legs.

She never remembered pulling the sword free of his body. It slid back into the scabbard, humming softly. Mhari lay still beneath the body of the man who had killed her father, violated her, would have inherited his high seat and Sain Scarp too. She looked up for a moment into the cold eyes of the *laranzu* ... then he was gone. He had never been there. Mhari wriggled out from under Narthen's body, seeing, as if her hands belonged to someone else, that they were smeared with Narthen's blood. She wiped them, savagely, on the silken nightgown.

Narthen's bodyguard burst into the room, shouting, "My lord!" He stopped dead at the doorway, staring down, wide-eyed, open-mouthed, at Mhari, in her blood-smeared gown, her hands dappled with gore. The sword hummed, high, shrilling, screaming.

Blood! Blood! Still I thirst, I am not sated....

"My lord!" yelled the man, ran across the room, throwing himself to his kneees by his dead master. "Oh, my dear lord.... Speak to me, speak to Haddell—"

Mhari shrieked, "He will speak no more to you ever!"

Haddell wrenched his dagger out of the sheath and came at her. "You! You hell-cat, I told him to beware—but I've got this—"

"Come on! Come, then," Mhari screamed. "You want some too?" The sword whistled, seeming to tug her along after it, slicing through Haddell's neck and nearly taking off his head. He lurched, carried along by his own momentum after he was dead, fell heavily to the floor.

The women, Beria and Lanella, came crowding, drawn by the screams, recoiled at the smell of death and the blood that seemed everywhere in the room; then ran, screaming. The sword seemed to tug at her, shrilling, *blood, blood, kill them too*. Mhari took one step, the sword held between her hands; then, coming swiftly back to sanity, stopped dead. *No. Enough. Enough for now*. Deliberately, she forced the reluctant sword back into the sheath. The women might not spread the alarm, but whether or no, there must be a moment to return to sanity. She could not, certainly, kill everyone in the castle, not even with an enchanted sword.

She washed her hands and face, stripped off the blood-soaked nightgown and thrust it into the fire, found, in a chest, one of her own old woolen gowns. Now she must somehow manage to get to the stable, find a horse, escape—at least free the messenger-birds.

She ran down through the great hall, hearing voices and babble.

"Didn't see anything, a death out of nowhere, no sword or anything . . . just a sound in the air and Haddell fell dead over the chief's body. . . ."

"Domna Mhari cut him down?"

"No, no, she couldn't have, there must have been someone hiding in the room, maybe one of the old lord's men who escaped and came back. . . ."

"Where'd she go? Where's she hiding?"

"Watch out, whoever killed the chief and his man, *he's* hiding somewhere. . . ."

Mhari hugged herself with a fierce satisfaction, snatched up a handful of cold meats and bread from the littered table, and a leathern bottle of wine, and ran for the stable. As she ran through the deserted hallway she caught up a cloak belonging to one of the soldiers, a coarse thing with untanned hide covered with curly white wool on the inside, and rough brown frieze on the outer layer. It scratched at her, and smelled strongly of wool, but it was warm.

It was snowing outside, a heavy flurry, and her feet crunched hard on an already-frozen crust of snow. She scurried into the stable, peered back to see lanterns everywhere, men spreading out, searching. She could never get through them. Not even by night, not with such a horse as she could find and saddle in the dark. She ran desperately, shinnied up the ladder to the loft. Sleepy cooings and cluckings greeted her from the coop of the messenger-birds; she wrenched at the door of the coop, windmilled her arms, urged in a harsh undertone, "Shoo! Shoo! Out, out, fly—!"

They poured out the round window of the loft, and she saw them silhouetted against the snow, whirling and wheeling briefly as a flock, confused by the sudden freedom; then, almost as if they were all controlled by a single intelligence, hovering in the air, then turning and flying through the storm—away, away, over the pass to Scaravel.

They will know, there, that something is wrong. They will come, they will rescue me . . . my only brother Ruyven, my cousin, my kinsman, my lover Rafael. . . .

Gasping with effort, she leaned back against the beam of the loft. The hay was so soft under her feet that she wanted to sink down into it, to sleep, sleep, sleep forever. . . .

"Look," someone shouted outside, brandishing a lantern, "there they go—all the birds! Someone's in the loft, men! Get him! Up there! After me!"

Her arms, her hands, were shaking with weariness. Mhari set down the bag of meats and bread that she had stuffed in her pocket, gripped at the sword with weary hands. She heard the scrabbling of feet on the ladder, saw the light of a lantern glimmering through the trapdoor. She backed away from the hole in the flooring, gripping the sword. The high shrilling was all around her, and she heard the hay rustle under foot as she moved.

"Up here," shouted the man. "After me—"

His head sprayed blood even before Mhari knew the sword was out of the sheath. His body fell, tumbling head over heels down on the clustered bandits below. Then there was silence, and after a time the lanterns went away.

The sword slid back, humming with pleasure.

Dim gray light stole into the empty loft; snow was drifting

through the window. Mhari rubbed snow on her face to refresh herself, her eyes hot and burning. Narthen was dead, and the bandits were running around in the courtyard like a hill of scorpion-ants when someone kicks out the side and stamps on the queen. A few of them went riding away; others were shouting, quarreling over who was to lead them now. One of the women, a sackful of silver plate lumped in front of her on a donkey, her skirt rucked up to her knees as she rode astride with her legs sticking out showing several inches of striped woolen stocking, jounced away down the hill. Mhari heard two of the bandits arguing about going after her, but then they began to fight over some plunder they wanted.

With luck they will all quarrel, fight, kill one another. I can lie low here until they go away. By tonight, the birds should have come to Scaravel. . . . Even if a full half of then fall to cold, storm, predators, the rest will alert them at Scaravel that something is wrong. . . .

She ate some of the bread and drank a little of the sour wine, grimacing and wishing it were water or milk. After a time she heard footsteps in the stable below her; but it was only someone leading out a horse, and she relaxed.

The high shrilling began in her mind.

Blood, blood, I will have blood. . . .

No, she told herself. Not now. She would conceal herself quietly here until they went away, there was no need for more bloodshed. Leaderless, Narthen's men would never agree on how to keep this place, and when the rescuers arrived from Scaravel, it would be short work to get rid of the few that remained. . . .

I thirst! I will have blood!

Mhari clenched her teeth, forcing the voice down, but against her will, her hand went to the sword-hilt. . . . It was in her hand, it was naked in her hand, and the high shrilling filled her mind, filled all the world. . . .

Draw me never save I may drink blood! You have sworn to pay my price of blood, blood, bloodbloodblood. . . . The humming was so shrill that Mhari thought it would deafen her. Sobbing, she realized that she was on her feet, that her steps were moving toward the ladder. . . .

"No! Oh, Gods, no, no . . ." she cried, half-aloud, but the sword seemed to tug, drag at her until she felt she would fall headlong through the trapdoor; blindly her feet went out, seeking without volition footholds on the ladder, leading her down into the courtyard among the quarreling men. The sword flashed. . . .

A man lay dead at her feet, then another. She felt herself lunge, felt her arms moving, killing without thought or volition. A man howled, fell at her feet. Another, his arm lopped from his body, lay screaming and screaming and bleeding until the screams died. Mhari felt herself retch, turned aside and vomited, but the high shrilling sound of the sword, feeding, filled all her mind and all the world. . . .

The invisible death flashed, played, struck again and again. . . .

Then the bandits, screaming in panic, turned and ran wildly from the courtyard, tumbling over one another. Some fled on foot, others stumbled to horses and fled that way, plunder forgotten, everything forgotten except the invisible death that came out of nowhere to strike them. Then the courtyard was empty and a young girl lay sobbing, empty and sick, on the paving stones, in the falling snow, her hands clenched, retching uselessly; and there was no sound but the full-fed murmur of the sword.

After a long time she got up and went inside the castle, where a few of the remaining servants who had bowed their head to the new master to save their lives, bowed to her and went to her chamber to drag out and bury the bodies of Narthen and his henchman.

Late that night a passenger-bird flew into the yard, and Mhari, hearing the soft crying, came and fed the bird, and took from its leg the tiny scroll, which read:

> If any survive at Sain Scarp; we are coming, we
> will be with you on the second dawn from this
> day.
>
> > Ruyven Delleray.

Mhari wept, holding the little scroll in her hand. *My brother, my brother still lives,* she thought, *and he will be here tomorrow. But I have avenged my father and my mother, and my sisters and brothers.*

. . . at her waist the sword shrilled.

No. My revenge is done, she whispered, but the high shrilling seemed to fill all of space. Without thought she heard it whirl in the air, clamped her hands in useless resistance.

The bird fell dead at her feet, head shorn from its body,

and Mhari, staring in horror at the bird's blood on the sword, burst into wild weeping.

She lurched on nerveless feet to the chapel, and laid the sword there, stumbling quickly away as if she feared it would follow her.

By the time the riders appeared over the brow of the hill, a small army of them, riding up with swords drawn and at the ready, the few remaining servants had scrubbed the blood from the cobblestones in the yard, and fresh snow covered the court with a smooth white blanket. Mhari ran toward them, seeing Ruyven at their head. He stopped, leaping down from his horse and sweeping her into his arms.

"What has happened? Ah, blessed Avarra, have they all gone? How did you escape alive? Are they all dead—mother, father—?"

Clinging to him, weeping, Mhari stammered out the whole story, of invasion, treachery, battle, murder, violation. Ruyven wept as he listened, then turned his face grimly to the battlement where Narthen's head hung, flanked by those of his men.

"And you—you, little sister—*you* avenged them all?"

She whispered, "Not alone. I had—had help of sorcery— one of our far kinsmen—" and, when she led him inside, haltingly told him all the story.

"And where now is the sword, little Mhari?"

"It lies in the chapel," she murmured. "Hidden again as it was first I went there."

"I have heard of this story," said Rafael quietly. "One of your forefathers, Ruyven, made compact with a spirit called *Chaos*, for vengeance. The legend goes that when any of Delleray blood cries out for vengeance he will come to their aid; the sword was forged and tempered with his own blood, and cries out for the blood of the enemies of his clan . . . but I cannot call to mind the rest of the tale. It is uncanny to deal with such things. . . ."

"Oh, it was horrible," Mhari wept. "It kept on killing . . . and killing . . . even when I didn't want it to, when they were all gone. . . ."

"Poor Mhari," murmured Rafael, taking her hand. "You have paid a dreadful price, and after all you suffered!" He drew her close, one arm around her waist, and faced Ruyven.

"*Bredu*," he said softly, "you have long known that Mhari

is of all women the most dear to me, as you are the most
dear of kin. Mhari has now no other kin; will you give her to
me in marriage?"

"Willingly," said Ruyven, taking his friend and his sister
into a great hug. "Nothing can end my grief for my kinfolk;
but there's no mending it, nor bringing them back from
death, and such as I am, I am lord of Sain Scarp and Delleray. And the wedding may be held as soon as you will."

Mhari asked, gasping with shame, "You would—you
would still take Narthen's leavings? I—I am soiled with him,
and stained with blood—"

"Ah, Mhari," Rafael murmured, drawing her close and
covering her hands with kisses, "you are even more dear to
me for all you have suffered; and as for the blood you have
shed, it was shed for the honor of your house and in vengeance for your own kin-blood. I am proud to have such a
wife as Mhari, the brave sword-woman of Sain Scarp! Will
you marry me tomorrow, so I can make you forget your sor-
rows?"

Lying at ease against his breast, she whispered, "I will."

All their kin had come for the wedding, and Mhari,
dressed in a simple gown of blue—it had been too plain to
attract the doxies who had dwelt in the castle in Narthen's rule
there—stood in the Chapel of the Four Winds at Rafael's
side. Ruyven, smiling, locked the bracelets on their wrists.

"May you be forever one," he said, and claimed a kiss
from his sister, even before her young husband took one.

Mhari, her husband's kiss on her lips, stood frozen. On the
empty altar a long, pale, blue glow was slowly spreading, and
she looked, terrified, into the eyes of the *laranzu* of Chaos.
The high shrilling in her mind drowned even Rafael's voice.

*Blood, I will have blood. . . . You swore that no price
was too high to pay. . . .*

"No! No!" she screamed, putting her hands up to her ears
to shut out the terrifying sound, but those merciless eyes filled
all of space, and she felt the merciless drag of the sword,
pulling at her hands, pulling, pulling, shrilling. . . .

"No," she screamed again, even as the sword swept up in a
great and terrifying arc, and swept down. Rafael, the joyous
smile of his bridal kiss still on his lips, fell without a cry.
Mhari, screaming, fought her way backward, staring madly

down at the body of her lover, his bridal finery all spattered with blood.

Ruyven cried out in horror. "Ah, Mhari, Mhari—ah, you fiend from hell, what have you done?"

Blood! I thirst! Blood, more bloodmorebloodmorebloodmore. . . .

Ruyven, his cry of outrage and dismay suddenly turning to terror, cried out, "Mhari—sister, sister, no—"

"No," she screamed. "No! Ah, no, you fiend from hell, I will not, I *will not.* . . . Too much, too much, let it be enough . . . not Ruyven, not Ruyven too. . . ."

Relentlessly, the sword went up, her hands fighting it, struggling away. "No," she cried piteously. "No! Ah, no! Spare me. . . ."

Ah, now I know the price, the only blood that will stop the death. . . .

Ruyven, white with terror, watched, ran forward to try to prevent the struggle as Mhari fought to turn her hands on the sword, drove it mercilessly down. . . .

Her own heart's blood spurting forth, she slid down and with her last strength, flung the sword away from Ruyven. . . .

In midair it stopped, glowing blue. Around it, *through it,* the figure materialized, tall, spare, redheaded like a *laranzu,* the eyes blue as copper filings in flame. Then he faded; and the sword lay, visible for a moment on the altar; then faded and was gone again. Ruyven swept his hand over the altar.

But the altar was cold and empty, and Mhari lay smiling, her face unmarred, and somehow her hand had fallen into Rafael's dead hand.

Between the Ages

Chronology has always been a troublesome business in the tales of Darkover. The three stories that follow could have been placed in almost any section, from the time of the early settlements and the first emergence of laran powers, to the final downfall of the Comyn. It was impossible to assign definite chronology to any one of them; after moving them from section to section several times apiece, I began to feel like the centipede in the old rhyme . . .

A centipede was happy quite,
Until a frog in fun
Asked him: "Which leg moves after which?"
Which raised his thoughts to such a pitch
He fell exhausted in a ditch,
Not knowing how to run.

And therefore, abandoning any effort to determine which leg moves after which (chronology in the Darkover novels was never my strong point anyway), I decided to bring them to you in a separate section.

About "Di Catenas" by Adrienne Martine Barnes, she says that it was an attempt to explore the early beginnings of that custom whereby bride and bridegroom wear double bracelets on their arms as tokens of their lasting tie; and therefore it must come quite early in the history of Darkover.

Susan Hansen's "Of Two Minds" could perhaps be assigned to the Ages of Chaos, since it quite possibly deals with the days of the breeding *program, but then, it could have happened at any time, for the birth of a child so handicapped as Mikhail could have occurred at any time after the* laran *gifts were known.*

And finally, Dorothy Heydt's "Through Fire and Frost" could have been placed at any time during the history of Darkover. Dorothy said about her story that we had heard a great deal about the Gods of Darkover, but ignored the tradition-based religion of the cristoforos, and she felt it time to present their side of the story. It was also her intention, she said, to present a story in which not a single character was redheaded, nor of the aristocracy, in which no one had laran *or used a matrix stone. And yet, for all that, the story comes out with a uniquely Darkovan flavor.*

DI CATENAS

by Adrienne Martine-Barnes

She twisted the bracelet back and forth on her wrist. No matter how she turned it, the hideous head of the serpentine figure, with its starstone eyes, seemed to stare at her. The body of the thing, for she had no name for the animal, was a rainbow interlace of some glassy substance over the chased metal, colors moving in and out in eye-aching curves. It almost seemed to flow along the bracelet, as if it were alive.

Alais was cold. She had been cold since they left her father's house three days earlier, riding to avoid the next assault of winter in the hills. Her feet were damp and her body ached from the bouncing gait of the stag-pony. But the bracelet was all she was conscious of. It was, she knew, a handsome thing, a masterpiece of the craftsman's art, but she had hated it from the day, seven years before, when it had been clasped on her sister's arm. It seemed, somehow, the final indignity, that she should be handed over to Enid's *relict,* and then bound with the self-same object which had turned her sister from a ray of golden light into a sickly shadow.

"Stop fiddling with that!" he snarled.

Alais jumped at the sound of his voice, her long, damp hair brushing across her cheek. She looked at her husband of four days and remembered how handsome she had thought him when he came for Enid seven years before. He was still handsome, in a florid way, though now his dark red hair was slightly streaked with white, and a tiny curved scar slashed one cheek. It made him look rakish, but tired too. The scar was a white moon against his skin, and there were deep lines, canyons running from nose to mouth, which had not been there before. But he still held his shoulders with the same insufferable arrogance she had found attractive and repellant when he married Enid.

If only my father was not such a fool, so determined to keep his blood pure. If only Roderick hadn't gone to find the

106

sea, which we sing of, but no one has ever seen except in dreams. Three years he has been gone. I know you are not dead, my brother, but for all the good you are to me, you might as well be. And mother didn't protest, even though this man killed my sister.

Her hand went back to turning the bracelet without volition. It hurt, not a physical pain, and not even her own, but a special agony which was Enid's. Alais was attuned to the voices of objects, a small talent among others, which she kept very much to herself, respecting her father's violent objection to any hint of the unseen powers which were treasured and sought in many of the hill families. Rodrigo Asturien dismissed all such matters as superstitious nonsense or, worse, evil, and married his children into such families as showed no evidence of *laran*.

Alais wondered how Enid had endured the thing, Enid who hated metal, who could not even bear the wonderful silvery hair clasp which had been a birthday gift one year. To Alais, Enid had been the most wonderful creature in the world, with her pale golden hair and gray eyes, her long legs which could outrun even the swiftest boy, her fearlessness and ready laughter. She had been a little jealous when Enid had married Bryan Aldon, a little sad at the separation, but sure that so beautiful a woman deserved so handsome a man. Alais thought her own flame hair and green eyes ugly.

She tried to turn the ugly face of the beast away. *Was that why you made her wear it, because you knew she hated metal?* Alais raised her eyes to study Bryan again. *You swore you would tame her, my wild sister, but you didn't. I heard you boast the night before the wedding, when I should have been in my room. But you only broke her. And now, because you are the richest man in the district, it has become the custom to put these things on a woman's arm, to mark her as servant to some man. Raoul Benjamin nearly beggared himself to get one for his new bride, and the Benjamins are rich. The servants make wooden ones, to ape their betters. I wonder you didn't have it fashioned for her neck. It's so hard to think. It makes me feel weak.*

"I told you to stop that." His almost golden eyes seemed to darken as he spoke.

Alais shivered, for the room was cold. Aldon House was almost deserted, which surprised her when they arrived. There had been a rheumy old man who took the ponies, and a doddering crone who opened the door. The fire on the hearth was stingy, and there were great webs festooning the beams in the chilly room. The corners of the wall hangings were moldering and the whole place smelled of decay.

It was a puzzle, as great a puzzle as Bryan's unseemly haste to bring her back to his home, before the wedding feast was quite consumed, almost. Alais liked problems to solve, from a recalcitrant waterwheel in the mill, to the spinning of the spiders in the feather-prod trees. If he had seen the place, her father would never have let her marry Bryan, for his pride was as great as his stubbornness.

The skin under the bracelet was red with rubbing. Alais moved her hand away, but it slid back across her lap to turn the thing almost immediately. "Go sit on your thumb," she answered rudely. Her words startled her, almost as much as they did the man across from her. Her brother always said, *Alais wouldn't say boo to a woodhen,* and it was true. She was as quiet as Enid was fiery. "Preferably in a snowbank."

Bryan bristled and leaned toward her. Alais rose and stepped away, reluctant for his touch, and knocked her chair aside. The cup of sour wine the old woman had brought fell onto the greasy stones and spilled out in a bloody puddle. She was filled with a trembling rage, part her own and part from the bracelet cutting her flesh. No, the thing was loose. Why did it seem to sear the skin where it touched?

He stood and caught her by the shoulders. She looked at his face, and at the curved scar. She suddenly knew that Enid had struck his face with the bracelet, and was horrified. A woman shouldn't offer violence to her husband, not ever.

He studied her with some intensity too. "You are shaking all over. Are you ill, Alais? Did you get chilled? There, there, child, I won't hurt you. I'm not a monster. Why do you look at me like this?" Bryan drew her against his chest and stroked her damp hair gently.

The tenderness in his voice and touch surprised her. His chest felt heavy and dead under her cheek, and she wished to draw back. Couldn't he feel the cold? Where were his servants? Was he mad, or just stupid? She tried to find the curious lines of color in his body, the lines which told her so much about the people around her, and there were none. She had never met anyone she couldn't "see," and it disturbed her more than anything.

"Please, Alais, don't go mute on me. I've had years of

silence already. Try to tell me." His voice went husky. "I will never understand how a woman can smell so good after three days travel, when a man stinks like something a Banshee would pass up."

He was indeed a little high, but Alais was used to that. Men alway reeked a bit. But his hands were touching her face and she felt his lips brush her brow in a light kiss. It was a practiced gesture, a little cunning and manipulative, and she stiffened. How wonderful it must be to have such power, that a caress could still a woman's mind. Was this the secret which made men the masters and women the servants? She hated the idea of being other than a reasoning being, of becoming a rutting beast, and drew her head back from his hands.

"You are very sure of yourself, Bryan. Why . . . did you choose me? Wasn't murdering my sister enough? Couldn't you have left me alone?"

"Murder? Is that what you think? Enid died in childbed, as women have done since time began. We did everything to save her. I had the best healers in the hills, the finest midwives. It was useless. I think she wanted to die. And I don't know why. Do you?"

Alais frowned. She looked at the room in its grand decay and wondered if it had been like that when Enid came. She had loved her sister, the child of her father's first marriage, as one adores an older sibling, but she had not known her. There were too many years between them, and Enid had been a curiously vague person, almost as if she were part of the forest which surrounded the house. She had admired Enid's constant rebellion, lacking enough courage to imitate it. "You broke her spirit."

"I . . . what? Alais, I am not a patient man, and I'm sometimes a little rough, or so my mother always told me, but I swear I never laid a hand on Enid in anger. Not even when she gave me this." He touched the scar. "She screamed at me, and clawed my face and arms, like a wildcat. It was like a madness."

"You didn't have to. Don't you know what this . . . accursed thing did to her?"

"The bracelet? What are you talking about?"

"Are you dull-witted or merely insensitive? Couldn't you feel what it did to her? It hurts me, and I can bear metal on my body. She couldn't. Why did you give her this? Tell me."

A strange expression crossed his face, as if some struggle warred in his mind. Bryan reached out and took the bracelet in his fingers. The tips of his fingers traced the scales along the body of the beast. "I was told to," he said, with some difficulty.

"Who made you do this?"

Again, the curious pause, the look of pain, before he spoke. "My cousin, Katria, the Seer, recommended it, before she died. Here, sit down." He righted her chair and took a shabby blanket from near the fireplace. He draped it over her shoulders and tucked her into the chair like a child. Then he refilled her cup and handed it to her. "You're white as death."

Alais's teeth chattered against the rim of the cup. She gulped down a large swallow and sputtered when a drop went down the wrong way. When she stopped coughing, she said, "I might have guessed that old witch's hand was in this somewhere. My mother always said she had a talent for vengeance. Don't look so dumbfounded. Bryan, you can't be that ignorant of the feud."

"It seems I am. Pray, enlighten me."

"My mother's father, Artros MacGowan, refused to marry Katria, though the match had been made by their families. He chose Caitleen MacAran. I don't know why. But they seem to have had a good marriage, with four sons and two daughters. All healthy too. And fertile. That seems to have stuck in the old fiend's craw. My mother called her *hada maleveo*."

"A wicked *fay*? But . . . that is ancient history. What has it to do with me or you or Enid?"

"It chafes so, and I can hardly think." Alais rubbed her wrist. "I don't wonder Enid went a little mad. No, Bryan, it isn't ancient history. Stories don't end when people die. You learn things at your mother's breast which you pass on to your children. But I wish I knew what she was up to. There is purpose in this bracelet. Can't you feel it?"

"No. To me, it is just a pretty piece of metal."

Alais sipped her wine and thought. There was a puzzle here, if she could only arrange the pieces aright. She closed her eyes and extended herself. The bracelet was a shining wall in her mind, confining her and breaking up the energy lines of her body. She could "see" beyond it, but only vaguely, like pale shadows instead of the bright clarity she was used to.

She "entered" the bracelet, and there was a sickening sense of confusion, a twisting, coiling madness. Alais yanked herself out of the thing, and forced her eyes open. She choked back the nausea which almost overcame her. She panted and her head and heart pounded.

"What beast is this?" she asked slowly.

"An old, fanciful creature—the *salamandre*. It is a thing of fire, an elemental. Why?"

"Fire? It would be. Katria gave you the pattern, yes?"

"She did."

"Who forged it?"

"The smith at Neskeya, Guilliume."

"He's dead now, isn't he?"

"Yes. This was about the last thing he made."

"Are you so bare of guile you never wondered why he died, or Enid hated this, or Katria designed it?"

"I never think of it . . . at all. You're right. It is almost invisible to me. In fact, it gives me a headache. When I think of it."

"Will you take it off me?"

All the color drained from his face and beads of sweat broke out on his brow. His hands clenched, then twisted and jerked. "Not while you live," the words whispered. The strong, broad shoulders shuddered and stooped forward.

Alais knew these were not *his* words, nor *his* voice, but something she did not understand. She wondered if she had ever "seen" Bryan at all, or whether he had been a remnant of a man even when he came for Enid, a garment in which Katria had clothed her malice. What, she wondered, had the old woman done to him? What special gift had she possessed?

Those gifts, or tricks, or powers, were causing a kind of war between the hill families. The families with gifted children wanted more, and the families without were divided between the stiff-necked conservatives, like her father, and those who would achieve some domination by marrying into clans with *laran*. The Aldons were a safe family, by her father's estimation, because they showed no evidence of any strange powers.

And then there were the crystals, the blue starstones, like the ones in the eyes of the beast on her wrist. These objects seemed to enhance the natural powers of some individuals. The stones were a gift of the beautiful folk, the legendary spirits of the trees. Enid's grandmother was supposedly one of these spirits, and Alais had always wondered if her father's distaste for mind seers and foretellers was not linked to his first wife. He even violated the code of the hills and would not give a *leronis* house room during a storm. "Let them use their powers to keep from freezing, if they can," he would say.

Old Katria had been known in the hills as a woman of great capacity. She was feared and hated, but never abused. Alais had seen her once, at the rabbithorn sheering festival, a raggedy old woman with wild eyes.

Some of the families, she knew, were now making a deliberate effort to understand the gifts which seemed to run in their bloodlines. Tests had been devised, but Alais had never been subject to them. Her father would never have permitted that.

But she had trained herself to use the little "tricks" for which she had no names. Following her mother's wise schooling, she never let her father see any of them, and such was the extent of Rodrigo's egotism that having declared that such things did not exist, for him they did not. With great difficulty she used one now.

Alais withdrew herself somewhat from her body. She felt as if she were sitting on a cobwebby beam, looking down at herself and Bryan. The bracelet tugged her back, making the feat almost impossible, and she could only manage it for a few seconds at a time.

The flickering sense of in and out of body "seeing" was dreadful, but she managed to look at Bryan. She studied the huddled form from boots to brow, seeking the color lines, and finally finding a tiny spark, like an ember, at the base of his throat. Something like a dense black veil seemed to cover him, and the spark flashed like a candle in the wind. If the bracelet trapped her, then something else bound him, and she knew she had to find out what.

She brought herself back together and touched the bracelet. Then she tried to really look at it again. The colored arches of the body seemed to swirl in front of her eyes, as if it did not wish to be looked at.

Alais nodded and almost smiled. She had hated the band because it had hurt Enid, thinking nothing of the decoration upon it. Now she knew the pattern was as important as the metal itself. Somehow it disrupted her body's energy lines.

She wrapped the blanket around her left hand and held the bracelet so that it did not touch her arm at any point. A kind of strength surged through her, like a spring flood in the hills.

Alais bent forward and tore a wide strip off the hem of her skirt. Then she began winding it around the bracelet, overlapping each turn until the metal was completely covered. She tore the ends with her teeth and made a clumsy knot, jerking it tight.

"What are you doing?" Bryan was watching her, his color almost normal.

"Just making sure I never cut your handsome face with this thing," she answered shakily. "Besides, it's ugly. Why didn't you get me a new one? I hate wearing anything of Enid's. It wasn't meant for me."

Bryan frowned, as if he listened to words in his mind. "But, it was. Unwrap it!"

"No!" She never wanted to feel that horrible weakness again.

He staggered up like a drunk and lurched toward her. Alais felt he was being dragged against his will. She reached up and twined her arms behind his neck, so he could not reach her wrists. He pulled her elbows down, broke her grasp easily, and fumbled with the meager knot.

Alais slipped her left hand under his shirt and found a leather thong. Without thinking, she jerked it with all her strength. On the second pull, it snapped, and she drew out a bare starstone, so dark it was nearly black. She hurled it away from her as he snatched her hand, sending it smashing into the stones on the hearth. There was a snapping sound, like an icicle breaking, and a glassy tinkle.

Bryan stood dazed. His eyes had a stricken emptiness and he swayed as he stood. Then Alais saw the spark in his throat blaze into flame, the lines of his life force coursing through his body.

He stared at her, bewildered. "Funny. I don't remember what I came over to you for."

"To take off the bracelet." She could sense the confusion in his mind.

"Was I? Why?"

"I don't like it."

"You don't?" He pulled the knot loose and began unwrapping the bindings. Then his fingers touched the exposed metal and he screamed and fell to the floor, twitching and tearing at his garments. Alais felt his agony and she bent to touch him.

"Ahh! No, no. I'm sorry! I didn't know. I'm sorry. Don't touch me. It hurts. Ah, how it hurts!"

Alais realized that the stone she had torn from his throat had protected him in some way from the bracelet. He was unshielded now, bare and naked, and Alais drew back. Then she ripped his belt pouch off and poured the contents into her lap. The tiny key seemed to squirm away from her and she fumbled to seize it. He had half unwrapped the bracelet, and the lock lay just under the *salamandre's* ugly mouth. The eyes seemed to dazzle her. The key wavered in her hand, blurring her vision. She tried to put the key in the lock and failed. The swirling in her mind was like a dust devil and she felt sick.

Finally, she closed her eyes and fumbled for the lock by touch. The very feel of the lock was cold and slimy, and it took her several tries. Finally, the bracelet opened and fell off into her skirts. With a swift jerk, she dropped it to the floor and brought her boot down on the object. She stood up and did a kind of dance, stamping on the bracelet as if it were alive.

Bryan was sitting up and watching her. There was no color in his face and he shivered all over. "It's cold in here," he said, as if discovering a new idea. "Why is the fire so tiny? There's hardly any wood."

"I don't know." She gave the bracelet one last stomp and heard a glassy crunch under her heel. "The place seems deserted."

"Deserted. Yes, it is. I remember now. They all packed up and left, when my mother died. I feel as if I had been far away, as if my life were a tiny picture on the wall which I have watched. Like a dream. I remember Katria putting the jewel around my neck, and then everything got . . . small."

"Get off the floor."

"Yes." He didn't move, but looked at the room. "It was very nice, once."

"Do get up, Bryan. I can't lift you." She was shaking with fatigue, but his bewilderment tore at her heart.

Bryan reached over and took the broken bracelet from the floor. He tore off the remaining rags and looked at the ruined object thoughtfully. "It seems to be dead. Poor Enid. I never knew it hurt her. And I'll never forget the pain. I wonder if the lock can be fixed."

Alais was horrified. "Why?"

He clasped the bracelet clumsily over his huge wrist. "No. It would never fit. I never want to forget what it did, you see."

Alais looked at his bowed head and understood that it was his way of showing remorse. She shook her head. Her father's hearty egotism and her brother's selfish curiosity had left her unprepared for guilt or sorrow in a man. She found it infuriating and pitiable.

"Bryan, have it melted down and made into a new one. There's enough metal in it for two, and . . . make two. We'll both wear them, to remember." She hated the thought of it, but anything was better than seeing him bowed and broken.

"Would you?"

"Yes, my husband."

He stood up and put one arm around her shoulders, hugging her to him. She felt the warmth of his chest and the beat of blood through his veins. He was alive again, and she found that she was glad. "I don't deserve you."

"No, you don't. But you are stuck with me anyhow," she said with a laugh to cover the joy in her heart. Then she saw that he was crying, and lifted her hand to wipe the tears off the scarred cheek. "You are a laggard in love, husband. It is four days, and I am still a maiden."

"Then let's hope the fire in the bedchamber is better than this one."

OF TWO MINDS

by Susan Hansen

There comes a point in every person's life when he is sure that his life will never change. Then it does.

My turn came early, when I was in my fifteenth year—a time when I dwelt in that wonderful netherland where I was expected to assume all the responsibilities of manhood, and none of its privileges. I was just Dawyd MacAran, son of the poor relations of a proud family. A feud had cleft my father from his noble brothers, and on that day he swore he would have no part of them. To Ian MacAran, pride was more important than wealth or prestige; there are those who would disagree with him and call him a fool, but I am not among them.

My father earned what little one earns in a small village in the Venza hills. My brother Robard helped him once he reached manhood; I proved to be much less useful, choosing to serve as apprentice to the old healer, Marguerida. My mother's energies were spent loving her husband and five children, and trying to feed us all. Liriel, my eldest sister, helped her care for the little ones, Alaric and Maellen. I wasn't much help, really, but I don't think I was ever really missed. On those nights when Marguerida rewarded me for a day's work with an evening meal, my mother would try to hide her relief. I never begrudged her that; the little ones were growing still, and one less mouth to fill was that much more for them.

Marguerida was growing feeble, and as the years of my apprenticeship passed, she grew slower, frailer, sliding slowly into senility. She once said that I had a gift for healing, and I suppose she was right, for as her decline became more and more apparent, people began to trust me more readily with their ills. I didn't care what gifts I possessed, knowing only my new-found joy in my chosen life's work. I had found my niche, and would remain there.

116

Or so I thought.

The *leronis* rode in on a chestnut gelding. The day was bright and warm, and the flowers were abloom with vivid colors. Her arrival created quite a stir. It was rare for any of the *vai leroni* to take notice of a humble village such as ours. Small crowds gathered to watch as she rode down the dusty, grass-scattered road with her small escort of two strong-look-ing bodyguards in fine livery, and a frail, young looking maiden on a brown chervine.

What could a *leronis,* a trained telepath-woman of the Comyn, want from us? As if to answer the silent question, she reined in her horse and addressed the crowd.

"I wish to speak to the elders of the village."

Within moments it was arranged. Soon after, with all due haste, her mission was explained to us. It appeared very simple, but made little sense. Her name was Melisande, and she hailed from the tower at Hali. Her task was to test the village children between the ages of ten and sixteen years for the telepathic gifts of *laran.*

Perfectly logical . . . but outrageous. Never had the *leronyn* of the Towers sought their own kind among the lowly settlements. It was understood that Comyn blood must be kept pure, untainted. For what purpose did they stoop to such depths?

I didn't expect an explanation, and when my turn came, after a dozen or so children had been turned away and a few told they had some unremarkable latent abilities, the *leronis* didn't offer to explain. She told me to sit down, to relax. She seemed somewhat bored by the whole business.

Settling down to concentrate, Melisande gently uncovered her starstone, the brilliant blue crystal used to amplify the psionic powers of the Tower-trained. It could be used for communication, locating lost objects or people, psycho-kinet-ics or healing. This much I knew from Marguerida, who for many years was midwife for the Altons of Armida, where such things were common. Most people feared the starstones as a sorcerer's tool; I knew better, but feared it nonetheless.

"Look into the stone," she directed. "Don't touch it—merely look, and tell what happens."

I obeyed. My eyes were seared by a blinding pain, and something seemed to *twist*. Tiny lights within the stone seemed to writhe and dance, and my stomach began to mimic their movements.

"I think I'm going to be sick," I said hoarsely, closing my eyes. With a mild air of triumph and surprise, Melisande covered her matrix, and the sickness went away. Bewildered, I thought, *what did that mean?*

"Don't be so frightened, child." The *leronis* smiled gently. "Can I ask you some questions?"

I nodded. She smiled again.

"Are you sickly? Are you often ill?" She absently fingered the chamois bag that held her starstone.

I shook my head. She looked slightly surprised. "No dizziness, disorientation, nightmares?"

That brought back some not-so-pleasant memories from when I was twelve. For months, my parents thought I was losing my mind, for I was plagued with headaches, visions, and voices, none of which I could explain. Fortunately, they had faded as the months passed, and by now I had all but forgotten them.

I related this to Melisande, who nodded as if she understood. Without another word, she measured some liquid from a crystal vial into a small glass.

"Drink it," she commanded.

A trifle hesitant, I sniffed it first, which told me nothing. I drank the stuff. The acrid liquid seemed to evaporate on my tongue. I waited.

Dawyd MacAran. Melisande's quiet voice spoke. But she hadn't spoken.

I stared at the *leronis,* too scared and confused to speak. She smiled faintly and nodded, and I heard her voice again.

Dawyd, you have laran. *Untrained, undeveloped, but with training you will be a strong telepath.*

I have come searching for a boy such as you, laran— *gifted, to serve Lord Marius, who sits on the throne on Thendara. Do you know of his son, Mikhail?*

I wasn't quite sure how to answer. I had heard much about him; he had been born a moron, blind, deaf, and mute.

Melisande's voice returned, heavy with sadness. *That is true. But he must have a companion now, to know and serve his needs. This is how you might serve Lord Marius.*

That much I understood, but why a pauper from the hills? Why not a Comyn son despaired of a decent inheritance by a dozen-odd elder brothers, noble, like himself? Even some lord's *nedestro* would be a more logical choice than I would.

Melisande had heard these thoughts and answered them.

There are those, Dawyd, who might use such a position to gain influence, power. For anyone of Comyn blood the temptation is there. We are not saints, you know. I sensed laughter beneath the thought. *Yet poverty and* laran *were not the only prerequisites. Do you think you are the only gifted child I have found in my travels?* She looked at me, half-serious, half-mocking.

After a moment, I spoke aloud for the first time in what seemed like hours. "*Su serva, domna.* I will come."

I left my village then, with Melisande, to go to the Tower at Hali. There they taught me to master my gift and make it into a skill. In time I was given a matrix, trained in its use, and then sworn never to take part in or allow its misuse. Even as I rode, escorted, toward the gates of Castle Hastur, the silken cord and soft chamois bag felt strange and unfamiliar to my neck. Little more than a month ago I had worn rags; now I wore fine livery, fit for a Comyn son.

A wizened servant met us at the gate, beckoned to a stable boy to see to the horses, and took the small sack that held my few belongings. He led me through the mazelike corridors and stairways to a large, richly decorated room. At a small table sat a tall, slender man with auburn hair graying at the temples and sharp gray eyes. At his curt nod, the old servant disappeared, and I was alone with Marius Hastur, Lord of the Seven Domains.

After a moment, he said, "Well, now, I don't bite, lad. Sit down." I obeyed.

He smiled. "That's better. Your ride has been long. Are you weary?"

I shook my head, and spoke for the first time. "No, my lord. The ride was not strenuous." My fear got the better of me, and I barely choked out the words.

Finally, Marius threw back his head and laughed. "You make me feel like I am an ogre, young Dawyd! Am I so fearsome?"

The tension broken, I relaxed. Lord of the Domains he might be, descended from the Gods, but face to face he was a man, tired-looking, but kind. "No, *vai dom*," I replied, trying to return his smile. "I am sorry."

"I was not offended, but that is not important. What is important is that you realize that you have accepted no easy task, child."

"I do, *dom* Marius." Tiring, yes, but how difficult could taking care of a helpless child be?

Marius continued. "Nor is it one I want you to take lightly. Whatever else he is, Mikhail is my only son." There was a world of pain in that voice. I couldn't bear it.

"He will be as my own brother born, Lord. I swear it."

Marius's eyes seemed for a moment to pierce through to my very soul. Then, rising abruptly, he commanded, "Well, then—it is time you met Mikhail."

Lord Marius led me to a rather inaccessible suite of rooms on the eastern side of the castle. Seated by a window was the most beautiful child I'd ever seen. His face was fair and unblemished, his features fine, and his hair deep red with glints of shining copper. What haunted me most, though, were his eyes. Gray and almost colorless, they seemed empty, expressionless.

We were very unlike in feature. Although he was underweight, Mikhail was sturdily built, where I was tall for my age and wiry. My own eyes were not gray, but bright blue, and my hair dark brown with only highlights of the red Mikhail possessed in abundance. Two people could scarcely be less alike.

Marius laid a hand on his son's shoulder. Like a cat, Mikhail spun around and well, I suppose the best word is *pounced* on Marius's hand, first sniffing it, then pressing it to his cheek. The child visibly relaxed. I stared, amazed at his swiftness. Marius withdrew and motioned to me to follow his example.

I hesitated, unsure. Marius waited, expectantly, and finally I laid my own hand on the child's shoulder.

Again, the swift response—only Mikhail was not so swift to relax. Instead, he frowned and repeated his motions. Then, as if he had filed the information somewhere in his brain, he released my hand.

Marius laughed. "And now that you've been properly introduced, I will leave you to rest; then you will be refreshed enough to dine with me tonight. We will talk."

With that, he left. Mikhail seemed quite content as he was, so I wandered into the room that was to be mine, feeling uneasy. Something had not been quite right about that last scene. I couldn't figure out exactly what it was, but something was strange . . .

Wait. All I could remember was Marius's veiled pain, worried reserve—and my own fear. After a time, when you're a telepath, the emotional aura around you becomes part of your memory, too, and I had none from Mikhail. No fear, no curiosity, not even boredom. Nothing.

I couldn't understand it. Even a moron should have emotions. Was it some sort of natural shield, some uncanny fluke, or could he really be that far gone?

Well, worrying about it won't change it, I thought. At least not tonight. I had about an hour before I was to dine with Lord Marius; I would use that time to bathe and make myself presentable. How odd, I thought; dirty and dusty as I was, clad in road-worn travel clothes (better than any I'd owned before but in dire need of washing nonetheless), I'd spent the last hour talking with a king. Well, I could rid myself of the dirt; the bath was luxurious, almost decadent, and there was a fine set of clothes spread out on the bed.

Once clean, I slipped them on to find that they might well have been tailored for me. A white, full-sleeved linen shirt, blue tunic that by coincidence matched my eyes, and brown breeches that fit into fine leather boots. I looked like a prince. I felt like an ignorant country boy dressed up like a prince.

An old nurse came to stay with Mikhail for the evening, and before long I was seated at Lord Marius's table. We were not in the enormous formal dining room, but in the small room where we had first met. The first part of the evening was spent exchanging polite inanities. Then, for no apparent reason, we both fell silent. The tension grew. Finally, Marius spoke.

"Dawyd, I said before that you have no easy task. This is true. I do not think you realize what it means to care for a child who can tell you neither why he weeps nor why he laughs. You'll clean him, feed him, dress him, and he'll not give you a thing in return. And you'll grow to love him, too, if you are the person I think you are, and Mikhail is not an easy child to love. Trust me, I know." His eyes were grave and sad. I felt his grief as if it were my own.

He looked at me somberly. "But whether you grow to love him or not, be kind to him. That is all I ask of you. Be kind, for the Gods will deal with you as you deal with my son. Camilla and I have felt their wrath; she has borne no living child since Mikhail. Perhaps blessed Avarra will let this one live." *Lord of Light, hear our prayers.* The unspoken words echoed as if he had spoken aloud.

Quietly, evenly, I replied, "I will not stand forsworn, *via dom*."

Marius smiled a little, wryly. "Ah, I believe you, *chiyu*. It was my own sore conscience speaking. My son is not what the world expects him to be, and despite power and riches I can give him little, not even time. I am seldom here to be with him, and Camilla's grief and guilt make it unbearable to care for Mikhail—which only multiplies her distress. She is again pregnant, and so fearful that she might miscarry that she barely stirs from her bed. She will soon be too old for bearing, the midwife says." Marius sipped his wine thoughtfully. "My nephew, Damon, stands as heir designate. The Council would never accept Mikhail." His simple words hung starkly in the air.

Suddenly, I realized how weary I was, and pushed my wine away. It is not courteous to fall asleep in front of a king, not even a kindly one. Marius rose.

"You have been a good audience, Dawyd, and now you must rest. Your task soon begins."

And so it did, but it was not all that difficult at first. Mikhail was passive, pliant; he seemed to care little what was being done to him, and less who was doing it. I really couldn't tell one way or the other, for there was no trace of rapport between us. He had some sort of natural barrier that I hadn't the skill to tamper with—so I left it alone.

Mikhail, as it turned out, liked to touch things, feel their textures. He could sit for hours exploring an object with his fingers, as if he were trying to determine its total meaning and purpose. That always mystified me. What went on in his mind, what there was of it, behind those empty grey eyes? I turned it into a game, giving him new things, which he would accept eagerly, to touch and feel. I'd give him familiar things as well, which, amazingly, he recognized. Once, I brought a *rryl*, letting him feel the vibrations run through the strings as I fingered different chords. He even learned to finger a few. He never smiled or acknowledged these gifts in any way, but somehow, I knew they pleased him.

All in all, it was a quiet, peaceful existence. I lacked nothing. I lived much better than I had ever lived at home. But after a time, I began to feel caged in; I craved companionship. Being with Mikhail filled my days, but often it was the same as being alone in the room. My frustration grew as the weeks passed.

Then the dreams began. They're hard to describe, for they involved no images that I can remember, much less relate. I suppose they seemed mostly like waves and waves of strong emotion, wordless frustration, pain, anger. Aching loneliness like a knifing pain constricting my throat, bewilderment, longing.

What was going on?

The feelings would fade by morning, and I would remember them more clearly than any normal dream. These disturbing experiences made me even more restless; I became irritable and snappish. Once, I even raised my hand to strike Mikhail when he accidentally knocked over a glass pitcher. He drew back, as if he could see my intent.

That shocked me back into my senses. I hugged him roughly in apology, and wondered what it had been that made him draw back so instinctively. Habit, perhaps? His nurses could have treated him so, and no one would have known. Whatever it was, I would not do as they had, therefore it wasn't important. But I knew then that I had to get out for a while before I grew too agitated to take proper care of him.

I asked an old nurse whom I trusted to stay with Mikhail for the day. I then invited Felix, the *coridom's* son, to accompany me. He was a rough, friendly lad about my age, and he would be pleasant company. I didn't give it a second thought, as I sincerely doubted that Mikhail really knew or cared who was with him. So long as the person was familiar, and cared for his needs, he was quiet and docile. So I kissed him on the forehead with the affection I was just beginning to realize I felt for him, and left.

All day I was uneasy. I returned that evening to find the old nurse, Gwynnis, in near hysterics.

"I've never seen the lad in such a state! All day long, wouldn't touch me, wouldn't eat—just sat there, quiet as a mouse, crying. Blessed Cassilda, what's the matter with the child?"

I was puzzled. He'd never behaved that way in my presence. I walked into Mikhail's room.

He was sitting there, playing with a scrap of yarn. There was no trace, not a sign of the scene Gwynnis had described. I looked at her frightened face; she wasn't lying. Something was terribly wrong.

I lifted Mikhail's chin in my hand and pressed my cheek to

his. "Hello, *chiyu*," I said, solely for my own benefit. It was becoming a habit, for it filled the silence.

With a fierceness I'd never seen in him before, Mikhail grabbed my hand and pressed it to his cheek. For what seemed like a long time, he held it tightly, warmly.

Bewildered, I gently withdrew. What could it mean?

That night, I dreamt again.

Fear. Abandonment. Loneliness so deep that it felt like an endless descent, falling, falling . . . a black pit of hollow pain. Impotent rage eating through defenses like strong acid. Despair—hopeless, unutterable, unbearable.

I sat up in bed with a start, fully awake. Still the frenzied emotions overwhelmed me, like thick smoke choking, suffocating me. Blindly, without thinking, I rose from my bed and followed some subliminal pull to the source of my distress.

I found myself kneeling by Mikhail's bed. He lay awake, motionless as a statue or a corpse, eyes open, unblinking. He barely seemed to be breathing. As I knelt by his side, the waves of pain nearly made me cry aloud. And I understood.

Laran. What kind of *laran* could a moron have? Why hadn't I realized earlier? The dreams had come only at night. Could he have known what he was doing?

. . . But a moron cannot know. There was too much coincidence. Too much. A moron cannot know.

Then Mikhail was no moron. He had been trying to communicate, in the only way, in the only language he knew—feelings. He reached out at night, when I could listen, when I wasn't dressing or feeding or cleaning him, taking care of him yet never really caring for him, worrying about how lonely I was and whom could I talk to.

The child had been trapped within himself, his unfortunately imperfect shell of a body, for over ten years. I put my arms around his frail shoulders, held him tightly. I was crying. I think he was, too.

"I hear you, Mikhail." The words meant nothing; the contact opened a blaze of rapport between us, and I felt the despair broken by a joyful hunger, reaching . . .

. . . blending . . .

I felt the wetness of his tears on my cheek and knew, perhaps with a flash of precognition, that this child in my arms would mean more to me than father, mother, or brother. "*Bredu*, beloved brother," I whispered, choking on my words.

We had no knives to exchange. But we could use the fine-honed blade of our *laran* to cut the bonds of his imprisonment.

Mikhail had much to learn.

THROUGH FIRE AND
FROST

by Dorothy J. Heydt

An icy wind poured down the mountainside, through the pungent-smelling trees, over Father Piedro's bare scalp and down his neck. Strange, an east wind in the middle of winter; the Heller Wind, just as icy and a lot stronger, should have been blowing out of the northwest and over his shoulder. But no wise man trusted the weather to do what it was supposed to. Doubtless it would shift back in a few hours.

Under this mild wind, the world was full of whispers: the rustling of the trees, the soft shuffle of the donkey's hooves through the fallen needles with their thin drift of snow, the murmuring of Father Piedro's prayers. Two hundred psalms sung in four hours and round again, keeping the prattling lower half of his mind occupied while his soul meditated on the holy mysteries that bound together the world and all that was in it—and, incidentally, that kept him warm even in the snows of Nevarsin.

He was a tall, gangling young man, his black hair tousled around his shaven crown, the scars of youthful skin trouble still visible on his cheeks. The sandaled feet at the ends of his long legs reached almost to the ground under the donkey's flanks. He had just completed his twentieth year, only just been ordained as Father of the *cristoforos,* and Father Master had granted him leave to spend the Midwinter Festival with his family in the world. His belly was still full of his aunt's spicebread, and his saddlebags bulged with bundles of healing thornleaf from her garden.

The donkey lifted its gray head and brayed softly, almost a whimper. Father Piedro brought his attention back to earth. "You smell something, little brother? So do I." The scent was stronger as the wind blew more gently: resinous smoke. Somewhere, the forest had burned, or was burning still. It had been a dry winter.

Any able-bodied man, even a monk, was bound to take his

126

place on the firelines at need; but where was the fire? He didn't know whether to pray to find it, so that he could help to extinguish so deadly a menace, or to give it a clear miss, so that he could continue on to Nevarsin without delay.

Cormac's Station was just ahead, its few mossy roofs becoming visible through the trees; he would give the alarm there—but surely it had already been given. The mountain men were not likely to lie asleep while smoke drifted through the trees. He slapped the donkey's angular backside just the same, and urged the little animal on to a reluctant half-trot.

There were no men in the road between the half-dozen rough huts of the settlement; no women collecting water from the little spring that trickled out of the rock to fall a thousand feet into the valley; not even the children who should have come out, curiosity overcoming shyness, to look at the stranger. The men might all be off on the firelines, but where were the others? Was there sickness in the place? He put his foot down the last handsbreadth to the ground, and swung his long leg over the animal's head. The donkey took another few steps before realizing that its rider had dismounted and it was time to stop. He bent his head to peer into the nearest hut. It was deserted. His foot struck against a wooden cup, abandoned on the threshold; it clattered across the floor. *Sickness,* he thought, *or else they feared the fire was coming this way, and then it veered off.* He looked into another hut. It was empty. He pushed open the door to the third, scraping on its leather hinges, and a voice inside cried, "Mikhail?" A woman's voice, shrill with fear or anger. He pushed the door wider and went in.

The woman lay on a resin-needle pallet near the fireplace, covered with a patched quilt. The quilt was stained with blood, but the woman seemed hale, though her face was very white against her dark hair. She had risen on one elbow and was trying to peer into his face, indistinct as it must be with the bright winter sunlight behind it. As he knelt beside her, she sank back onto the mattress. "You're not—I'm sorry, Father. For a moment I thought you were my husband."

"I'm Father Piedro. Are you all right, my daughter? Where are the others?"

"I'm Catriona. The men are on the firelines. Mhari and the others, they left yesterday. The fire was coming. But then it didn't come."

"They *left* you here?"

"I was in labor, I couldn't travel." Her eyes closed for a moment. "It hurt so much. I couldn't walk, I couldn't even stand. I *made* them go, or they would all have died with me. But the fire didn't come, and in the night I had my baby." She tugged down the edge of the quilt, and Father Piedro saw the matted dark hair and flattened face of a newborn infant. "Isn't she lovely?"

"Lovely," he agreed. To him the baby was identical to his sister's new son and as ugly as a half-drowned mudrabbit. But every child was beautiful in its mother's eyes. He tried to remember what little he had read about the care of mothers and infants. The Father Healers didn't teach midwifery. "Did you tie and cut the navel cord?"

"Yes, and burnt the afterbirth in the fire. And then we just stayed in bed. Her name is Alanna. My husband—" She broke off, her eyes wide, and outside in the road the donkey screamed. Piedro rose to his feet, his head brushing against the underside of the thatch. The smell of smoke was strong in all their nostrils. The wind had changed.

"This east wind was sent out of mercy," he said, "to let you bear your child alive. Now the fire is coming on again, and we must move quickly. Can you get up?"

"Yes, I was up this morning, getting clean linen." She rose to her knees. "I need some now. Alanna's wet, or worse." She reached for a little pile of folded fabrics: the baby's breechclouts, carefully collected out of every worn rag the settlement could find her. "But I don't think I can walk far."

"You needn't. You'll ride my donkey." He half-turned from her as she deftly cleaned the baby's tiny body and tied the new breechclout in place. It wasn't really fitting for him to watch, and yet he had always wondered how the things fastened.

He looked around the hut for anything worth salvaging, but Catriona's kinswomen had stripped the place. There was part of a bannock and a leather bottle of sour beer on the hearth, and he picked them up. They might be needed before they reached the next settlement.

"Do you have warm clothing for the baby? A fur sack? We'll be going through the snow to Maclidan Keep. Yes, and give me the rest of the clouts. No, not the soiled one, not in my saddlebags full of simples. You'd better take my arm." He lifted her to her feet and led her out of the hut into the road.

The smell of burning resin was strong now. The donkey stood trembling in the middle of the road, his ears laid back, the whites of his eyes showing, almost ready to bolt. "All right, little brother. We're getting out of here." He tucked the baby's clouts into the saddlebags, and helped Catriona to put her foot into the stirrup.

She mounted easily enough, but then rose at once in the stirrups with a shocked look on her face. "Ai! Father, it hurts to sit down."

"Then sit on one hip," he said firmly, feeling his face flush red hot. From what little he knew about the mechanics of childbearing, he could well believe the woman's bottom parts were sore, but she couldn't stay here to recuperate. "Swing your other leg over and ride side-saddle like a *Com'ynara*. That's right." He returned to the hut to get the baby, securely tucked away in a leather bag with a tiny hood for her face. The fur around the opening was shabby and the leather well-worn. Alanna could have been the dozenth or the fiftieth baby in the little settlement to have used it. As he picked her up, she opened her eyes. They were a strange blue-green, like his little nephew's eyes, but deeper: the color of thunder-clouds, or perhaps of the sea that none of them had ever seen. She wasn't really looking at him, but her eyes were dev-astating. He suddenly realized that he was in the presence of a real person, not just a kind of egg with legs, but a human being in her own right, even though small enough to hold in his arms.

"Hello," he said softly. The baby stared past his nose at whatever it was she saw. "Hello, Alanna." She sneezed, a tiny sound like an exasperated mouse, and he laughed and carried her out of the hut.

Catriona had managed to settle herself in relative comfort on the donkey's back, her quilt folded under her and her heavy cloak around her. He put the baby into her arms.

"There you are, little one." She rubbed her nose against the baby's little button and made a foolish sound like a drunken dove. Alanna gurgled. (Piedro felt like a rejected suitor.) "Isn't she lovely?" she said again.

"Beautiful," he said, meaning it this time. "In a dozen or thirteen years you'll have to keep the lads off with clubs." *What a way for a priest to talk*, he thought. He took the donkey's reins and led it up the road. The beast needed no urging at all.

He tried to calculate how much time they had. With the wind out of the northwest again, the fire would rise straight up the mountainside till it reached the timberline and starved for fuel. How long that would take depended, not only on how fast the fire could burn, but on how far down the mountain it was to begin with. He had planned to reach the little shelter at the timberline by dusk, a matter of two or three hours; but that was walking, not trotting. Not that they could run all the way up the mountain. But then, Catriona and Alanna together didn't weigh as heavily on the donkey's back as he had. He realized with a sense of frustration that he had no way of finding out ahead of time whether they would escape the fire or not.

And therefore, it clearly wasn't his problem. It was a matter for Blessed Cristoforo, Bearer of Burdens, or for the Archangel Rafael who cared for helpless children. *He has given his angels charge over thee, lest thou dash thy foot against a stone. The fire shall not consume thee by day, nor the cold by night.* All Piedro had to do was to trust in them and keep the donkey moving. He lengthened his stride a little. Soon he was singing again, his lower mind busy getting from one psalm to the next, his upper mind contemplating the Holy Archangels. Some part in between kept him on the road.

The trees thinned out; the snow grew deeper underfoot. A bowshot's length away the trees ceased altogether before a pile of snow-covered rubble at the foot of a small and dirty-looking glacier. "Praise the holy one, you his children, praise his name; from the sun's rising to its setting, praise the—" Piedro came out of his meditations, breaking in the middle of a psalm, to realize that they were almost clear of the timber and safe from the fire. But he also realized that he heard a crackling sound, not so far behind him. Something was crashing through the trees: an animal? No, it was above his head, breaking branches as it went like an impossibly huge bird— and then he tugged at the donkey's bridle, shouting "Hold on!" and pulled the frightened beast out of the path, in among the trees, five feet from the road, ten feet. Above their heads a great tree was falling, a great-grandfather of trees, dead at the roots and tinderous about the trunk, snapping branches as it fell. Little flames sprung up all round it. Piedro scrambled among the trees, dragging the terrified donkey behind him, unsure of the path but hoping that uphill was the way to safety. The light was increasing ahead of him, and for a moment he feared they were surrounded by the flames, but then he found himself stumbling through the open, the trees behind him, the fire behind him, reflecting from the snow-field.

"Are you all right, my daughter? What about the baby?" *Daughter*, he thought wildly. *She's older than I am.*

"We're all right, Father. Alanna, if you'll believe me, is still asleep."

Piedro looked over his shoulder: the fire's glare mingled with the fire of the setting sun. The trees behind were catching, but it was clear that they had escaped. A hornbuck came plunging out of the forest, its coat singed; it shied away from them and leaped away across the foot of the glacier. And snow began to fall.

First a few flakes, drifting crazily in the updrafts from the fire, till its warmth melted them into raindrops that fell sizzling into the fire. But a dark cloud was rolling overhead, and the snow fell thicker and heavier as they watched, half-melted flakes clinging together in clumps that hit the snowy ground with audible little *plops*, a fall of slush rather than of snow, wet and dirty from smoke and ash. The fire's advance slowed and faltered. The blazing twigs on the nearest tree were snuffed out one by one. The roaring of the flames died away, leaving the mountainside in silence but for the faint patter of falling slush.

"Thank you, Holy Rafael," Piedro said. "Most of this isn't even killed, and will grow back in the spring."

"Perhaps they found a *laranzu* to being the snow," Catriona said.

"Maybe," said Piedro. He didn't care to argue the relative powers of men and angels. "If they did, he's a good one. Look at it coming down! We'll never get over the ridge to Maclidan Keep tonight; we'll shelter in the cave." He led the donkey across the snow-covered rubble to the scarp of rock that marked the bottom of the pass. Here, longer ago than anyone remembered, strong men had piled three slabs of rock together to give a rudimentary shelter: a roof and two walls against the foot of the scarp. There was barely room for all of them with the donkey. As Piedro had hoped, the tree boughs that earlier travelers had cut for bedding were still there, dried now, but better to lie on than snow or rock. He put Alanna, still encased in her bag, in a bed of tree needles and helped Catriona to get off the donkey. She slid to her knees and lay down beside her daughter. Alanna began to whimper, and Catriona opened her tunic and put her to the breast. Piedro took the quilt from the saddle and spread it over them.

"Don't get settled yet," he said. He fumbled in the near darkness for the saddle girth. "If my little brother will do as he's asked, I'll make you a lovely warm pillow." He persuaded the donkey to kneel, and settled Catriona against its flank, Alanna in the crook of her arm. In one of the saddle-bags was a small bag of grain for the donkey, and he spread it out under its nose. In the other bag were Catriona's bread and beer, and—he burrowed deeper under the sweet-smelling thornleaf—a packet of his Aunt Adriana's honeycakes. He found it by smell and feel; the sun had now set and the darkness was almost absolute. "Liriel is nearly full tonight," he remarked. "When she rises over the mountains we ought to have a little light. In the meantime, we can eat." He settled down beside Catriona against the donkey's side, divided the bannock and one of the honeycakes, and set the bottle down between them.

"I don't suppose we can make a fire."

"I'm afraid not," he said. "There's nothing to burn but the litter underfoot, and I'd rather keep that between us and the rock. Nor would it last long. We'll huddle together like three little donkeys and keep warm that way."

They sat together for a time, with no sound but a faint munching—the donkey with its oats and the two adults with the scarcely softer bannock—and the damp snuffling sound of Alanna taking in her own supper.

"Mmmm," Catriona said indistinctly, her mouth full, the scent of honeycake strong in the air. "This was never baked in a monastery."

"No, I brought that from home," Piedro said. "My Aunt Adriana has a great gift. Her cooking is the only thing in the world that I really miss at St. Valentine's."

"Really?" said Catriona in a surprised voice. "I would have thought—well." Clearly she had decided not to say whatever had been on her tongue. "Why were you thanking the holy Rafael? Is he good with fires?"

"He's the patron of children," Piedro said. "It's told in the Book of Burdens that once when there was pestilence in the Dry Towns, the hold Rafael took on human shape and went to rescue two children, Tobias and Sara, who had been left orphans. They were to be sold as slaves. The Dry-Towners saw the angel as a beautiful young man, and thought to sell him for an evil purpose. But when they threw him into the compound, he picked up the two children in his arms and walked straight out of their midst unseen, and left the gates locked behind him. And he brought the children into the hills, and recovered a debt left to Tobias's father, to provide for them, and he found fostering for them, and then disappeared. And when the children grew up, they married each other."

Catriona did not answer. There was a little moonlight in the shelter now, diffused by the tumbling snowflakes, and he saw that she was asleep, curled up against the donkey's warm side, Alanna asleep in her arms. Carefully, not touching her, he pulled the folds of her tunic over her breast. He tucked the quilt securely around them, and settled down to watch the snow fall. He would do better not to sleep himself. He went back to the psalms.

But he couldn't keep his mind on his prayers. He kept turning to look at Alanna, motionless in her mother's arms. Father Colin had taught him all he knew, all that a man without *laran* could learn, but almost nothing about infants. He had the vague memory of being told they sometimes died without warning, simply stopped breathing. Catriona was snoring faintly, but he could hear no sound from Alanna at all. He touched her cheek with his fingertip; it was cold. *Well, of course it's cold,* he told himself sensibly, *it's snowing out there and not far above freezing in here.* But he bent over in near-panic just the same, and put his ear near Alanna's face till he could hear the tiny sound of her breathing. Then he sat back again, trembling with relief, and told himself he was a fool.

He really didn't know anything about children, not little children. Boys came to St. Valentine's, as he had, at the age of ten, when they were already almost reasoning beings. His brothers and sisters had been tiny like that once, but he hadn't paid any attention to them, nor to his sister's baby. Clearly he had been missing something.

He leaned along the donkey's bony back and peered over Catriona's shoulder. Alanna's tight-shut eyelids might have been carved out of translucent wax, one delicate stroke of the chisel apiece. Her mouth was shaped like a hunter's bow, a tight-strung recurve bow for a hunter the size of his thumb. Her inconsequential lower lip twitched, as if she dreamed of nursing. So very small. She had pushed one hand up to her face; her fingertips were visible through the hood opening, tipped with nails like pink flower petals. *I could never have invented those little fingers,* he thought, *not if I tried for ten thousand years. Only a god could make something as perfect as that.*

Then her face crumpled, and her mouth opened with a thin scratchy wail like an indignant kitten or a very distant banshee. She had just been fed, so he couldn't understand it. Perhaps Catriona hadn't enough milk yet? A goat's real milk didn't come in until the third day after she had kidded, but the kid didn't need it till then. If Alanna needed something more than the firstlings her mother could give her, he didn't know what he could do. Could she drink melted snow? The faint sound of her crying made it very hard to think.

"If it cries," said a woman's voice in his memory, "you feed it." His mother's voice, he thought, or possibly Aunt Adriana's. "If it isn't hungry, you bubble it. If it's wet, you change it. There's not much else it needs."

He picked her up and held her upright against his shoulder. She drew in a fresh breath and cried again. He patted her back, awkwardly, not sure where the leather sack left off and Alanna began. "I think I understand you," he said. "They're in the saddlebag, and if you don't mind smelling of thornleaf, and I can't think why you should—" he laid her down again. She hiccupped, glared at him, and continued to cry. Catriona must have been exhausted from the previous night's labor, to sleep so soundly. He found a clean breechclout in the saddlebag. It seemed fairly straightforward, with bits of cord to be tied on each side.

The leather sack was fastened by half-a-dozen bone buttons down its front. He unbuttoned them and hauled out a double handful of warm damp baby. She squirmed and twisted in his hands. Her head lolled forward on her chest, and he quickly put her down on the edge of the quilt.

The hem of her woollen gown was drawn up with a cord, enclosing her feet in a second bag. The cord was wet and difficult to get untied. Inside the gown the breechclout was sodden, and the cords even harder to untie. There ought to be some easier way of fastening the things, he reflected as he tugged and Alanna complained, considering that they would almost always be wet when the time came to untie them. Maybe they should have buttons, like the sack. He would ask Catriona about it when she woke. The knot came loose, and he tossed the wet clout outside to freeze. He might be able to dry it later, but he wasn't going to put it in his saddlebag wet if he could help it. He still hoped to get that thornleaf to Father Colin in usable condition. He turned back to Alanna and discovered that what he'd heard was true: little girls were shaped differently from little boys. How clever, how simple: a smooth shape like an almond's shell, no more. One of nature's inspired designs; though some day she would have trouble making water in the snow. He put the clean clout under her bottom and tied it around her waist.

Never to lay hand on any unwilling woman, the lower part of his mind reminded him nervously. *Never to look with lewd thought on child or pledged virgin.*

Shut up, he told it. *There's no offense here to Alanna's modesty, or mine.* He tied the gown around her feet. It was cold by now, and she started to whimper again. *If Alanna's father were here, he'd change her clouts for her, now wouldn't he?* "Come here, child. Let's keep your feet warm." He loosened his tunic and slipped her inside. He settled back with her little weight on his chest, her head tucked under his chin, and thought about Mikhail, a forester of Cormac's Station. Did the man realize his blessings? No, of course not, he had been out on the firelines since before Alanna was born. Piedro hoped he was all right. Perhaps he would be at Maclidan Keep when they got there. How delighted he would be. Sons were more important to a man in the world, of course, but surely no man could help but love such a perfect little daughter.

The donkey turned its head around and brayed, not too loudly, but Alanna jerked as if she had been struck. "Hush, little brother," said Piedro, and stretched out his free hand to scratch behind the animal's ears and pat its velvety nose. Its breath was warm on his fingers, like Alanna's on his neck. He wrapped his arms around the little bundle in his tunic, and sighed. *I am the picture of a fool,* he thought. *I have just been granted the right to be called "Father," precisely because I have vowed never, among other things, to have any children. And now look at me.*

Not that he really yearned for physical fatherhood. Or he didn't think he did. Certainly his imagination shrank from the

idea of begetting Alanna on Catriona's mysterious body. And
a man in the world had to spend most of his time working in
farm or forest, not in the home tending children; that was a
woman's job. And yet, and yet—all the work of the world
and all the holy work of the monastery, prayer and music
and reading and history and even the instruction of the no-
vices, seemed stale and drab now, on this night, with this
little child in his arms. *Peace, prattler,* he told himself. *You'll
feel much more like yourself in the morning.* And he began
to sing again, taking up where he had left off. "He raises the
weak from the dust, and the poor man from the midden, to
set him with the lords of his people." Only Father Gabriel's
ten years' patience had made even a passable singer of him,
but Alanna seemed to enjoy it. Perhaps the low notes tickled.
"He makes the barren woman to keep house, the joyful
mother of children."

"Father, I'm thirsty."

He glanced down at Catriona. The leather bottle lay between them, empty. "Here, take the baby; I'll get you some
snow." He put Alanna in her arms, tucked the quilt around
them, and went outside.

A stiff wind was blowing, but the snow had almost
stopped. The clouds were drawing back across the sky, re-
vealing Liriel's bright disk overhead and Mormallor dim and
yellow on the horizon. Piedro scooped up a double handful
of clean snow and took it inside. Catriona, bred in the mountains, knew how to take it in little sips, not throat-freezing
gulps.

"Thank you," she said at last. "Father, you sing very
nicely, but who is your song about? Does the Bearer of Burdens make it his care to provide us with lots of little burdens
of our own?"

He laughed. "I'm not sure. A lot of the old psalms don't
name names. Perhaps it's the holy Archangel Rafael again,
providing for children by giving them mothers."

"Anyway, I wasn't a barren woman. I've borne four other
children, and two of them are still alive."

"I doubt the holy poet had you specifically in mind." He
settled down beside her again. "That psalm goes back to the
beginning of time, anyway."

"Father, haven't you ever wanted to be married?"

He stared at her in astonishment. "Daughter, have *you*
ever been tested for *laran?*"

"Of course not, I'm no *Com'yn* by-blow. Doesn't it fret you, that you can never lie with a woman?"

"Not really," he said, shocked into plain speech. "I've never done it, after all. They say that the rebellion of the flesh only dies half an hour before we do—or maybe it's half an hour after. But it's hard to feel rebellious with flesh that's nine parts frozen, and by the time the novice is enough in the mold that he isn't frozen, the flesh is tamed and doesn't rebel much."

"And you never wish you'd stayed home with your family?"

He looked out of the shelter, where the growing moonlight shone on snow like new milk. "We'd better get moving. The wind's pouring in from the west and if we stay here we'll freeze, but it's blown the snow away and we can get over the ridge." He got the donkey to its feet and saddled it, while Catriona buttoned up Alanna's sack and folded her quilt. He loaded the donkey and led it out of the shelter and up the trail at a brisk pace, and in fact the wind was strong and bitter out of the west. But anything was better than staying in the shelter and continuing that conversation.

The trail wound narrowly between rock walls, mere accidental cracks where the mountain had seemed to present a solid front. Here it was dark, the moonlight never reaching the bottom of the chasms, but they were protected from the wind. But when they came out onto the cliff face, where the long trail wound down the mountainside to Maclidan Keep, the wind struck them like a giant's hand. It had shifted again toward the northwest, the true Heller Wind with snow on its breath, and either the path would keep free of snowdrifts long enough, or it wouldn't. Another matter to refer to the holy Archangel Rafael, while Piedro and the donkey concentrated on keeping their footing.

While the moonlight lasted, they made good time, Piedro's sandals shuffling over bare rock and the donkey's small hooves clicking behind. But then the light dimmed, and Piedro looking back over his shoulder saw clouds slipping across Liriel's face, and Catriona's anxious eyes beneath them.

The snow began quietly, a few big flakes drifting ahead of themselves on the wind. They struck face or sleeve or rock and fell away without clinging. Other flakes followed, smaller but just as dry, crunching like powder underfoot, as likely to be blown away from the rock as onto it. They diffused what was left of the light rather than obscuring it, so that Piedro was in effect walking in a narrow gorge again, between a dark wall of rock and a smoother wall of dim violet moonlight. But only one of them would support him if he stumbled and fell against it.

"Father, are we going to make it?" Catriona asked after the first hour's descent.

"I have every hope that we will," he said. "We're halfway down the trail already; beneath that there's only the Stair."

"Should I get down and walk?"

"No. The donkey's firmer on its feet than you are. Is the baby all right?"

"She seems to be. I've got her under my cloak and she's not too cold."

Piedro walked on without answering. The Stair at the foot of the trail, whose last steps came up against the walls of Maclidan Keep, was a collection of broken granite blocks, steeper than the trail, but with easier footing to be found. But to find it one needed light, and between the setting of Liriel and the rising of the sun there was going to be more than an hour of darkness.

His feet were actually on the Stair before the light died. He took the next three steps from memory, before the image of the rough granite vanished from his eyes in the blank white phosphorescence of the snow. After that he had to pick his way, slowly sliding his feet along each step till he found its edge, testing the drop to the next step, finally lowering his foot onto it. Twice he found no step at all below the one he stood on, and had to work his way back upward and across before trying to descend again.

The second time he stopped to catch his breath, leaning against the donkey's shaggy head. He mustn't let himself give up. If he went on working his way downward carefully enough, he would eventually fetch up against some part of Maclidan Keep's curtain walls and could make his way to the gate. Or in an hour the sun would rise. He tried not to remind himself that the wind was growing colder, cold enough perhaps to fell even a monk if he got tired enough. There was nothing to do but go on. He had neither the breath to pray aloud nor the concentration to pray in silence. He didn't know what he might ask for, anyway, nor what it might accomplish. He was walking not through snow and rock but through the wills of higher powers, and he could only acknowledge that he was in their hands and keep moving as they permitted. He led the donkey a dozen paces sideways along the shelf they stood on, and then began to descend again. And he heard a voice.

"Hey, man! Not that way!"

Piedro stood still, not believing what he heard. Footsteps, crunching through the snow, and the voice again: "There's nothing down there but a hundred-foot drop. Come on. Give us your hand." Piedro stretched out his hand, and felt it clasped: a man's broad hand, strong but smooth-skinned, like the hand of a nobleman, and warm.

"Who are you?"

"Your fellow servant. Mind this next step, it's a long one."

Piedro made a long leg to the bottom of the step, and guided the donkey down it. Catriona was a rough-textured shape, huddled in her cloak, clinging to the donkey's neck. Seeing nothing but the blank white of the snow, he followed the lifeline at the end of his arm.

The hand holding his was astonishingly warm. Only by the strength flowing back into him could he tell how close to the edge he had been. If this astonishing stranger had not materialized out of the snowstorm, he might—he didn't like to think of it. No decent monk feared death, but what would have become of Catriona and Alanna? "We live under the Rule in exceptional freedom," he remembered the Novice Master saying, "but a man in the world, with wife and family, has given hostages to fortune." He thought of Catriona and Alanna lying at the bottom of the Stair, and his heart turned over. "It's all right," said the voice out of the snow, as if he had spoken aloud. "Bear left here."

He bore left and felt the wind slacken; he had come into the lee of something high and solid. The cliff face? No, by all the angels, it was the wall of the Keep. "Twenty paces will take you to the gate," said the voice, and the warm hand let go of his.

"Thank you," Piedro called into the wind. "Who are you?" But there was no answer. He tugged at the donkey's bridle and made his way toward the gate.

The men at the gate gaped at him, appearing out of the snow in the dark before dawn, a mere sandal-wearer and alive. They led him, donkey and Catriona and all, through the great doors. The hall was packed with people, the inhabitants of a dozen villages burnt out or threatened by the fire. Most of them were asleep. The warmth of the three wide hearths felt like midsummer. Piedro unwrapped Catriona's hood from around her face, and was relieved to see her straighten up and look at him. "I'm dreaming again," she said. "I thought you were talking to somebody in the snow."

"I was," he said. He helped her slide off the donkey and make her way to the hearth. There was an old woman there, caring for some tired women and sleeping children. She put Catriona on a pallet by the fire and gve her a cup of soup. "Father, I'm fair pleased to see you," she said. "Are you a healer? We have some burns here, and some frostbites, and six or seven people all numb because they don't know what's become of their kin."

"I'm about two-thirds of a healer," he said. "Father Colin isn't finished with me yet. I'll do what I can. Have somebody get the saddlebags off my donkey."

Catriona unbuttoned Alanna's bag, to let the warmth in. "So who were you talking to?" she asked. "The holy Rafael again?"

"Perhaps I was," he said. "Whoever it was, he appeared out of nowhere and led me to the curtain wall. Probably one of the rangers belonging to the Keep."

"No road," said the old woman, giving Piedro another cup of soup. "There are none of our people out there. But they say there's a *laranzu* over the ridge at Corbie, come to bring down the snow on the fire. They can do strange things, walk in the overworld and I know not what else besides. He'll have sent his mind out to find you and bring you in; that'll be the answer."

"Maybe," said Piedro. He drank his soup, which he didn't really need. He remembered the warmth flowing out of the stranger in the snow. But he wasn't going to argue the relative merits of *laranzu'in* and. . . .

But now there was a great bellow in the air, rather like a lovesick Ya-man calling Catriona's name, and she was snatched up in the embrace of a huge black-bearded man. Mikhail, for it was obviously he, sank down onto the pallet with his wife, nuzzling his prickly face into her neck and weeping. Piedro hurried to pick Alanna up before someone sat on her.

She was awake again, looking almost at Piedro with her blue-green eyes. "Your father, my dear," he told her. "I'll make you acquainted later." He found a spare foot of hearth-ledge and sat down.

There were two older children sitting at his feet; they had waked at the sound of Mikhail's enthusiasm. There was a little girl of about five, who was crying, and a boy of about nine, who was trying to comfort her. They both had a look of Catriona. Finally the boy took his sister over to where their parents still sat embraced on the pallet, and helped her to climb into Catriona's lap. Then he came back to Piedro.

"I'm Brion, Mikhail's son," he said. "Thank you, Father, for taking care of Mama."

"I was happy to," he said. "This is your new sister, Alanna."

Brion gave her a brief glance. "I already have a sister. Oh, well."

"How old are you, Brion?"

"Eight. But I passed for ten today, on the firelines." He held up his arm, showing Piedro a nasty burn on the back of his hand and forearm.

"You shouldn't have done that. Even though you're big for your age. Let me get something on that burn."

"It doesn't hurt much."

"If you're going to do a man's work, you need to obey like a man and do what your healer tells you. Ah, thank you, daughter." The old woman had brought his saddlebags. (*And this "daughter" is old enough to be my grandmother*, he thought, *and what do I care? The holy Rafael brought me out of the storm!*) "Let me dress this burn and then I'll go to the other ones. Brion, what's your sister's name? The other one."

"Marguerida."

"Marguerida, would you like to hold your baby sister?" He settled Marguerida beside her mother on the pallet and put Alanna on her lap.

The little girl smiled like an enchantress. "Oh! The baby's *cu-u-u-ute.*"

"Quite right," he said, and went back to Brion. He found the kit of salves and bandages at the bottom of the saddlebags, and dressed the boy's arm. "Keep that clear and I'll look at it again in a few days if I'm still here." The sun was rising at last over the Hellers, light pouring down onto the slopes below Maclidan Keep: a valley and a hill and a valley, and then the great ascent to Nevarsin.

"This way, Father, if you're ready." He followed the old woman across the hall to where a man lay moaning with a burn all down one side of his body.

"Father, make it stop."

"Gently, my son. This will numb the pain."

Father Piedro knelt to his work, hardly thinking now of his encounter in the snow, though he would have to tell Father Master about it later. His sons and daughters needed his care. *Many are the children*—the line went through his head. *Many are the children of the barren, more than of her that hath a husband.* He would have to rephrase it.

"Daughter, I'm going to need sterile water. Do you understand me? Boil water and cover it and let it cool."

Many are the children of the vowed, he thought, *more than of him that hath a wife.* No, that wasn't right. It needed a disyllable in the first line. He would think of one. He would have time.

In the Days of the Comyn

The most familiar period of Darkovan history—at least, to me—is that in which the Seven Domains were ruled by the Comyn Council in Thendara. Several of our contributors have laid their stories in this familiar time.

One of the things I looked for in contributions to this volume was originality—an unexpected use of laran, *perhaps. In "Cold Hall," Aly Parsons shows us a new and different, but altogether high-minded and moral, use of* laran *powers . . . or is it? Midwinter Festival is a typical time of license in the mountains; only this one was different. . . .*

In general we receive more stories about the Free Amazons than any other subject—in fact, we get more Free Amazon stories than all other stories combined. Unless the stories have something different or unusual about them, they seem to be very much of a dreary sameness. Lynne Holdom, however, in "The Way of a Wolf," shows a Free Amazon in an alliance as original in its way as the very different Susan Shwartz story in an earlier section of this volume.

In the first of these volumes, The Keeper's Price, *the title story dealt with Hilary of Arilinn, a young Keeper forced inexorably, by poor health, to leave the Tower where she has made a life for herself. But what can lie ahead for a failed Keeper? In "The Lesson of the Inn," I have tried to carry on Hilary's story, and describe what happened to her on the inevitable day when she faced the wreckage of her life.*

And with a complete change of mood, Phillip

*Wayne, in "Confidence," tells a brief but grip-
ping tale of a Tower-trained youth whose confidence—and very survival—are severely tried
when he is attacked and captured by mysterious
enemies.*

THE WAY OF A WOLF

by Lynn Holdom

The rain was starting to turn to sleet when Liane n'ha Janella's horse threw a shoe. She cursed aloud, using all the oaths she had learned during her time on the Windriver Campaign. She hadn't wanted to cross the lands of the Leyniers and Lanarts at all, much less alone, since before she had joined the Sisterhood, she had been a *nedestro* of Serrais. It was the soldiers and *laranzu'in* of Serrais that had caused the devastation so evident all around her. Still there was peace of sorts now and she did wear the white sash of a neutral messenger. The urgency of her message alone forced her to travel through lands she privately considered "enemy territory," even though she personally had never fought here on any side.

At the moment she had to consider her horse. Smoke rose between the stunted trees over to the west. Where there was a village, there was, with any luck, an inn and a smithy. Her Serrais heritage was not evident in her looks. Her short-cropped hair was deep brown rather than the blond or red-gold typical of Serrais—or Ridenow as it was now coming to be called.

Wet snow was beginning to stick when Liane arrived at the village. This made the uneven cobblestones even more slippery and her horse stopped to nibble at a few tufts of grass peeking bravely through the snow. A wind was rising and rakishly angled shutters were banging and clattering. Almost half of the houses surrounding this end of the square were dark with smokeless chimneys while some obviously inhabited houses sported broken windowpanes.

The pump handle was broken as well. Liane sighed. She pulled her heavy red cloak more tightly around her and walked, head bent, to the far end of the square. There was an inn there with an attached stable, and, Avarra be thanked, a smithy.

Getting food and water for the two of them was Liane's first priority. She walked into the inn. A thin, dour, dark man stood behind a long table in the entranceway. "I would like a room for the night and stable room for my horse who also needs a new shoe," she said politely.

The man looked her up and down in a way she didn't like but had become accustomed to. "We don't serve your kind here. Come to steal the few children we've got remaining?"

Liane was astounded but knew it would be fatal to lose her temper. "I just want shelter for the night, a hot meal and the same for my horse," she said evenly. "I'll be leaving in the morning."

The man looked as if he wanted to spit. "Leaving with our daughters, no doubt. We know you *bre'suin* well." He walked over to the swinging door that led to the tavern. "Rory, Cathal, Mikhail. There's another of these unnatural women come to call. Show her what we do to her sort in High Pines Forst."

Before Liane could leave or even draw her dagger, several men—more than the three called—came into the entranceway and dragged her out into the snow.

"This'll pay for Camilla," one of the men shouted. He threw a snowball well mixed with pebbles which hit Liane in the shoulder. Soon snowballs, rocks and other debris were in the air. Liane, with all her training, was helpless against such an attack. She was being hit hard repeatedly. She slipped and fell to the snow-covered cobbles. "Merciful Avarra," she said softly. "Did I come to this forest to die?" Her urgent message would not get to Arilinn after all.

"Stop!" A voice range out across the square. "Is this a pack of wolves come down from the Hellers to feed I see before me?" The crowd parted. Someone dressed in blue knelt beside Liane, putting a rolled up cloak under her head.

"*Dom* Gervase," one of the men said. "She's the one took Camilla away to her death come back to steal another child. We're dealing with her so's she'll never do that again."

Dom Gervase's deep blue eyes looked steadily into Liane's. Then he stood up and turned to the crowd. "Do you know she is the one responsible for Camilla's death? She has admitted it?"

"You know no one'd admit to something like that," a man said testily. "But she's wearing the same clothes she did before."

"I see," *Dom* Gervase said. He looked down at Liane. "And you, what do you say?"

"I have never been in this forst before, or even in this area. All I want is shelter for myself and my horse before traveling on to Arilinn. I would never harm a child. I am a soldier, not a butcher."

"Is there a difference?" *Dom* Gervais said softly. Then he beckoned to one of the men. "Cathal, take the horse to the stable. Whatever the truth of this—and I suggest we send to Neskaya for a *laranzu* to find that truth—the horse is not guilty of any crime. As for the rest, it is cold and it is snowing. Get to your homes before you freeze. I will act as surety for the woman provided she gives me her oath not to try to escape." He knelt beside Liane again. "Better do so," he whispered, "or your life will be over. I could not hold them back. No one could."

Liane was no fool. She gave her oath. So there was a life between them. But how, the thought came quickly, would she ever get her message to Arilinn on time?

Dom Gervase lived in a sturdy stone house down a close in back of the inn. Liane was escorted into a large cheerful whitewashed room dominated by an enormous fireplace. It evidently served as both kitchen and living quarters. "Through there," *Dom* Gervase said, pointing to a heavy panelled door, "is the room where I usually see my patients. However, we'll stay in here where it's warmer as you've been soaked through." With that he sat Liane down on a straight-backed wooden chair near the fire where the contents of a huge metal kettle gave off a tantalizing odor. Liane realized that she was starved.

Dom Gervase followed her glance. "I normally have a woman here to help me but she's off attending her daughter who's dying, as she was in Aetheling Wood right after the Altons dropped that oily abomination on it. Now she's coughing up blood like all the others. So you'll have to make do with my cooking. We'll eat right after I make sure your ankle's only sprained, not broken." With that he looked into his ring—it was a starstone, Liane realized suddenly—and ran his hands over her body, not quite touching her clothing. "Nothing broken. I'll bind your ankle. Then all you need is a hot bath and some rest. You were lucky."

"Thanks to you." Then Liane remembered the accusation against her. "Just who was Camilla and how did she die?"

Dom Gervase spooned some stew from the kettle onto two plates. "Camilla was the innkeeper's daughter. She used to help out there. Everybody liked her. One day a woman of your Sisterhood came to town. When she left the next day, Camilla disappeared as well. Later Camilla was found dead and the body mutilated." *Dom* Gervase tasted the stew. "Not bad but it needs more salt. Now where was I? Oh yes, with you they apparently mistook the uniform for the person. The *laranzu* will discover the truth and you will be free to go on your way."

"But my mission to Arilinn is urgent. I can't wait a tenday for a *laranzu* to come from Neskaya."

Dom Gervase ate silently for a long time. Then he sighed. "With this snow you cannot go anywhere tonight. In any case you need sleep." After the meal he showed her to a small room behind the chimney. "This is the lying-in room and quite the warmest room in the house. You can sleep soundly. The door latches from the inside."

Liane felt a great sense of relief. *Dom* Gervase did not seem the sort of man who would rape, but past experience had taught her to be wary of even the kindest seeming man. Yet *Dom* Gervase was a puzzle in other ways. What was someone of noble birth—that was obvious in his speech and bearing—doing living in this half-deserted forst without even a servant? And even more puzzling, she realized suddenly, was the fact that he spoke the pure Casta of the Plains of Valeron.

By the time she awakened, *Dom* Gervase had porridge ready along with mugs of the sour ale that Liane didn't like but had become accustomed to as it was standard soldiers' fare. The sun shone across the oak-beamed table. A hungry Liane sat down eagerly.

"A messenger has gone off to Neskaya," *Dom* Gervase said as he spooned porridge into the earthenware bowl. "If the weather stays fair, you should be on your way in six or seven days."

"That's far too long. Couldn't you send to Arilinn for a *laranzu*? It's closer."

Dom Gervase sat down across from her. "You would honestly expect a *laranzu* from that Serrais-controlled Tower to be trusted by the people here? The *laranzu'in* are responsible for the devastation and death in this area. It was difficult enough to get them to trust any *laranzu,* even one of

Neskaya. Even that was only possible because the Keeper at Neskaya, Varzil, has pledged that Neskaya will produce no weapons of war."

Liane couldn't see the objection. In her experience a former foe often became an ally in the next campaign. "Still . . ." she began.

"Still, I do not expect *you* to be horrified by weapons of war or the past policies of Serrais. After all, you deal in war and sell your services to the highest bidder. You do not even have the feeble, but very human, excuse of fighting to protect your home and kinfolk, which if I'm not mistaken would be those of Serrais," *Dom* Gervase finished for her.

Liane had had enough of *Dom* Gervase's slurs. "What would you have me do? Stay at home to be the plaything of Lord Serrais's sons whether I would or no—just as my mother was? Then have those same sons refuse to call a child even *nedestro* because they could not be sure of whose siring she was? No!" she said banging her right hand on the table so hard that the dishes clattered. "I decided I would have some say in my life, not be a prize for jeweled dandies to fight over." She looked him right in the eye, "But then you were a nobleman yourself so you wouldn't see anything wrong in that now, would you?"

She waited for the explosion but *Dom* Gervase was a long while before speaking. "I see," he said so softly Liane was not sure he had spoken at all. Then *Dom* Gervase took a couple of swallows of ale and continued. "All you are saying is that in a world of wolves and sheep, it is better to be a wolf. I could argue the point but. . . . However, you forget that when the sheep are gone, the wolves turn on each other to slash and tear."

"Damn right, I'd rather be a wolf," Liane said angrily. "No one would be a sheep by choice. Only a simpering coward or a fool is unwilling to fight for what he wants."

"As Lord Serrais's sons took what they wanted?" *Dom* Gervase said softly. "Yet the herding dog, the best protector of sheep, was once a wolf."

Liane suddenly remembered something. "We could easily end this farce," she said, getting to her feet. "You are a *laranzu* yourself and could testify to the truth of what I say. Or have you some reason of your own to keep me from reaching Arilinn?" Liane said angrily.

Dom Gervase ignored the second accusation. "I, a *laranzu?* Whatever gave you that impression?"

"The stone in your ring. It is a sorcerer's stone, is it not?"

"Oh." *Dom* Gervase lifted his right hand and looked at the ring as if seeing it for the first time. "Yes, I have a matrix— that is its proper name—and did learn something of its use at Dalereuth Tower when I first came to manhood. I know my limitations, however; I cannot set truthspell. My talent is healing. Had I been a woman, I would have gone to the Holy Isle. As I am a man, I studied among the monks at Nevarsin. It was very peaceful there," he stared into space remembering . . . "I would have stayed there except that I am not a *cristoforo* and I had set myself a task."

"What task?"

Dom Gervase refused to be drawn any further. "I have to attend a woman at her lying-in. There is no midwife to do so. I leave you here alone in the trust that your soldierly honor will keep you from breaking your oath to me. Oh, and you might clear off the table and wash up, if your soldierly pride allows it." With that he walked out the door.

Liane did as he asked then prowled the room like a pent animal, considering her situation. True, she had given her oath and there was a life between her and Dom Gervase. But wasn't her oath to the Sisterhood just as important? They were counting on her to get to Arilinn. Why couldn't Dom Gervase see that? Probably because, despite his noble birth, he was a coward who hid out at Nevarsin studying healing rather than learning the martial arts customary for one of his caste. He had even wanted to go to the Holy Isle! While Liane did not deny that the women on the Holy Isle did important work, a strong woman would learn to protect herself and fight her own battles, not sit back and depend on Avarra to do so. The Gods helped those who helped themselves, as the old proverb went. So what was an oath to such a one as *Dom* Gervase worth? As much or more than the oath of loyalty to the Sisterhood? Probably, almost certainly, not. Yet she could not take any oath lightly. She trembled at the thought of it. She still had one more day before she had to leave in order to get to Arilinn before it mattered, so she would just have to use the time to get *Dom* Gervase to release her. After that . . . well she'd see.

All afternoon Liane sat and watched as a motley crew of the sick from the surrounding area paraded in and out. There were old women with rheumy eyes; old men too bent and crippled to work; worn looking young mothers who snatched their deformed children away when Liane would have come over to speak to them. Deformity—that was the thing that struck Liane the hardest. Weren't there any healthy children? *Dom* Gervase was especially attentive to a small redheaded boy, probably the *nedestro* son of some petty mountain lordling. He looked normal except for a harelip. At least he could run and play, which was more than most of the other children were able to do.

"Why all the deformity?" *Dom* Gervase said in answer to Liane's query as they sat and relaxed after the evening chores were done. "I don't know. There were so many things done in the battling here that it's hard to know what to blame. All anyone can do is hope that some people will remain healthy and outlast it. Now you begin to see why I hate war and soldiers. I have had to deal with too many of their leavings."

"That's not honest war," Liane said. "It's one thing to fight with swords and knives but this. . . . Give me a sword as a weapon. In such a battle both parties are in equal danger of death. Only cowards fight otherwise." Even as she spoke the words, Liane regretted them. This was not the way to win release from her oath.

"But are both parties in equal danger?" *Dom* Gervase asked gravely. "If you and I were to battle with swords, I can assure you that I would be in the greater danger."

But that would not be so if you had the interests and training normal to one of your birth, Liane thought angrily. The man was actually parading his lack of honor before her. Then she quickly checked her annoyance lest *Dom* Gervase have the socerer's power to read thoughts. However she believed him when he said he was not truly gifted that way, for all the sorcerers Liane had ever heard of were redheaded, while *Dom* Gervase's hair was the black of a moonless night. Still, it did not do to take chances.

"Can't you see any virtue in soldiering at all? Doesn't it pain you to know that people will die if I do not get my message to Arilinn?"

"All death pains me," *Dom* Gervase said softly. "But lack of trust is what makes men fearful and ready to kill. No one will risk going unarmed lest he be killed. And how can you trust anyone who would break an oath?"

Liane could not answer that. She just stared into the fire. She agreed with *Dom* Gervase but she owed her allegiance to something higher in this case. Her oath to the Sisterhood came first. She would leave for Arilinn in the morning.

Even after years of campaigning, Liane found it difficult to awaken in the gray pre-dawn and dress silently without a fire. There was something eerie and threatening about the most innocent places in the half-light. This time the feeling was intensified because Liane felt she was doing something wrong in leaving. The only thing that would have made her feel worse was staying and letting people die for want of her message. Luckily this was not farming country where pre-dawn rising was the rule. Here honest folk would still be in their beds. *Dom* Gervase was still asleep; at least the door to his chamber was shut. (Her one fear had been that someone would call for a healer in the night.) She managed to leave the house without any problems and slowly made her way to the stable through the deserted streets. She just hoped that her luck would hold and she would find no one keeping guard in the stable.

As she had hoped, so it proved. The stable was deserted except for three horses, one of which was hers while the other two seemed about to expire from extreme old age. Good. No one would be able to follow her—not on those horses.

By the time the sun was clear of the horizon, Liane was well away from the forst, climbing the steep winding trail toward Cluthra Pass, which, in theory, separated the lands of the Lanarts from those of the Ridenows. Liane fumed inwardly. She had a nagging sense of discomfort—her whole escape had been much too easy—that she knew would not leave her until she left the Lanart lands. Unfortunately the nature of the trail prevented her from traveling with any speed, while thick stands of fir and overhanging rocks prevented her from seeing any distance. It was an excellent spot for ambush. But if her luck held, she would be through the pass by noon.

As she was negotiating a difficult spot where the trail narrowed and the ground dropped sharply, Liane heard a high piercing shriek. The horse reared, almost dislodging her. Liane held on and spoke softly to calm him. She did not want either of them to tumble to the valley far below. Then the cry came again. And again. At first Liane had thought it was a banshee bird but then realized with horror that it was human—that of a woman or child.

She walked the horse to a wider spot where she could tie it to a tree. Then, knife in hand, she headed uphill through the trees toward the source of the cry. Urgent message or not, she could not ignore this. For a moment she had felt the sharp pain of a stabbing in her groin. Suddenly the trees thinned. There in a clearing was a small redheaded child being attacked by a snarling wolf. As Liane rushed to the child's aid, she saw that it was not a wolf that she faced but an extremely dirty and unkempt man.

"Stop!" she cried sharply. The man turned toward her. Liane felt a wave of madness engulf her. Then it was gone and light flashed on steel. The man had a knife! "Run, child! Go home!" The boy's clothing was tattered and bloody. There was blood all around on the ground and there were bright red spatters on the dirty snow which still remained in sheltered spots.

"Stay out of this, bitch." The man's speech was slurred. Was he drunk? He turned back to the boy, who had not moved. Why not? Was he too frightened, or too weak? Again the light flashed. The boy screamed.

Liane walked across the clearing. "Let the boy alone." The man turned angrily toward her and again Liane felt a wave of madness, this time combined with lust. She fought to stay calm. If she did not, she could easily die here.

"I told you to stay out of this, bitch." The man's eyes were wild. "Now you die along with the boy. Only one proper place for a dagger when dealing with a bitch." He laughed insanely at his own wit. The hills echoed with it. He turned to Liane and again sunlight flashed.

Liane had no trouble blocking the man's downward thrust, for he was not really skilled at knife fighting. What amazed her was the brute strength behind the blow which momentarily numbed her arm. He was much stronger than any man she had fought before. But then madmen often were exceedingly strong.

It soon become clear that the man's strategy was to wear her down rather than to make a quick kill. It might just succeed. He knew his limitations. While he was not skilled in attack, he was cunning enough to prevent Liane from making any hits, as his reach was longer than hers. He seemed to

know instinctively just how close he could come to Liane
without danger to himself. What he was doing was working
himself into the frenzy of a rabid dog. He was certainly sali-
vating like one.

The two circled again and again in the clearing. Out of the
corner of her eye, Liane noticed the boy still had made no
move to get away. Why not? Merciful Avarra, she was buying
him the time to do just that. However Liane could not concern herself with the boy. It was all she could do to keep herself alive.

"Die, bitch, die," the man said over and over again as if it
were some sort of ritualistic chant. He came closer and closer
but not so close that Liane could get a solid hit. "But before
you die, bitch," he said in that strangely slurred speech of his,
"gotta stick it up your. . . ." he finished with the most obscene of soldiers' slang. They continued their deadly circling
dance.

Suddenly the frenzied man's eyes went blank. He fell forward, knocking Liane to the ground. She got quickly to her
feet to resume the attack. However, there was no need for
that. The man was dead. An arrow protruded from the base
of his skull.

Liane jumped behind a rock. Then she remembered the
boy. "Come here," she called. As he moved to obey she
grabbed his arm and pulled him roughly to the ground. He
started screaming again. Liane tried to soothe him as she
looked around. The archer must be in the trees farther up the
mountain. There was no telling who his intended victim had
been.

Then the trees parted and a man carrying a crossbow
started downhill toward her. It was *Dom* Gervase! She
watched as he walked slowly to where the dead man lay.
"There is no need to hide from me, Liane. I would not harm
you. I would never have harmed Cathal except. . . ." He
stood silently beside the body, then knelt down and put his
fingers to the arrow shaft and quickly pulled them away as if
burned. For a brief moment Liane was one with *Dom* Gervase and felt all the emptiness, grief, and horror that so
overwhelmed him that he walked quickly to the side of the
clearing and was sick. He would have to live with his guilt
the rest of his life.

"I didn't know you could shoot like that, *Dom* Gervase,"
the boy said. He tried to rise but fell back to the ground.

"He's lost a lot of blood," Liane said, somewhat unnecessarily, considering the bloodiness of the boy's tattered clothing, not to mention the bloodstains on the ground. "He has a deep wound in his groin," she added, knowing this but unable to explain just how she knew.

Dom Gervase hurried over. He took off his cloak and laid the boy on it. "I hoped I would be in time to save Domenic. Right now we have to stop the bleeding."

Liane had seen the aftermath of too many battles to misunderstand. The two worked silently together. "I think it's stopped for now," she said finally.

The healer nodded. Only then did he answer Liane's unspoken question. "Once, in what now seems like another life, I was a master archer in the army of Lady Aillard, a kinswoman of mine. I still retain my skill though I do get some practice every so often killing small game for the stewpot. Did you think I would condemn something without knowing it?"

Liane was silent. She was too busy rearranging all her ideas about this man.

"You were to have been blamed for Domenic's death just as another of your Sisterhood was blamed for Camilla's," *Dom* Gervase's voice broke into Liane's thoughts.

"And you knew who the real murderer was all along," Liane said, some of her old anger returning. "You kept me in the forst on a pretext!"

"I *suspected*, I did not *know*." *Dom* Gervase's voice was firm. "The *laranzu* was needed to uncover the truth. If, as I strongly suspected," he caught her eye and grinned, "you left before his arrival, the stableman would be forced to act." *Dom* Gervase looked off into space. "As he was."

Then he looked down at the boy lying on the ground. He turned to Liane. "Your horse is nearby, I hope?"

"Downslope."

"Then you will help me get Domenic back to the forst where I can attend to him more thoroughly? Surely you can delay your trip to Arilinn that much more, considering that you cared enough to come to his rescue in the first place?"

Liane could hardly refuse, nor did she really want to.

Together the two of them got the boy back to *Dom* Gervase's snug house in the forst. There Liane was further delayed as she attempted to reassure an almost hysterical woman that her son was going to be just fine thanks to *Dom*

Gervase's excellent care. "You are fortunate to have him here," she concluded.

"I know, I know." The distraught woman wrung her hands. "That man is very special, one touched by Avarra, for greatness. Why Lord Lanart in the next valley was the man who ordered the destruction of *Dom* Gervase's town and murdered all his kin, and does *Dom* Gervase come here bringing destruction? No, he comes as a healer. He is special, I tell you. The chosen of Avarra, for certain. Oh, I do hope Domenic will be all right," she said as the door opened and Dom Gervase entered the common room.

"He'll be fine," said *Dom* Gervase sympathetically. "Why don't you go in and see him now. Just remember he's very weak from loss of blood."

The woman left. Liane was glad to be rid of her babbling. She looked questioningly at *Dom* Gervase, who was wiping his hands on a damp cloth.

"I did not intend you to learn that," he said finally.

"But why?" It made no sense.

"The chain of hatred must be broken somewhere." The sunlit room disappeared and Liane was in a darkness roiled by the waves of madness and rage that possessed a man at the death of his town, his kin, and especially his small son. The laughter of the frenzied stableman rang out. All these ebbed slowly, giving way before the solitude, meditation and discipline found in a cheerless monk's cell. Only when the last remnants were completely purged, had *Dom* Gervase discovered his talent for healing.

Then her thoughts went to her unknown father who had been too proud to acknowledge the child he could not be sure he sired; to the joyless home of her girlhood, where her mother had broken under the blame accorded her for her own rape and the daughter was blamed for her very existence and every crumb begrudged her. And what of the Sisterhood? What had she found there? A rough camaraderie but no one whom she would miss or who would grieve at her death. She found herself shivering despite the warmth of the room.

"I must go to Arilinn," she said when she had calmed herself. "I owe that to the Sisterhood. But I will be back. That I promise. I will even give my oath on that—for what it's worth." She tried, unsuccessfully, to force a laugh.

Dom Gervase walked with her to where she had left the horse. "It will not be easy, you know," he said as he held the reigns while she mounted. "Your Sisterhood will call you coward, or traitor, or worse." He smiled grimly. "Welcome to the life of a herding dog."

"I would still rather be a wolf," Laine called as she waved and rode away. "But the world goes as it will and none of us truly has any choice. Not in these days." She headed for the mountain trail. She was in a hurry to reach Arilinn. The sooner she got there, the sooner she would return. With luck, she would be through Cluthra Pass and well into Serrais territory by sunset.

COLD HALL

by Aly Parsons

Fredrik Ardais surveyed the Great Hall sourly, thinking that for a Festival the night seemed overlong. The older folk had long since withdrawn with the children, tactfully leaving the young adults to pleasure themselves without undue chaperonage. Perhaps, he mused, the musicians were at fault. There had been a superfluity of ring-dances, while dances for couples had been far too rare.

Seeing Colryn look around, Fredrik took two quick steps forward to paxman's position by his lord and cousin. Colryn Ardais grinned at him quizzically. "Why such close attendance during Festival in our own hall? The City Guard hasn't trained you to be social? I thought you'd have found a distant cousin to get close to."

And you," retorted Fredrik, "should be properly retired with your lady by now."

"Ah, I'm not yet tired," returned Colryn absently, then raised an eyebrow at Fredrik, whose unguarded thought ran, *And she has quite exhausted herself.* Colryn glanced at the wilted, panting Lira as she left a ring of women and dropped heavily onto a low-cushioned bench.

Fredrik had been favorably impressed by Lira when she welcomed him to Castle Ardais two days before, but now, in light contact wth Colryn, his judgment was tempered by Colryn's perceptions.

Lira was leaning indelicately against the wall. Her auburn hair was escaping its green-jeweled pins and untidy strands were plastered to her neck. Her dark green gown was low-cut to the extreme and the fine neck chain that disappeared into what bodice there was made the gown seem flauntingly immodest.

With an impatient shrug, Colryn turned away. Fredrik's own brow rose. Cautiously barricading his thoughts, he reflected, *Despite his father's poor health, Colryn seems to have*

158

no care for doing his duty and getting himself an heir. His marriage must be as dull as this party.

Keeping pace behind and to the left of Colryn, Fredrik had to consciously relax. The throb of his starstone against his chest was finally quieting, but it had been intruding too much upon him this night.

Fredrik and Colryn reached the refreshment table in time to see a serving bowl upended and wine forcefully dumped on the head of a guest. Colryn grabbed the victim's arm as he sputtered in surprise and rage and tried to strike his offender. Fredrik pulled the culprit back out of range, saying, "Auster, how could you?"

The drenched man muttered, "Six-fathered whoreson! Honor thy fathers, don't deny 'em. That's what I say."

Colryn reproved mildly, "Speak softly of my father's sister in this house, kinsman."

The man shook his head confusedly. "I speak ill of no lady—I speak only to this whoreson."

Auster muffled a yawn, then remarked offhandedly, "He'd been talking that way for long enough—I thought it time he became as sodden on the outside as he is on the inside."

"Filthy six-fathered . . ." the man numbled after Auster as the boy moved down the table to a plate of honeycakes. Auster tossed his head, setting his lank fiery hair swinging carelessly.

Colryn motioned to a guard and politely requested that he accompany the drenched man to a guest chamber and see he was attended to, diplomatically avoiding ordering his guard or censuring his guest on Festival night. He wrung the pale wine from his sleeves as he and Fredrik gazed after Auster, who seemed to be eating his way down the table. Fredrik remarked, "His use of wine as a weapon shows considerable restraint. He accepts common talk easily enough."

Auster, a table-length away, turned and swallowed a last bite of nutcake. His chin lifted and his eyes glinted. "Common talk from common folk is not hard to ignore. Especially when there is no choice!" He flung this last phrase bitterly at Colryn; then smiled sweetly at Fredrik, made a courtly bow, as of leavetaking, to both of them, and strolled up to the next table.

Fredrik shivered slightly. "He is not yet reconciled to the denial of his request to go to Nevarsin."

Colryn scooped up a honeycake Auster had overlooked.

"Father thinks his work here is more important than sending him to the monastery to escape the scandal of his mother's shame. After his last fight, Father ordered him to bear himself with dignity and quit trying to battle flapping tongues with fists." Colryn chuckled. "If Father hears of tonight's wine bath, I'll wager he'll be most amused at Auster's manner of preserving his dignity at the expense of the drunk's—who had not much dignity to lose anyway!"

Seeing Auster pick up a wedge of crumbly cheese and reach for a slice of nutbread to place it on, Colryn added, "Father might gladly have packed him off to Nevarsin if he had known the boy would eat his weight in food each day!"

Fredrik saw that Lira's childhood *breda*, Camilla, had joined her, and the two were evidently sharing some joke, their heads together, their shoulders shaking. Fredrik, his eyes on the dark beauty at Lira's side, cocked his head at Colryn and suggested, "Shall we beg a suitable tune from the musicians and snare some partners?"

Colryn asked, with strange concern, "Am I still presentable?"

Fredrik was startled into looking his cousin up and down appraisingly. With a straight face he answered, "Why, if I were your lady I'd dance my way into the closest dark gallery with you."

A faint flush appeared in Colryn's cheeks. "You dance in your gallery and I'll dance in mine." He stepped to the musicians' screen and rapped out a common dance rhythm. Fredrik looked on with disfavor. At the great balls in Thendara it added a touch of luxury to have the best musicians in the seven Domains discreetly out of sight; here in the Hellers he thought it affected and offensive to hide the local talent—besides, he enjoyed watching musicians play.

Colryn set out across the hall, following a drunkard's path to avoid the dancers, and Fredrik mock-danced behind him, leading an invisible partner. Halfway across the dance floor he caught Camilla watching him, laughing at his antics. Fredrik found himself hoping that his boredom was ended and the party saved for him. He whirled himself and his imaginary companion around several times, while managing to keep his eyes and grin brazenly focused on Camilla. Then he sprang to catch up with Colryn, reaching his side just as he stopped before the two young women.

Suddenly, Fredrik gasped and spun around to face the

dance floor, his body half crouched and his dagger near drawn. His skin was prickling as his eyes raked the oblivious crowd, searching for the source of the attack that had come——or, he questioned himself, was an attack imminent?

Alerted by his motion, Colryn had turned a bare moment after Fredrik. Colryn, his eyes narrowed, scanned the crowd. "What is it, cousin?" he demanded.

Fredrik, his sensitivity increased, felt a wave of amazed derision from Camilla and impatience from Lira. He knew his tension and confusion must be evident to Colryn, but nothing seemed to be amiss. Uneasy, yet embarrassed, Fredrik resheathed his dagger and half turned, too wary to turn his back on possible danger.

Lira wrinkled her nose and asked, "Have you been drinking all night, Colryn, that you reek so of wine?"

Over the beginnings of Colryn's protests, Camilla mocked, "If so, he has had a close companion. One who prefers his women invisible and knifes them if they are too forward! Or is it that you cast a glamour to make any woman willing, and have not learned the trick of removing the spell?"

Her tone added to Fredrik's discomfiture and several ripostes flashed through his mind. But neither bawdiness, defensive outrage, nor explanations seemed appropriate, so he merely grinned. Colryn, who had caught some of those thoughts, began to chuckle.

Looking from one man to the other, Lira's eyes filled with angry tears. Camilla glanced swiftly at her, and then rose to her feet, clasping Lira's hand and drawing her up too. Camilla looked past Fredrik and she said, "Come, my lady. We have left your guests too long."

Fredrik did not block their way. He was not sure if he imagined or heard the thought passing between the two: *Let us leave these boors.*

Colryn sank down in the spot his wife had vacated and rested his chin on his hand. He glanced up beseechingly at Fredrik and asked, "What did we do?" His anguish was clear to Fredrik. *Married a halfyear—we liked each other the few times we met before we married, but we have been strangers since. Even desire to live together is quenched by our squabbles. . . .*

Fredrik ached with his friend's misery, but he was too tense and restless to sit down. "Colryn . . ." he temporized. He was concerned about Colryn's problems but he *could not* turn his mind to them now. He swung around and surveyed the room again.

Colryn touched his shoulder and he jumped. Then, rudely grasping Colryn's arm, he marched him along the wall and into a small alcove. Fredrik stopped with his back to the side wall of the alcove and let out a deep breath. Colryn stared at him. "*Bredu,* what is the matter?"

Fredrik shook his head. "I felt as though the Compact were broken and archers at the ready were hiding in the balconies—all aiming at you—at us! Of course I know that such cowards' weapons are not truly here, but something. . . ."

With a shock of dismay he found that his left hand was already tugging at the cord around his neck, pulling the small leather pouch out from concealment beneath this shirt. He felt cold panic rising as he turned to face the hall. Then his emotions dissolved and he felt himself an onlooker, calmly gazing over a stranger's shoulder as that stranger—*with my own hands*—opened the drawstring and carefully prodded the insulating silk within to move it aside. Tilting the pouch, he slid the matrix crystal into his cupped hand. As he looked down into the depths of the stone, he knew the lights within it were already pulsing in time with his own inner rhythms. He merged with the stranger, feeling the calmness he brought back spreading throughout his body.

His awareness expanded to encompass the living presences about him. He knew that Colryn, mildly curious, was watching him, but with thoughts centered on Lira. Where wine had flowed too freely in the hall, some halfhearted fights were starting. Elsewhere, minor disagreements were being masked by icy politeness. A concentrated busyness, startling at this hour, he quickly identified as the cooks and kitchen servants. For all the energy of the dancing, a queer lassitude seemed to be affecting the party crowd.

A wave of hostility swelled and he turned his face to its source. Three men dressed in the crimson and gray of Ardais were heading toward him. He realized that in the blue light from the matrix, he was clearly visible despite the dimness of the alcove. The guards' suspicion and fear hammered at him and he hastily insulated the blue jewel and thrust it back into concealment.

"What are you doing there?" the leading guard asked harshly. "What sorcerer's tricks are you working on the guests of the lord Ardais?"

Fredrik felt Colryn move to his side and felt safe in ignoring the guard's challenge while he attempted to consolidate his impressions. There had been something odd. . . .

Colryn spoke authoritatively, drawing the full attention of the guards to himself and distracting Fredrik. "*Dom* Fredrik is my guest—and he seeks an enemy of Ardais."

"*Vai dom!* I did not see you there. If you require privacy. . . ."

The guards looked ready to retreat, but Colryn held them there with a gesture. "What did you discover?" he asked Fredrik.

Fredrik was sure his face was turning red, and he did not know how to reply. Slowly he said, "I . . . found no threat, but still. . . ." He touched a finger to the back of Colryn's hand to facilitate communication. "*Something is wrong. I know it. But I am unskilled at matrix work. Perhaps if you tried. . . .*"

Colryn frowned and broke the contact. He spoke aloud, "There is no present danger. My cousin has felt some danger here, but whether it lies in future or—perhaps you glimpsed the midwinter battle in my grandfather's day, when bandits rode in disguised as guests? In any case, Eduin, Hjalmar, please make the rounds of those on duty: make sure all are alert, but raise no alarm. Radan, stay near us as we tour the hall."

As the two guards moved away, Fredrik saw Eduin shake his head and clearly overheard his muttered comment: "Past, present, future—who cares? Trouble will come when it comes. Why warm a cookpot when the trap is empty?"

Fredrik bit his lower lip and began to carefully scrutinize the many entrances, recesses, and balconies. Radan dropped back out of earshot and followed the young nobles as they moved along the wall. After one all-encompassing look around, Colryn watched Fredrik's face. Colryn commented quietly, "During our times together in Thendara, I never knew you to use your matrix. . . ."

Fredrik said tightly, "I never felt such a need to use it before. Why wouldn't you scan the hall with yours?"

"Why, I caught most of what you sensed—which seemed normal enough. Didn't you know I was 'listening'?"

"You seemed so distracted." Fredrik realized, tardily, that just as he had been overhearing, and trying to suppress, Colryn's thoughts of Lira, Colryn must have been sharing the impressions he received.

Colryn persisted. "I thought you might have found something in the moment I turned my attention to the guards. If not, why are you still so troubled?"

Fredrik raised a barrier to contain his growing shame and fear. Reluctantly, he answered, "I don't know. Perhaps the matrix itself has caused my unease."

Colryn stopped in the entrance of one of the long galleries and faced him. He reminded, "You were uneasy before you took your starstone in hand."

Fredrik studied the floor. In unconscious imitation of the older guard, he muttered, "Past, present, future—the matrix muddles time and space." His familiar fears brought out fine beads of sweat on his face and body. He wished he could escape the directness of Colryn's gaze.

Colryn touched his arm, saying gently, "It is a tool to be used, as you must have been taught at the Tower."

Fredrik stiffened. "I remember little of my time there," he said evasively. "Between bouts of threshold sickness, I played games with the matrix . . . learned to control my thoughts and barricades. But my parents requested my return as soon as I was out of danger. After losing two daughters and a son as each reached adolescence, they've kept me rather close." He shrugged slightly. "Now that my younger brother has passed the threshold safely, I may risk myself in such foolhardiness as traveling here in midwinter weather."

Colryn scoffed, "Not much risk, knowing the combined experience of your escort! Ricard and Gwynn could tiptoe across glaciers under the beaks of banshees. And that withered Amazon guide—surely she's been around since the mountains' very birth!"

One corner of Fredrik's mouth twitched up in acknowledgment of Colryn's raillery and he shifted to move on. But Colryn's hand on his arm again halted him.

Colryn's voice, though soft, acquired a slight edge. "*Bredu,* I was told how threshold sickness had ravaged your family. What has that to do with whatever's disturbing you now?"

Fredrik pulled away, unable to meet Colryn's gaze or withstand his touch. If his barricades were breached, his distress was sure to reach every telepath in the castle. Colryn was waiting with unrelenting patience. Unevenly, Fredrik resumed speaking.

"As the Tower, I heard their thoughts so often. . . . None seemed to believe I could survive—or do better than live on for a time as my sister had, mindless. How can I know I've survived that period *unscathed?*" His voice had begun to rise. He swallowed, then went on in a forced whisper. "I could not stop myself from using the matrix this time. What if the motives and *laran* it adds power to are somehow—twisted?" Finally raising his eyes to Colryn's face, Fredrik was startled to find impassiveness instead of the ready sympathy he expected.

"You were at the Tower five years ago. Am I the first to whom you unburden yourself?" Colryn's tone was incredulous and it stung Fredrik into responding with a mute nod.

Without hearing it, Fredrik knew Colryn's next word was *fool.* "A Keeper, or better yet, a good monitor, could have allayed your fears at any time—you could have made full use of your *laran* these past years unhindered." His thought eased through Fredrik's wavering defenses with companionable derision, *I have touched your mind and you are no monster.* Fredrik felt his fears dissipating under Colryn's intolerance of them. A stillness settled between them and Colryn said quietly, "Would that my troubles were so easily solved."

He turned his look upon the hall and, following his gaze, Fredrik saw Lira standing still in the middle of a circle of dancers, her gaze locked to Colryn's. A mutual loneliness and unhappiness was mirrored in their faces. Neither moved toward the other.

"Go *to* her," urged Fredrik.

Colryn raised a hand as though to reach toward her, then dropped it laxly. He turned back into the gallery. His thought, again clear to Fredrik, rang sorrowfully within him, *It is no use.* Like wrapping a fur cloak tightly about himself, Colryn drew his barriers into place, locking his thoughts and emotions into privacy.

The guard moved even with Fredrik to follow Colryn. Fredrik impulsively asked in a low voice, "What do you know of a trouble between *Dom* Colryn and his lady?"

Radan responded without hesitation. He had guarded Colryn and Fredrik when they were inseparable companions through their childhood. "Only what all the house guards have seen and heard. They are very formal with each other and at times barely civil. One is often heard to criticize the other, and yet they seem to crave each other's company. It is most strange."

"Indeed," murmured Fredrik. He could do no more than be prepared to listen whenever Colryn next tried to discuss his problems. Colryn had wanted to talk earlier, but . . . Fredrik's pace lagged as he tried to weigh his earlier sensations of danger. An inner chill permeated his reverie, compelling him to pause, attention fully on his surroundings.

After the warmth and light and noise of the Great Hall, the gallery was cold, dark, and still. Isolated sections were illuminated by the romantic glow of flames through pierced metal and colored glass. Colryn passed through the warm glow ahead, his hair and ornaments gleaming momentarily; then he was swallowed by the dimness beyond. Radan followed, his head turning from side to side. The echoes of their boots on stone changed subtly. Fredrik moved forward, senses tingling. He noticed that the wall near the cresset was patterned by a mural. The opposite wall fell away beneath an arch which was framed by two images in muted colors, somewhat larger than life. *Hastur and Cassilda,* he noted automatically. Within the recess, the curved shape of a divan caught the light. He glanced swiftly away, but as he passed it he knew the recess was empty. Fredrik hurried to overtake the guard and Colryn.

During their quick search of the areas surrounding the hall, they came upon two female guests asleep in chairs, an empty jug between them. Just within the entrance to another gallery they found one forlorn young man whose cheek carried a reddened handprint. Other than that . . . "The galleries are empty!" Fredrik stated the obvious.

He realized this had disturbed him before, when using his matrix. He had unconsciously expected to touch, and ignore, the usual licentiousness of any festival night. But high spirits had been reserved for renewing old acquaintances; even mild flirtations had been few. Seeing now what "sparkle" the party lacked, Fredrik exchanged puzzled looks with his cousin and received the sardonic thought that perhaps Colryn's troubles were contagious.

Looking distractedly about him, Fredrik saw Auster swipe a tray of sweets from a servant and balance it on one hand, rummaging it with the other. Spotting him just as the music paused, Colryn exploded irritably, "Zandru's hells! The lad eats like a Keeper!"

Auster froze and the wooden tray slid sideways unchecked. The crystal dishes shattered and the confections rolled or crumbled. Auster blinked and looked down, dropped to his knees and began to clear the mess.

Colryn made a disgusted sound and turned away, but Fredrik moved to stand over Auster. He looked down thoughtfully at Auster's hands, unsteady as he gathered pieces of glass and pastry.

"You are nervous, cousin," Fredrik said softly. He crouched down, ostensibly to help, but more to try to glimpse Auster's face.

"Leave me alone, *cousin*." Auster mouthed the last word as a curse.

A dainty foot in dyed green leather toed a pastry into the pile. Lira, holding her skirts against her legs to keep them out of the sweets, inquired, "Why so harsh, Auster? He only seeks to aid you. Let it be now. . . . The servants are coming with brooms."

Fredrik rose, then handed Auster a cloth napkin.

Lira said lightly, "I was just coming to tear Colryn from your side and say our good nights. This company seems about danced out, but unless Colryn and I start movement toward bed, we may all be partying through breakfast time."

Colryn had walked on, but he came back on hearing Lira's voice as though drawn to a lodestone. Fredrik watched them smile tentatively at each other and wondered if they were too tired now to bicker. They were a handsome couple: Colryn, his lordly dignity tinged with shyness, and Lira, prettily tousled and sleepily relaxed.

Fredrik felt Colryn's delight as Lira permitted him to place an arm around her shoulders, as she touched his cheek tenderly while he gave her an apologetic hug. His hand slid beneath a loop of auburn hair to the nape of her neck. Fredrik looked away from the intimacy of that caress, striving to break the contact between Colryn and himself.

Auster was smirking at the couple in a mood Fredrik could not understand. Auster thrust a thumb beneath the lacing of his tunic and curled his fingers inside his shirt's open collar. Fredrik looked back at the couple as something *shifted* in the atmosphere and he felt his skin prickle, his senses leaping to full alertness.

Colryn's awareness of Lira surged into Fredrik. Her perfume warred with the scent of holiday spices in the air; the cosmetics on her face were markedly evident; her hair was straggly; the back of her neck felt clammy. . . .

Lira gave a muffled exclamation and ducked away from Colryn's arm. She took two steps backward and stood still, her back stiff, her cheeks flaming. "How dare you maul me so in public! Have you no sense of propriety?"

Her words reverberated within Fredrik, echoed between his and Colryn's minds. Colryn's anger sprang full-blown; without moving, he was suddenly looming over her.

"Slut!" he returned. "Were you taught manners in an Amazon Guildhouse, to entice and then refuse a man so? But no! Even Free Amazons are said to act more seemly!"

She gasped in indignation, then looked about uncertainly, both hands to her chest as though to cover herself.

Colryn's unreasoning rage beat within Fredrik's mind, and he raised his hands to his head. Even Lira's distress was perceptible, and quickly growing more intense as his receptivity of her emotions increased.

"Stop it!" grated Fredrik between clenched teeth. "Stop it, both of you!" Contact with Colryn seemed to have stripped away his defenses, and now he couldn't shut either of them out. He swung about to find Auster gone and somehow that added to his pain. Superimposed on his view of the room was Auster's smirking face; he knew that though he could not stop the couple's emotional storm, he *could* remove that smirk. The only place Auster could have disappeared so fast was into the nearest gallery. Fredrik bent his head and plodded slowly toward the entrance. He felt Colryn, then Lira, look after him, concern on his behalf blunting their other emotions.

A cold current of air met him as he stepped inside, and he was finally able to break the link with the couple. He walked gratefully into the coldness, feeling it soothe away the fire inside his head. Auster had opened a casement and was leaning into the chest-high opening, silhouetted against the moonlit brightness of fallen snow outside. Snow was being sprayed upward by gusts of wind, and the rush of air was loud enough to cover the sound of Fredrik's approach, strong enough to carry Auster's quiet laughter.

Fredrik reached around Auster's slim waist and divested him of his dagger. Stepping back, he tossed it to skitter noisily on the uneven stones of the floor behind him. Startled, Auster spun around, one hand reaching for the missing hilt. Fredrik crowded him back against the sill, intentionally showing the gleam of his own knife.

"Who—?" Auster's question cut short as Fredrik's right

hand gripped his throat. Auster wrenched his head back and cried, "Let me have my knife and I'll fight you fair, you—"

Fredrik gripped him more securely, growling, "What makes you think you deserve a fair fight? Keep still, coward, and you won't feel a thing."

Auster was held leaning backward, his feet almost off the floor, his shoulders crowded into the embrasure. He made an awkward grab at Fredrik's knife arm, but Fredrik's sure left hand avoided Auster easily and drove the knife toward Auster's chest. As the point of the knife slid between the lacings of Auster's tunic, Fredrik ripped it downward, slicing through the leather cord.

Behind him, Colryn called, "Fredrik, have you gone mad?"

Fredrik gave a short reproachful laugh, exulting silently, *Any madness here is not my own!*

Auster made a more frenzied effort to escape, but there was little he could do in his awkward position. As Auster let out a strangled sob, Fredrik released his throat and grabbed the roll of his shirt collar. Again the knife ripped clothing instead of flesh, tearing a good part of the left side of the shirt's front so that a large flap of cloth hung down in folds. Then, grabbing Auster's arm, Fredrik pulled him free of the opening and pushed him savagely against the near wall.

Lira's voice was cold as the snow. "Fredrik, what have you done? Auster has never provoked a fight!"

"That I'm sure of," said Fredrik calmly: He closed his hand about the loose piece of cloth and was not surprised to see Auster flinch, half stunned though he was. Turning his hand over, Fredrik opened the cloth upon it, reverse side up. A small pocket of silk was sewn there, with a thin strand of metal thrust through it. Holding the shirt fabric beyond the silk, he sliced the uppermost line of stitches and flipped the triangle of silk back. A blue jewel, trapped in a coil of copper wire and securely pinned to the cloth was thus revealed.

Auster twisted convulsively, snatching the cloth and hitting Fredrik's arm away. Then he dived through the opening he had created, careless of his unguarded back. Fredrik snorted contemptuously and shoved his dagger into its sheath.

Radan and another guard, who had followed Colryn and Lira in, caught Auster after a brief struggle. The boy looked groggy and barely able to stand, though the guards had not been hard on him. Radan asked, "Did he steal this, then?" and reached for the pin. Fredrik, Colryn, and Lira all cried,

"No!" in tones of such apprehension that Radan froze, his fingers near the dully gleaming jewel.

In the momentary silence that followed, Auster's teeth could be heard chattering as he trembled violently in the grip of the guards, his eyes shut tight, an expression of dread on his features.

Colryn spoke quietly, "Move back, Radan, and do not touch the jewel." He gestured to a nearby doorway and said, "Bring him in there and let him sit down."

Lira and Fredrik brought lights into the room and the guards withdrew, taking up posts outside the heavy curtain.

Fredrik heaved a sigh of relief and commented, "No one deserves murder in return for churlish pranks."

Auster was seated, his forearms flat on the table before him, his fingers spread. He looked, thought Fredrik, as though ready to spring up. Auster whispered, "I thought you meant to. . . ."

"I was your victim for only one night. If you wish mercy, beg it of Colryn and Lira," Fredrik said dryly.

"I will neither beg nor make apology," Auster mumbled. "I have done nothing but avert indecency in this house." He leaned his weight on his arms, his eyes half closing, then blinking alert again. A sequence of faces flashed through Fredrik's mind—each reflecting Auster's view of an inviting smile shifting through distaste to disinterest. Auster started, then glared directly at Fredrik. His thought flared, *You'd never have known, but there were so many . . . I got so tired. . . .* A repetitive image rippled through Fredrick of a hand tapping on the musicians' screen and he realized that Auster had requested the many ring-dances. Fredrik withdrew before Auster's weary efforts to close him out.

Fredrik gently clasped one of Lira's hands and touched his other hand to Colryn's. Their bewilderment and faint surmise ran into him. They looked into each other's eyes and their wonder filled Fredrik. He realized that this was the first time the couple was in clear contact with each other's thoughts. Grimly, Fredrik overlay their budding joy with his view of Auster reaching for the matrix and the subsequent change in the couple's perceptions. Auster had magnified people's faults with his "anti-glamour," and he had probably damped any strong emotions he found undesirable.

Lira reacted first, sending a swift impression of her own suspicions, now confirmed, which she had refused to entertain. She concluded, *I convinced myself that any growing boy might eat so much. . . . He's been stuffing himself to replenish the energy he used against us!*

Colryn roughly broke the contact, his face hardening as he confronted Auster. "Your dirty tricks made my wife a stranger to me and threatened our marriage bed. You unlawfully interfered with the lives of many here tonight. . . . If our guests knew of your crime they would clamor that your *laran* centers be destroyed! This is how you repay your lord, my father, for treating you generously, giving you responsibilities enough to build your sense of worth in this household? Only your age will protect you from the harshest penalty. . . ."

Auster bowed his head before Colryn's anger, and Fredrik watched the pinned matrix flash into sparkling life, then fade to its former dullness.

Colryn switched to a more reasonable tone in midsentence. ". . . but I suppose you are too young and inexperienced to understand the passions that make life interesting. . . ."

Lira and Fredrik exchanged glances, then both burst out laughing. Colryn looked at them, frowning, then grinned self-deprecatingly. "He did it to me again!"

Auster raised his head slowly and looked from one side of the room to the other, his features lax; then carefully laid his cheek to the table and closed his eyes.

Looking at the defenseless boy, the gray circles around his eyes, Fredrik could not renew his former grimness. "Poor lad. The whole party's kept him so busy tonight that he had no energy left for a fight."

Lira smiled gravely at Colryn. "I fear we cannot make up the misunderstandings of a halfyear in a single night, but," her smile intensified for a moment, "we can make a beginning." She turned grave eyes on Auster. "We'll let him rest and finish this tomorrow. He must be near shock from overtaxing himself. I don't know where he came by his matrix, but we should send him to a Tower to learn the proper use of it—not to mention the responsibilities and conduct it entails."

Fredrik offered, with a wry smile at Colryn, "I could accompany him—and finish my own training."

Colryn acceded, "He evidently has strong *laran*, and even Father would agree that with proper training he'd be more useful working in a Tower than as a menial for Ardais." He grinned rather crookedly. "The Tower would not approve his talent at enforcing chastity. But later, if he is still minded to go, he'd be welcome at the monastery to practice his perversion usefully."

THE LESSON OF THE INN

by Marion Zimmer Bradley

Hilary Castamir rode head down, her gray cloak wrapped tightly about her, the cowl of her cloak concealing her face. She did not turn to look her last on Arilinn.

She had failed. . . .

She would never, now, be known as Hilary of Arilinn, or grow old in the service of the most ancient and prestigious of the Towers of the Seven Domains; revered, almost worshipped. Keeper of Arilinn. Never, now. She had failed, failed. . . .

It would be Callista, then, who would take Leonie's place when the old sorceress finally laid down her burden. *I do not envy her,* Hilary thought. And yet, paradoxically, Hilary knew that she did envy Callista.

Callista Lanart. Thirteen years old, now. Red hair and gray eyes like all the Altons—like Hilary herself, for Hilary too had Comyn blood. Why should Callista succeed where she had failed?

Leonie had tried to soften the blow.

"My dearest child, you are neither the first nor the last to find a Keeper's work beyond your strength. We all know what you have endured, but it is enough. We can ask no more of you." Then she had spoken the formal words which formally released Hilary from the vows she had sworn at eleven years old. And half of Hilary was shaking with craven relief. Not to have to endure it anymore, never again to await, in helpless terror, the attacks of pain which swept over her at the time of her women's cycles, never again to endure the excruciating clearing of the nerve channels. . . .

Or worse than that, again and again, the desperate hope that this time it would be only the cramping, spasmodic pain, the weakness that drove her to bed, sick and exhausted and drained. *That* she could endure, she had endured; she had patiently swallowed all the medicines which were supposed to help it and somehow never did; she never lost the hope that this month the pain would simply subside as it did in the other women. But every month there was the terror, too, and the guilt. *What is it I have done that I ought not to have done?*

What have I done? Why do I suffer so? I have faithfully observed all the laws of the Keepers, I have touched no man or woman, I have not even allowed myself to think forbidden thoughts. . . . Merciful Avarra, what am I doing wrong that I cannot keep the channels pure and untainted as befits a virgin and a Keeper?

All the training she had endured, all the suffering, all the terror and the guilt, the guilt . . . all gone for nothing. And there was always the suspicion. Always when a Keeper could not keep her channels clear there was suspicion, never spoken aloud, but always there.

The channels of a virgin, untainted, are clear. What is wrong with Hilary, that these nerve channels, these same channels which in an adult woman carry sexuality, cannot remain clear for unmixed use of laran? Even Leonie had looked at her in sharp question, a time or two, the unspoken doubt so clear to the telepath girl that Hilary had burst into hysterical crying, and even Leonie could not doubt the utter sincerity of bewilderment.

I have not broken my vow, nor thought of breaking it. I have faithfully kept all the laws of a Keeper, I swear it, I swear it by Evanda and Avarra and by the Blessed Cassilda, mother of the Domains. . . .

And so, in the end, Leonie had had no choice but to send Hilary away. Hilary was almost hysterical with relief that her long and agonizing ordeal was at an end; but she was still sick with guilt and terror. Who would ever believe in her innocence, who would believe that she had not been sent away in disgrace, her vows broken? Sunk in misery, she did not even turn to look her last on Arilinn.

Seven years, then, gone for nothing. She would never again wear the crimson robes of a Keeper, nor work again in the relays . . . as they crossed the pass, there was one narrow space where they had to dismount and walk carefully along the narrow trail while the horses were led along the very rim of the chasm; and as she looked down into the dreadful gulf dropping away to the plains a thousand feet below, it came into her mind that she could take a single careless step, no

more, it would be so easy, an accident, and then she need
never again face the thought of failure. No one could ever
look at her, and whisper when she was not in the room that
here was the Keeper who had been sent from Arilinn, no one
knew why. . . .

One single false step. So easy. And yet she could not summon up enough resolution to do it. *You are a coward, Hilary
Castamir,* she told herself. She remembered that Leonie herself, and the young technician Damon Ridenow, who had
sometimes come to help Leonie with the clearing of her channels, had praised her courage. *They do not really know me;
they do not know what a coward I am. Well, I will never see
them again, it does not matter. Nothing really matters. Not
now.*

Toward mid-afternoon, as they came down into a valley
outside the ring of mountains which shut the Plains of Arilinn
away from the outside world, they stopped at an inn to
rest the horses. Her escort said that she would be conducted
to a private parlor inside the inn, where she could warm herself and have some food if she wished. She was weary with
riding, for she had risen very early this morning; she was glad
of a chance to dismount, but when the escort, in automatic
courtesy, offered her his help, she had scrambled down without touching him, so skillfully that she had not even brushed
his outstretched hand.

And when a strange man in the doorway held out his
hand, with a soft, polite, "Mind the steps, *damisela,* they are
slippery with the snow," she had drawn back as if the touch
of his hand would contaminate her beyond recall, and had
opened her lips to flay him with harsh words. And then she
remembered, with a dull sensation of weariness. She was not,
now, wearing the crimson robes which would protect her
against a careless touch, even a random look. Her gray
hooded cloak was the ordinary traveling dress of any noblewoman; even though she shrouded her face deep within it, it
would not wholly protect her. It seemed, as she went through
the hallway to the inn, that she could feel eyes on her everywhere.

Do all men, always, watch women this way? she wondered.
And yet no man's eyes had rested on her for more than a
moment, as they might have rested on a horse or a pillar; it
was only that they looked at her at all, that their eyes were
not automatically withdrawn as they had been in Arilinn

when she rode forth with the other women of the Tower, that everyone did not step aside, as she had been accustomed to their doing, waiting for her to pass.

In the room to which the servant conducted her, she unfastened her cloak and put back the hood, she went to the fire to warm herself; but she did not touch the jug of wine which had been sent to her.

After a long time she heard a soft sound at the door. A woman stood there, round and plump-bodied, enveloped in a capacious apron; she might have been the innkeeper's wife or daughter, or a servant. She said with soft courtesy, "I will make up the fire freshly for you, my lady," and came to put fresh logs on it. Then she blinked in astonishment. "But you are still wearing your cloak, *damisela*. Let me help you." She came, and Hilary started to recoil, automatically . . . no human being had laid so much as a fingertip on her garment, not for years. Then she remembered that this prohibition no longer applied to her, and stood statue-still, suffering the impersonal touch of the woman's hands, removing her cape and the scarf around her neck.

"Will you have your shoes off as well, my lady, to warm your feet at the fire?"

"No, no," said Hilary, embarrassed. "No, I will do very well—" She stooped to unfasten her own traveling-boots.

"But indeed, you must not," said the woman, scandalized, kneeling to draw them off, "I am here to serve you, lady—ah, how cold your feet are, poor little lady, let me rub them for you with this towel. . . ." She insisted, and Hilary, acutely embarrassed, let her do as she would.

I did not know how cold my feet were until she told me. I have been taught to endure heat and cold, fire and ice, without complaint, even without awareness . . . but now that she was aware of the cold, she shivered as if she would never stop.

The woman took a steaming kettle off the hob of the fireplace and poured something hot into a cup. "Now drink this, little lady," she said compassionately, "and let me wrap you in your cloak again. It will warm you now. Here, put your feet up to the fire like this," she said, drawing a footstool around so that Hilary found herself deep in a chair with the soles of her feet propped up to the blazing fire. "Have you dry stockings in your saddlebags? I think you must have them on, or you will take cold." And almost before Hilary knew it, her feet were toasty warm in dry stockings, and she was sipping at the hot spicy brew which, she suspected, had had something a good deal stronger than wine added to it. A sensation very like pleasure began to steal over her.

I have not been this comfortable in a long time, she thought, almost with a secret guilt, *a long long time*. Her head nodded and she drowsed in the heat. Some time later she awoke to discover that a pillow had been tucked behind her head in the armchair, and someone had covered her with a blanket. She had not slept so well for a long time, either.

The thought began to stir faintly in her consciousness. *I have been taught to be indifferent to all these things, indifferent to pain, cold, hunger, isolation. Such thoughts are not worthy of a Keeper. I learned to endure all these things*, she thought. *And still I failed. . . .*

Outside in the hallway she heard soft voices; then there was a tentative knock on the door. Quickly Hilary turned her skirt down over her thin knees. *Even if I am no longer a Keeper*, she thought, *I must behave as circumspectly as one, lest my behavior give them cause to think I was sent away from Arilinn for something I have done.* She got to her feet and called, "Come in."

The leader of the escort sent by her father stood hesitantly in the door, saying diffidently, "My lady, the snow has begun to fall so thickly that we cannot go on. We have arranged to remain here for the night, if it please you."

If it please me, she thought. But the words were only formal courtesy. *What could they possibly do if it did not please me? Try to force their way through the storm, and perhaps lose the way or be frozen in a blizzard?* She did not look at the man; her face was turned away, as always in the presence of strangers, and she longed for the protection of her hooded cloak, hanging on the chair to dry. She said with aloof courtesy, "You must do as you think best," and the man withdrew.

Later she heard voices along the hall.

"Look, I don't care who the *vai domna* is, unless she is the Queen's own self or Lady Hastur. Once and for all, we are crowded and overworked down here, with the storm and all these travelers; no one has leisure to go back and forth along all these corridors with trays and special meals now. The worthy lady can just haul her honorable carcass down to the common room like everyone else, or she can stay in her precious private parlor and go hungry, for all I care."

Hilary's anger was purely automatic. How dared they speak like that? If a Keeper of Arilinn chose to honor their wretched little inn, how dared they refuse her the protection of her privacy? Then, dully, Hilary remembered. She was no longer Keeper, no longer even a *leronis* of Arilinn. She was nothing. She was Hilary-Cassilde Castamir, second daughter of Arnad Castamir, who was only a minor nobleman on a small-holding in the Kilghard Hills. She remembered, dimly, like something in a dream, something her father had said to her. It had been the year before she went to Arilinn, but already she had been tested and had begun to dream of being one of the great Keepers. She had been about nine years old.

"Daughter, the servants and vassals have tasks much harder than ours, much of the time. You must never needlessly make their lives harder; it is not worthy of a noblewoman to give orders only for the pleasure of seeing yourself obeyed."

Hilary thought; *I need nothing, I will tell them I am not hungry, then I can remain here in peace, untroubled. They need not spare anyone to wait on me.* But there was a good smell of cooking all along the hallways, and Hilary reflected that in order to tell them this, she would need to go down to the common-room anyhow. And she had breakfasted early, and scantily, and had had nothing since except the drink the woman had given her. She put her light veil about her head, and went along the passageway to the common-room.

As she came in, the woman who had waited on her before came toward her; Hilary stopped in the doorway, overcome by shyness and the impact of the crowded room, more people than she had seen in one place in many years; men, women and children, strangers, all overtaken by the storm. The woman led her quickly to a small corner table, apart from the others, where she could sit in the shadow of the projecting fireplace and not be seen. The four men of her escort were eating and drinking heartily, laughing over their food and wine; the leader came and inquired courteously if she had everything she needed. She murmured a shy assent without raising her eyes.

The woman was still standing protectively beside her. "My name is Lys, my lady. Will you have wine, or hot milk? Food will be brought to you in a moment. The wine is from Dalereuth and quite good."

Hilary said shyly that she would rather have hot milk. The woman went away and after a while a great fat woman, swathed to the neck in a great white apron, came around, lugging a huge bowl the contents of which she ladled out onto every plate. She passed Hilary's isolated table and ladled out a great dollop of whatever it was onto her plate, then passed on to the next table. Hilary stared in consternation. It was some kind of stew, great lumps of boiled meat and some kind of thickly cut coarse vegetables, white and orange and yellow.

Hilary was rarely hungry. She had been ill so much that she almost never thought with any pleasure of food. When she had been doing heavy and strenuous work in the matrix screens, she was ravenous and ate whatever was put before her without tasting; not caring what it was, so long as it replaced the energy her starved body needed. At other times she cared so little for food that the others in her circle tried hard to think up special dainties which, delicately served, might tempt her fickle appetite just a little. This stew from the common dish looked appalling. But it smelled surprisingly good, hot and savory, and after all she could not sit there and seem to disdain the common fare. She took a bite, squeamishly, and then another; it tasted as good as it smelled, and she ate it all up, and when the woman Lys came around with her hot milk she stirred honey into it and drank all of that, too, surprised at herself.

While the adults in the room were busy at eating and drinking, two young children had come and knelt on the hearth, their tartan skirts spread around them. One of the little girls had opened a little bag she carried and spilled out some small cut and colored pebbles. Hilary knew the game; she had played it with Callista, to try to divert the homesick child in her first loneliness. As they cast the stones, one of them fell on the edge of Hilary's green skirt; they looked at her, too shy to come and fetch it, and Hilary bent down and held out the small carved stone to them.

"Here," she said, "come and take it." It did not occur to her to be shy with the children.

The taller of the little girls—they were about six and eight, with long tails of white-blond hair down their backs—said, "What is your name?"

"Hilary."

"I'm Lilla, and my little sister is Janna. Would you like to play with us?"

Hilary hesitated, then realized that in the darkness of the room, they probably took her for a child like themselves. Rising early at Arilinn that morning, she had simply tied her hair at the back of her neck without bothering to do it up. The little girl urged, "Please. It isn't so much fun to play with only the two of us," and it reminded her of something Callista had said once. She smiled and sat down on the hearth beside them, carefully tucking in her skirts. Lilla said, "You can have first turn if you want to, since you are our guest," and at the child's careful politeness, she wanted to giggle. She thanked Lilla and shook the toys out on the floor.

After a time the woman Lys came back to clear away the plates and mugs, and looked startled to see Hilary on the floor with the children. Recalled, Hilary looked around for her escort; they were wrangling with the housekeeper, near the door. The children scrambled to their feet. Lilla said politely, "My mother will be looking for us. Thank you for playing with us. I must take my little sister to bed," but small Janna came up, held out her arms wide and gave Hilary a moist kiss and a hug.

Hilary, too shy to return the kiss, felt tears start to her eyes. No one had kissed her in so many years. *My mother kissed me, in farewell, when I went to the Tower. No one since, not even my mother when I visited her, not my sisters; they had been told of the taboo, that I was to touch no one, not with a fingertip. Callista did not kiss me when we parted. Callista, who will be Lady of Arilinn. Callista will make a good Keeper; she is cold, she finds it easy to keep to all the laws and rules of the Tower . . .* and again she felt the weight of her guilt and shame, the weight of failure. For a few minutes, playing with the little girls, she had forgotten.

The escort and the innkeeper were still arguing, and the woman Lys broke away from them and came toward Hilary. She said, "Lady, my master cannot displace any guest who has bespoken a room before you. But I have offered—it is mean and poor, lady, but the room I share with my sister and her baby has two beds; I will share my sister's bed and you may have mine, you are very welcome." And as Hilary hesitated, "I wish there were some place more worthy of you, lady, but there is nothing, we are so crowded, the only alternative is to spread your blankets in the common room with your soldiers, and that a lady cannot do. . . ."

"You are very kind." She felt dazed by many shocks. She had eaten in a room full of strangers, played with strange children, now she was to share a room with two strange women and to sleep in a servant's bed. But it was preferable, of course, to sleeping among her soldier escort. "You are very kind," she said, and went with Lys, only half conscious of her escort's look of relief at this solution.

The room was dark and cramped and not warm, but floor and walls were scrubbed clean, and the linen and quilts heaped on the beds were immaculate. Between the two beds was a cradle, painted white, and on the other bed, a woman sat, holding a chubby baby across her lap and dressing it in clean clothes. Lys said, "This is my sister Amalie. *Domna,* I must go and finish my kitchen work. Make yourself at home; you can sleep there, in my bed." Hilary's saddlebags had been brought and shoved into the cramped space at the foot of the beds, and Hilary began to rummage for her nightgear. The woman with the baby was looking at her curiously, and Hilary murmured a shy formula of greeting.

"It is most kind of you to share your room with a stranger, *mestra.*"

"I hope the baby will not keep you awake, lady. But she is a good baby and does not cry very much." As if to give her the lie direct, the baby began to wave its small fists and shriek lustily, and Amalie laughed.

"Little rogue, would you make a liar of me? But she is hungry now, my lady, she wants her supper; afterward she will sleep."

"I have heard that it is good for them to cry," Hilary said timidly. "It helps their lungs to grow strong. How old is the baby. What is her name?"

"She is only forty days old," Amalie said, "and since my husband is a hired sword to Dom Arnad Castamir, I named her for one of the lord's daughters; Hilary."

So the baby is my namesake. Couldn't the woman do better for her child than to give her the name of a failure, a disgraced Keeper? But she could not say that. She said, "My name is Hilary, too," and held out her hand to the chubby screaming child. The fist waved, encountered Hilary's finger and gripped it surprisingly hard. Amalie was unfastening her dress; she was thin, but Hilary was surprised to see her breasts, grotesquely swollen, it seemed, to the point of deformity. The nipples already oozed white. Amalie lifted the baby, crooning.

"There, you greedy puppy," she said, and the small rosy mouth fastened hard on the swollen nipple, the crying choking off in mid-scream. The baby made small gasping noises as she sucked, waving her clenched fists rhythmically, in time to the sucking gulps. Hilary had never seen a woman nursing her child before—at least, not since she was old enough to remember.

"I heard them say in the inn that you were coming from Arilinn," Amalie said. "Ah, you must be happy to be coming home to your mother, and she will be happy too. I think it would break my heart if some day my daughter went so far from me." She stroked the baby's forehead with a tender finger, brushing the colorless curls away from the tiny face. "They live such sad and lonely lives in the Tower, poor ladies. Were you very unhappy there, very glad to come away?"

Not a word or whisper of disgrace. Nothing but, you will be glad to be coming home to your mother. *My mother,* Hilary thought. *My mother is a stranger; she has become a stranger to me. And yet once we were close . . . as close as that,* Hilary thought, looking at the woman with the child at her breast. *My mother need not be a stranger now. Perhaps, when she knows how hard I tried, she will not blame me for my failure . . .*

The baby's fists were still clenching and unclenching rhythmically as she sucked, her toes curling up with eagerness. The woman's eyes were closed. She looked happy and peaceful. Suddenly Hilary felt a pain in her own breasts, a cramping down through her whole body, not unlike what she felt at the time of her recurrent ordeal, only now, for some reason, it was not particularly painful or even unwelcome. It was so intense that for a moment she thought she would faint, and clutched the bedpost; then quickly she turned away and began to rummage again in her saddlebags for her nightgown.

She got into bed, and lay watching the nursing, feeling strangely drained. The pain had gone, but her breasts felt strange, tense, as if she could feel the nipples rubbing hard against her thick nightgown. The woman finally drew the baby, sated and blissful, from her breast, fastened up her nightgown, and carried her to Hilary where she lay in the strange bed.

"Would you like to hold her for a minute, *Domna?*"

Hilary held out her arms, and Amalie put the baby into them; she held her awkwardly against her own meager breasts. Full and sleeping, the baby squirmed, nuzzling her mouth against Hilary's nightgown, and the woman laughed as the little flailing hands closed on Hilary's breast.

"You will find nothing there, greedy one, and you are as full as a suckling pig already," she scolded, teasing, "but a year or two from now, well, she would have better luck looking there, perhaps, lady?"

Hilary blushed, looking down at the baby in her arms, drawing her finger over the soft little head. It felt like silk, feathers, nothing in the world had ever felt so soft to her. The soft sleeping weight against her body made her feel depleted, with a pleasant exhaustion. When Amalie picked up the baby to tuck her into the cradle, Hilary's arms felt suddenly cold and empty, and after the light was out she lay listening to the soft breathing of the women, and the child, feeling the curious ache in her body. What must it feel like, to nurse a child that way, to feel that hungry tugging at her breasts? She felt her nipples throbbing again. She had never been conscious of them before, they had simply been there, part of herself, like her hair and her fingernails. She put her hands over them, awkwardly, trying helplessly to calm the aching; she felt cold, an empty shell, shivering, finally pulling the pillow toward her and hugging it tight, in an attempt to quiet the strangeness she could not calm. Suddenly, exhausted by strangeness and fatigue, she slept.

When she woke the room was filled with sunlight, and Amalie and the baby had gone, and Lys was saying apologetically, "I am sorry to waken you, my lady, but your escort sent to say you should be ready to ride within the hour."

Hilary sat up in bed and blinked; she had slept unusually long and late.

"You can wash yourself here, lady, I have brought you some hot water. I will bring your breakfast if you like."

"I can come to the common-room for breakfast," Hilary said, "but I will be glad of your help in lacing my gown." She gave Lys a gift of money before she left. When the woman protested, saying it was unnecessary, she said, "Give it to your sister, then, and tell her to buy something pretty for the baby."

On the steps of the inn, crowded because the unexpected guests of the storm were readying themselves for departure, and the courtyard was thick with horses and men, she suddenly heard, around the corner, a man's voice.

"Who is the pretty young lady in the green gown and the gray cloak? I saw her last night in the common-room, and again this morning, but I do not know her by name."

It was one of the escort who answered. "She is the lady Hilary Castamir; we are bringing her from Arilinn. I have heard she found the work there too hard and too taxing to her health, so she is going home to her family."

Now it will come, Hilary thought, braced for the indecent jests about a Keeper who found it too difficult to keep her virginity, the rude speculations, the talk of broken vows, disgrace . . . but the first speaker only said, "I have heard that the work there is difficult indeed. It would have been a great pity for such a young woman to live all her days shut inside a Tower, and grow at last as gray and gaunt as the old sorceress of Arilinn. She is only a pretty girl now; but if I am any judge, one day she will be one of the loveliest women I have ever seen. I hope the bride my father one day chooses for me will be even half so lovely."

Hilary listened, shocked—how dare they talk of her this way? Then, slowly, it dawned on her that they were actually complimenting her, that they meant her well. She wondered if she was really pretty. It had never occurred to her even to think about it. She knew, in a vague way, that most women cared a good deal about whether men thought them pretty; even those women in Arilinn itself who did not live under a Keeper's laws, the monitors and mechanics and technicians there, went to great pains to keep themselves prettily dressed and attractive when they were not working. But she, Hilary, had always known such things were not for her. She dressed for warmth and modesty, she wore the crimson robes from which all men turned away their eyes by instinct, she had been taught to give no time or thought to such matters.

The women in the Towers, those other women who need not live by Keeper's laws, they know what it is to think of men as the men think of them. . . .

Hilary had always known that the women and men in Arilinn lay together if they would, had been aware in the vaguest of ways that the women found pleasure in such things; but she, a Keeper, a pledged virgin, had been taught, in all kinds of ingenious and demanding ways, to turn her thoughts elsewhere, never to give such a thought even a moment's mental lease, never to know or understand what went on all around her, to numb all the reflexes of her ripening body. . . . Hilary stood paralyzed on the stairs, motionless under the impact of a thought which had just come to her; remembering the curious pain in her breasts last night as she watched the nursing child.

I have denied myself all this. Even the pleasures of warmth and food. I have taught my body to feel nothing, except pain . . . that I could not barricade away, but except for the pain I could not deny, I had refused to know that I had a body at all, thinking of it only as a mechanical contrivance for working in the relays, not flesh and blood. I leaned to feel nothing, not even hunger and thirst. And perhaps the pain was the revenge my body took for letting it feel nothing more than that . . . for allowing it no comfort, no pleasure. . . .

The leader of her escort came and bowed.

"Your horse is ready, lady. May I assist you to mount?"

She started to mount without assistance; in the old way. Then she thought, in surprise, *Why, yes, you may.* She said, with a smile that surprised him, and herself, "I thank you, sir." Momentarily, and from habit, she tensed as he lifted her, then relaxed, and let him lift her into the saddle.

"Are you comfortable, my lady?"

She was still too timid to look at him, but she said softly, "Yes, I thank you. Very comfortable."

As they rode out of the courtyard, she put back her hood, luxuriating in the warmth of the sun on her face.

I am pretty, she thought defiantly. *I am pretty, and I am glad.* She looked back at the inn, with a warmth akin to love, and for a moment it seemed she had learned more in the single night there than in all the years that had gone before.

I can kiss a child. I can hold a baby in my arms, and think about what it would be like to hold a baby of my own, to have my own baby at my breasts. I need not feel guilty if men look at me and think I am pretty. And tomorrow I shall see my mother, and I shall throw myself in her arms, and kiss her as I used to do when I was a very little girl.

I can do anything.

Poor Callista. She will be Lady of Arilinn, but she will never have any of this.

I am free!

By the time she rode up out of the valley, she was singing.

CONFIDENCE

by Phillip Wayne

Consciousness returned to him slowly.

The pain blotted all. As it cleared, some of it came back to him. The fall from the mountain pony into the deep canyon below.

Grab a bush! Sink into the snow!

Reflexively, his hand closed on the material beneath him.

Cloth? He shook his head, trying to clear it. Identity came back to him. *Dom* Manuel Rodrio . . . something . . . Elhalyn y Hastur.

His head was still a jumble. A red curtain hung over his eyes, obscuring his vision.

"Well, are we finally awake?"

He turned toward the sudden voice. "Who are you?"

"They call me Vraga the Rock." The woman chuckled. "And who might you be? All cold and half-exposed in the Hellers when I found you?"

"I am Manuel Elhalyn y Hastur. I was out riding when the storm hit and my pony threw me. How long have I been here?"

His vision was clearing. The woman sounded much older than she looked. No more than thirty, he guessed. She wore men's clothes, with a red spotted bandanna tied around her head. As she spoke, she held the point of a thin dagger to her lips.

"About a day." She leaned back in thought. "That name sounds like you are *Comyn*. Now who would believe that?"

"Everyone in the Hellers knows my family."

"I know the Elhalyn. But I know something of the Comyn too. By the time they reach twenty . . . and don't try telling me you are younger than that . . . they already have their starstones. Where is yours?"

His hand went to the pouch at his throat . . . should have been at his throat. *It's impossible. If it was torn from me I*

187

would be dead. Merciful Avarra! What has happened to my starstone?

"Don't try to pretend. We both know no Comyn could live without his starstone." She laughed again. "Now who really are you?"

Manuel shook his head again. *It's true. If I were really Comyn, I would have it. But I am Comyn! Where is my stone?*

He shook his head. "I don't know. May I get up?"

"If you are careful. I would not move around too much, for your own safety. Some of my *servicin* are very protective of me. They might get the wrong idea if they thought you were a bandit." She drew a finger lightly across her throat.

Servicin. The word rolled into his head like a stone in one of the Drytown rattles. It was slang, only used by some of the less honest of the bandits that roamed the Hellers in midwinter.

Around him, he could see three solid walls of earth. They were windowless and without ornament. In the fourth, a thick wooden door stood a few paces from a roaring fireplace.

"Could I get something to eat?"

She walked over to the kettle in the fire and ladled soup into a bowl she picked up from beside the hearth.

He watched her walk, noting the slight limp of her left foot. *Something about her . . . I know the name from somewhere. Where?*

"What were you doing in the Hellers, *vai domil?*"

To Manuel's ears, the diminutive sounded on the border of insult.

"I am in the Tower. I came back for more training in the sight." *Or did I? I have no matrix.* His hand went to the lump on his head. *I am not even sure of who I am! Did the fall do something to my mind? If I were who I think I am, I would have a starstone.*

"I went into the Hellers . . . I can't remember why. There *was* a reason."

Vraga the Rock looked at him skeptically. "I think you are a spy, I do. Sent here to spy on us. Simple, hard-working folk that we are, trying to scratch a living out of these hard mountains."

My father was talking about her just before I went to the Tower. Why can't I remember? He felt the back of his neck prickle.

There was a knock at the door.

"Enter!" Her voice seemed accustomed to command.

The man came in with his sword drawn. He glared at Manuel as he bent down to whisper in Vraga's ear. She nodded and then motioned him back through the door.

I remember! My father said she was an outlaw when he was a child in the mountains. How is that possible? My father is nearly fifty, and this woman is only thirty. Or is this also a product of the lump on my skull? Impossibility on impossibility! None of this makes any sense!

Vraga leaned back against the door, the point of her dagger occasionally touching the tip of her tongue. *Like a cat watches a mouse,* Manuel thought, *just before his leap. What does she want?*

The soup was dark, and smelled of meat. He watched reflection in the liquid as it wavered. *I wonder,* he thought grimly, *if the me on the other side of the soup sees my reflection also. I look so disheveled. I remember the copper mirror in my mother's apartment. Now there was a clear image, not like this, in a bowl of soup.*

"What do you want from me?" he asked finally.

Vraga smiled, and again flicked the tip of her tongue against the point of the knife. "What do you have?"

Manuel spread his hands in front of him. "Only what you see. But my father will ransom me, if that's what you have in mind."

Vraga flipped her wrist. The motion was almost casual, but it sent the knife hurrying past Manuel's ear and into the wall behind him. He felt a small, wet patch along the top of his ear and put his hand to it.

There was a smear of red.

"I hit what I'm aiming for, and don't forget it. If I had wanted that blade between your eyes, that's where it would have gone. Now I want to know who you are and why you were in the Hellers, and I want to know now!"

"I *told* you, I am *Dom* Manuel Rodrio Elhalyn y Hastur. My pony threw me and you found me. There is no more to it!"

He saw the other knife in her belt, but her hands were well away from it. As he spoke, he backed slowly toward the wall. *If I can get that dagger, I will at least have a fighting chance.*

He felt the cold earth on his back, and his hand came along the wall in a swift motion. He turned his head to find

the knife, and heard a quick whistle. His hand was around the
hilt, but his sleeve was pinned to the wall with its mate.

"Sometimes, people carry a knife in a back sheath, too.
Can't be too careful. Now I think you had better not move
until I get those other two knives, or I may have to throw too
fast and miss."

As she approached him, she kept one hand on the remaining dagger on her belt.

He watched her. *No one is that accurate. It isn't possible.
That small limp, very like Arianna, one of the matrix workers at the tower. Physically, too, they are very similar. I think
there is a key there. Where?*

"Thomaso!" she called out. The door opened once again.
"Tie him. Then we will question him again. He does not respond well to kindness, so I will try other methods." The
tongue flicked out again onto the point. "Perhaps not such
gentle ones."

She walked to the hearth and set two of the daggers down
with their point in the coals.

She sat him in a chair, and Thomaso did his work both
quickly and well. Manuel was unable to break the ropes
which secured him to the chair.

She pulled one of the knives out of the fire and spat on it.
The saliva sizzled but she shook her head and put the blade
back in the coals.

It's all so impossible! he thought. *Vraga has to be older
than my father, but she is not. My matrix can't have been
lost, but it was. No one could be as accurate as she is with a
knife, but she is. None of it makes any sense at all.*

Vraga pulled the knife out again. The tip glowed dull red.
She shook her head and put it back in the flames.

*What in Zandru's seventh hell is going on? What was it my
father used to say . . . "If it doesn't smell like a cralmac,
then it's not, no matter what it looks like."*

Manuel eyed the fire, feeling the heat of its flames in his
face. *Let me start over, and see what this smells like. First, it
is impossible that my matrix was taken from me, so I must
still have it. But I can't feel it!*

*I wish my hands were free! Second impossibility . . . that
woman cannot be Vraga. She was dead before I was born. Is
she Arianna then? No, this must be real! I can see it, feel it,
taste it, even smell it.*

But, if she is Arianna, then I must still be in the Tower. But why would the Tower do this to me?

Arianna-Vraga pulled the blade of one of the daggers from the coals. "Now, you will tell us what you were doing in the Hellers, and this time it will be the truth. Or perhaps you would like to feel how it is to have an eye burned out."

"I can't tell you anything!" He screamed at her.

The knife point lowered toward his cheek. He could feel the heat from it. It touched, and he screamed.

The pain was intense, but momentary.

Why would the Tower do this? I came to learn to use the sight. Is this a test of it? Is this only an illusion controlled by the matrix circle in the Tower, to test how well I have learned? If it is, then by Avarra, I can break it!

Vraga-Arianna leaned in close. He could smell her breath. "I am not going to ask many more times."

He fought to believe that he had not lost the matrix. *It is still there, around my neck. If it were not, I would have died. It must be still there!*

The hot blade came down on his other cheek. He screamed again.

"Are you still going to tell that story about being one of the Elhalyns? We know truth when we hear it!"

I must know it to see it. Why can't I believe that I still have my stone? I am not dead. I must have it.

He tried to let his consciousness sink down, as he had so many times before, but found nothing.

Even an illusion can kill, if it is believed. All logic says that this is not real. I must not believe it! My matrix lies at my throat, where it has always lain. I must believe that to survive.

Once again, he let his consciousness sink down. He felt it! *It is there!*

He felt the merging; the sweet, silent, thunderous merging with the power of the matrix. *There are threads here—control threads! I was right. I am being controlled!*

Even as he detached them, he could see the blade of the dagger, shimmering with heat as it reached toward his eye. Carefully, he separated each one and let it fall into the void. Vrada and her knife shimmered, and then faded as the last fell.

Around him stood the Tower working circle.

Arianna held out her hand to steady him.

He leaned on her. "What would have happened if I had failed?"

The Keeper looked at him strangely. "We would have sent your body home to be buried with honor. Would that not have been proper?"

Someone embraced him, and he fell asleep.

The Empire and Beyond

Readers of the Darkover saga are likely to take sides, very violently, pro-Darkover and anti-Empire; although among Darkovan fans a rather healthy backlash seems to be starting, indicating that the Empire is not all bad and that perhaps Darkover is not completely perfect. That tension of balanced forces, of cultures in conflict, often brings out the worst of either side—or the best. This conflict and tension is explored to the full in Patricia Mathews's "Camilla," a story of adventure, conflict and character, which reintroduces an old friend for readers who have read The Shattered Chain *and* To Keep the Oath; *Camilla n'ha Kyria, Renunciate, Free Amazon—and, in this story, Terran Agent.*

Another old friend returns in Millea Kenin's "Where the Heart Is." At the end of Sword of Aldones—*or of* Sharra's Exile, *if you prefer—Lew Alton leaves Darkover with his wife and his daughter Marja, never to return. Many readers have asked what happened to him, on whatever strange world he found, and what happened to Marja; Millea Kenin tells a tender and convincing story of Marja Alton, who inherited her father's* laran *and found it a pathway to exploring the minds—and hearts—of an alien species on a world which was not yet her home.*

And yet other old friends—David Hamilton and Jason Allison—return to carry on the story of Project Telepath, when the Empire agrees to explore Darkovan laran, *and comes up against a most unusual form of psychic power—and a complete skeptic, a man who never believes in*

193

*anything he cannot experience. In Lynn Mims's
story we meet the skeptic, and find out why.*

*And finally, just because every anthology
should leave you laughing when you say good-
bye, we present the most unusual story ever submitted to a hapless editor.*

*In putting out the requirements for this anthol-
ogy, I rashly stated that I would give priority to
very short stories, and (because we received so
many grim tragedies) that I hoped some of the
contributors would submit a humorous story or
two.*

*Well, the title story of this collection reem-
phasizes the old saying,* Be careful what you ask
for—*you might get it. Millea Kenin, whose short
story* "Where the Heart Is," *had already been accepted, brought* "A Recipe for Failure" *to my
women's circle one night, and began to pass it
around. One after another, the entire membership exploded into helpless giggles. Then they
handed it to me.*

*So here, by special permission of Anne Mc-
Caffrey, we present a story which is not—well, not
entirely—a Darkover story. But I did say, at one
time, that there had once been dragons on Darkover, and so, probably, it serves me right.*

CAMILLA

by Patricia Mathews

Prologue:

Slowly, carefully, Alicia Crowley of Mapping & Exploration raised a long-barreled blaster at the tall, weedy man across the campfire from her. "Kireseth," she said with the dead calm of shock. "All right, Roger, hands up."

Roger Benson hesitated and gauged his chances of jumping the gun. The scene was fantastic: pink flames against an indigo sky, a violent moon riding the crests of mountains higher and wilder than any found on Earth, a broken plastic crate spilling golden dried hallucinogenic flowers across the cordovan sands; and Lish, utterly prosaic in black leather, jacket open to reveal a rainbow iridescent tunic, an ashen streak across her aristocratic cheekbones the only sign of strain. Lish, holding a gun, the most fantastic scene of all.

"And drop your gun," she added, rising slowly, gun steady, bleeding a little inside. "Hands out in front."

Roger smiled weakly. "Now, Lish, you can't imagine. . . ."

Gun in hand, she picked up a length of wrapping cord. "You've always been a gambler, Roger, and this time you lost." She came close enough to the outstretched hands to wrap the cord around them. Roger lunged. She fired, and the stench of burning flesh and synthetic fabric filled the night with Roger's screams of pain. She retreated and went for the aircraft's first-aid kit as Roger howled curses and screamed his pleas for help. She tossed him a small vial from a safe distance.

"Painkiller. Take three, sit down, and put your hands in front of you." Her gun did not move. She waited until he obeyed, his features became slack, and his eyes closed. The normal dose was one tablet.

The next thing Roger knew, they were airborne. He was fastened into the passenger seat of Alicia's aircraft by the emergency crash webbing. His shoulder felt as if it were on

fire. There was turbulence, and the craft felt as if it were flying heavy; the crate of kireseth must be aboard. The crate of
evidence that would see him barred from the planet and in
for five-to-ten of Rehabilitation. Experimentally he jiggled his
bonds.

"Hold still, Roger. We're running into some upper air turbulence," Alicia said absently, most of her mind on keeping
the dangerous overloaded craft aloft. She was a skilled pilot,
but the hills of Darkover, as the planet was known, developed
some hellish cross-currents. Somewhere over the range the
Drytowners call the Black Hills, she lost her battle and forced
the craft to some sort of rough landing, her beacon broadcasting all the way.

The telephone buzzed in the quarters of the Assistant Terran Coordinator in Carthon. Sleepily she answered it, and the
voice of her security officer said, "Maggie? Dave. There's a
plane down in the Black Hills, and we won't be able to count
on native Search & Rescue this time." He sounded young and
frightened.

"Why?" she asked sharply, pulling on her pants and shirt
and checking the clock. Three o'clock in the morning! What
idiot was making a night flight in this region?

"It was carrying contraband, I think, and if there's even
the slightest chance. . . ."

"Yes."

"Besides, it's Drytown country; the Darkovan teams won't
risk war by going into it. By the same token, we can't ask the
Amazons. And the pilot was Lish Crowley; I wouldn't trust a
Drytown team to pick up a female officer, Mag."

"Dave, you're absolutely right." She turned up the light
and looked out at the city of Carthon, a city so old, the true
Carthene despised Drytowner and Domains alike as newcomers.

There was one person who knew the Drytowns and was
willing to risk an expedition like this. Now all she had to do
was haul this agent out of a very comfortable retirement and
persuade her to take on an assignment of extreme danger, on
the budget given the Assistant Coordinator's office in Carthon. Camilla n'nakyria, they called her. She had broad,
green acres in the hills behind Carthon where she raised fine
horses and finer cats and lived in a long-cherished solitude.
One could sometimes find her at Amazon House when she

was in town; more likely she would be at the purdah gaming house called the Veil, also known to Terran Intelligence as the Diana Club. And thank the Goddess, the Assistant Coordinator thought with sincerity, that Intelligence had bought its female staff a very expensive membership on the grounds—quite true—that all the gossip in Carthon passed through the gaming rooms of the Diana.

She left her office at the first hour that seemed reasonable, was checked into the club by a white-furred nonhuman guard with a lisp, and let an attendant take her overcoat. Darkovan cloaks and Drytown veils hung next to it in the closet. She settled into the comfortable chair with the name Terran Intelligence on it and let the bartender bring her a whiskey sour. The bartender was a young woman who spoke all three languages fluently; costumed, like all Diana Club servants, in voluminous trousers tucked into soft, low, ankle boots; a neat jacket; and a full-sleeved embroidered blouse. Not the dress of any one of the four cultures one could find here—Terran, Drytown, Darkovan, and Amazon—but acceptable to all. Idly the Terran woman thought she'd one day prove what was so obvious, that Intelligence owned the place.

A lean hand reached across the table to the chessboard on it and moved a pawn. "Good day, Margala," a dry voice said. "What brings the Terran Empire here at this hour?"

Margala looked up at a lean woman in her middle forties with the face of one who has lived hard and the expression of one who is now living very well. She was simply and expensively gowned, although her hair was short and brushed back. "I never thought I'd see you in a dress, Camilla," she counterattacked, then said, "We have a plane down in the Black Hills, with Alicia Crowley aboard. I'm trying to get up a rescue party."

"I am no longer for hire," Camilla said, sipping her Darkovan cordial. "I have everything I need: my horses, my cats, and my land."

"In the name of the Goddess, Camilla."

Camilla's face was cold and deadly. "You do not demand that I help the Terran Empire in the name of the Goddess, Margala!" she said softly, and a long, thin dagger was in her hand.

Margala shook her head. "I don't demand it for the Terran Empire," she told her old riding companion and nemesis. "I demand it for Alicia Crowley, a fellow woman, who will die or be carried off to some Drytown harem—if she's lucky—or to the brothels of Ardcarran, unless you help her. She appealed to me—"

"In the name of Terra Imperia—"

"And I appeal to you."

Camilla let her lifelong codes struggle with the urge to keep her comfortable solitude. "If I agree, when do we go?"

Margala shook her head. "Your pilot will be someone from the Medical Examiner's office, Security and male. You know it's suicide to send someone obviously female into Drytown territory. You, of course, are a mistress of disguise."

Camilla's smile acknowledged a hit. "Send me this boy you would saddle me with. I'll be ready to leave at dawn."

Margala stood up and took Camilla's hands. "Thank you, oath-sister."

"Don't thank me. This is going to cost the Terran Empire dearly.

Bobby Ffoulkes had never seen an expanse of land that great except on posted government reservations. The thought that it was all private property struck him as obscene. He flew over the rail fence, his nerves expecting an automatic warning signal even though he knew this world wasn't up to that technological level. There was no automatic guidance either; he had to fly visually and by the map.

At last he saw a complex of unpainted wooden buildings and resisted the impulse to radio for permission to land—there were no radios on this world. Carefully he set down and got out, proud of his piloting.

A dry voice said "Well, *chiyu,* did you need to come in with all jets blasting and terrify my cats? I have two breeding queens about to kitten."

Bobby gulped. "Very well, ma'am," he said, remembering his orders. *Very important native personnel; do not antagonize.* Angrily he wondered if those orders went both ways. Camilla! Whose bad joke was it to give this hardened old agent the name of the Lady of the Camellias? She looked as if she could be hell to tangle with. He followed her, watching her pick up one of the cats gently, and thought that they were the only thing in the world that could possibly want to get that close to her.

Camilla laid down the cat and moved her head toward a door; behind the door was a small office and a brazier with a pot of *jaco* brewing. Bobby had never learned to like jaco; he accepted a cup and loaded it with milk and honey. Camilla watched him with narrowed eyes. "So you are the one the Terrans decided I must travel with."

"Oh, don't worry, ma'am!" he said with a jaunty assurance he did not feel. "I've worked with women agents before; you won't have any trouble with me treating you as an equal partner. I'm liberated." He looked at her like a puppy waiting to be patted on the head, hoping for her approval.

Her face exploded in incredulous anger and she stood up, hand on the table. "Get this straight, *chiyu*. I do *not* like men. All they do is get in the way when there's a job to be done. Now, if you can work for me without expecting me to flatter you, cater to you, wait on you, and without trying to take over the mission, I'll allow you to come, simply because you know how to fly these Terran machines. But I refuse to cross the Drytowns unless I can count on you not to make trouble. Understand? I suggest you answer with either *Yes, ma'am* or a swift return to Margala's office with the suggestion that she send me a human being. Do you understand?"

What got her so fired up? the young Terran wondered, anger struggling with self-conscious tolerance. *Probably nobody's paid her any attention in years, she's so plain. Oh, the sacrifices we make for the Empire.*

Camilla waited. If the Terrans wanted this expedition badly enough, they'd let her do it on her own terms and send her either three good Amazons who spoke Terran and could fly an aircraft, or someone who'd been around long enough to have some sense knocked into him. Not this patronizing, self-important puppy. She thought of Buck Kendricks; she and the Space Force man heartily disliked each other, but they could work together. Kendricks had learned his business over the years. Puppy seemed crestfallen and shocked, as if no woman had ever offered him hostility, let alone contempt, in his life.

Bobby Ffoulkes looked up at Camilla again and decided, correctly, that she was hoping he would quit. That did it. "Yes, ma'am."

Camilla loaded her gear into the rear of the aircraft as if it was commonplace to her. She wore low boots, tight-wrapped breeches, and loose-sleeved shirt and overshirt, all in shades of orange and brown. She carried a Terran-made communicator and two knives. She stowed her gear and caught Bobby looking at her. "Fly the place, *chiyu*," she said, not unkindly, and leaned back, head and back against her bedroll. Bobby wondered briefly what she was thinking.

He loaded his own gear by slinging it into the back, and climbed into the cockpit. Camilla's sharp voice interrupted him. "Stow it, *chiyu*. We haven't got all day."

"Ma'am—why don't you call me Lieutenant Ffoulkes," Bobby asked, disgusted to find it sounded plaintive even in his own ears.

"The Terrans gave you that title, not I," she answered, not moving from where she sat. She lit a small, sweetish cigarette while Bobby wondered resentfully if she was just going to sit there and not lift a finger to help. He stuffed his bedroll into the nearest locker and jammed his bag in after it under the Darkovan woman's gimlet eyes. When it was all over, he looked at her reproachfully, as if expecting praise. All she said was, "That'll do—for now."

As he started to return to the cockpit, she said, "*Chiyu*— on the trail we each carry our own load, or else it's share and share alike. An Amazon girl of fifteen would know more than you do, but it's not your fault. However, you'll have to learn, and damned fast; we can't afford dead weight on an expedition. Fly the plane."

He climbed into the pilot's seat and started the engines almost mechanically. He couldn't call off the mission now without a downcheck on his record; failure to complete a mission for inability to work with native personnel was especially damning. But once he was safely back at headquarters and told the A.C. what a bitch this Camilla was—and if she didn't listen, he'd go clear to the Legate. Satisfied, he checked the instruments and took off.

"A little hasty, but it will do," Camilla said critically.

Bobby Ffoulkes was a good pilot; his only fault was that he was a little too aware of it. Once the plane was aloft, he was in a mood to talk.

"I wonder why there are no native pilots? Are they just not interested? Or is it that all those generations of a low-technology culture have simply ceased to breed mechanical aptitude? . . ."

"Ask the Terrans," Camilla said curtly. "So far, they're the only people giving flying lessons around Carthon. If you don't mind, *chiyu*, I'm tired of chatter and have the rest of this mission to think about. I advise you to do the same."

Alicia Crowley's plane had crashed into the side of a low dirt hill, covered with scrub dryland vegetation and weeds. The crash webs had protected them from the worst of it, but her entire body was bruised, and there was a severe gash in her leg where the sides of the plane had caved in and broken. Roger, in the next seat, looked unpleasantly dead, but she could hear breathing, rather shallow, from his side. The first-aid kit was scattered all over the back of the plane. The crate of kireseth had fallen through a cargo hatch that now dangled, door on one hinge, from a bent and buckled hole.

The beacon was still broadcasting, and that was good news, unless Roger was in with a ring of smugglers who were watching for just this. Alicia laughed a little; that was a plot out of teledrama, not likely on personnel-short Darkover. For sure, the natives wouldn't pick up the signal; the Drytowns thought Terrans were a figment of Domain imagination, and Terra was not about to enlighten them. The Drytowners near Carthon, who knew better, also knew better than to tangle with the Empire.

That was evasion. Forcing herself to unfasten the crash web, she took stock. She could stand up, and even walk, that was the first thing. The rations were all over the place, but the little plastic bags they were in were mostly intact; they wouldn't starve. Salvaging the antiseptic and some bandages from the first-aid kit, she tended her cut. That would have to do until she could get to a doctor and have it stitched.

The water was low. The crash had broken the water tank, causing a leak about a third of the way up. They'd have to drink what they boiled their freeze-dried rations in, and use almost none for any other purpose.

They had shelter and food. They could probably burn the brush for fuel if they took care not to start a forest fire. The plane was completely dead; when she tried to start it, it made a feeble grinding noise, and then quit. Probably the impact had cracked the starting system. The radio didn't work.

Roger had a head injury. Uncharitably she thought that damaging Roger's brain was like bringing sand to the Drytowns. She mopped down his face with a very, very little bit of the water; he stirred feebly and tried his bonds again. She thought of the length of time he had been in the seat, drew a gun, and cautiously released him. He looked dazed; she took him by the arm and led him toward the plane's sanitary facilities. She even let him lock the door behind him. Then she set the flush valve to NO, and inside the head, the sign lit up: "We are over a populated area. Do not flush. Close lid behind you." From inside she heard the blessed sound of Roger laughing.

The *rf* locator's steady hum had gone from inaudible to subliminal to the very verge of audibility, and Bobby wondered when Camilla would order him, harshly, to turn that damned thing off. When she didn't, he decided that she must not have normal human ears. Perhaps her hearing had grown as calloused as her hands and as hardened as her face. *They don't feel things the way we do,* he thought vaguely. "We're getting there, ma'am," he said hopefully.

"I can hear that," she answered, and lit the second of her funny native cigarettes.

"That smells good, ma'am," he said then. "Mind if I try one?"

"The little boy would try women's vices?" she asked with almost a smile. "Not now, *chiyu.* Perhaps later. Does your machine say how far we have to go?"

Rebuffed, Bobby resolved not to share his six-pack of beer with the old witch. "Not in so many kilometers, ma'am, but we have a range. Can you read a map?"

Camilla only smiled at that absurdity and leaned over the seat, reaching out with one thin finger at the hills to the south and west. "I hope you aren't planning to go that way," she said, "or we walk from here," her finger landed on a point far short of the marker that indicated the downed plane, "on in."

Suddenly Bobby turned around. "With all due respects, ma'am, I'm flying this plane," he snapped.

"Very well," she said, and went back to her seat in the back.

That put her in her place, Bobby thought with satisfaction, and turned the plane south and west. His satisfaction lasted for several hours.

A very frightened Bobby Ffoulkes clung to the aircraft steering gear and wrestled the plane against the high and turbulent winds of the Black Hills. The corner of his mind that held his rather shaky pride kept running the expected scene with Camilla, as soon as they were on the ground. At least she had the sense not to exercise her taste for bawling him out while he was trying to land. But his inner mind was very badly on the defensive. Who could have expected her to know anything about flying conditions in the Black Hills?

She would say he had refused her advice because she was a woman, or because she was native. It wouldn't help to admit he'd refused it because she was forever on his back; the last thing he needed was a downcheck for immaturity.

Why didn't she say something?

A high wind buffeted him from the right; he overcorrected, and nearly tore a wing off as he banked steeply to avoid a hillside. Correcting the correction, he muttered a few things under his breath, saw a smooth stretch of dirt ahead, and headed into it. From the rear of the plane, Camilla spoke for the first time in several hours. "Land at the far end. It's soft sand down here."

"Yes, ma'am," he said, and there was no anger in it at all. Pulling up slowly, he skimmed the sand until he could see for himself where the texture changed, and very carefully reduced speed and set down. The motor idled a few minutes and died; Bobby sat there shaking. Then he said sincerely, "Thank you, Camilla."

Camilla nodded. "Bring water for three days," was all she said.

They wore Drytown headcloths and the breeches worn by men of the Domains. Camilla added a shabby Drytown shirt-cloak and weapons of the style of the Domains. For Bobby she had a very shabby Service jacket with the buttons and insignia ripped off. He looked at the disguise dubiously. "Why don't we wear native gear? Wouldn't it be less conspicuous?"

Camilla nodded, and in a dialect he could scarcely follow said, "Who was thy father, water-brother? And what is thy father's tribe? Oh? I have not heard of a Jalak-son-of-Yussoph around the Wells of Shieth. Who gave thee leave to drink from the wells of the tribe? . . ."

"I see," Bobby said at last. "It's one big kinship network, and you can't plug into it at random. I can see I don't know anything about the Drytowns." He looked at the map and frowned. "It doesn't look like good hiking country. Are you sure you know a way through these hills?"

"Several ways," she said. "Bring the maker of squealing

sounds to guide us; it works line-of-sight, but its vision is better than ours."

"Yes ma'am," he said in startled respect.

They made up bedrolls and packs and started off. Bobby bit his tongue on an assurance that he would try to keep his pace down to one she could match easily, and after a while was glad he'd had the sense to keep his mouth shut. It had never crossed his mind that a woman twenty years older than he could set a pace like that.

His mistake in the air bothered him badly. After a while he said, "I'm sorry about the plane. I mean, about not listening to you. I didn't realize you knew. . . ."

"Just don't try to prove your points when the dice are really thrown, *chiyu*," she said dryly.

"I wasn't trying to prove anything."

"It's just that you don't need a woman to tell you what to do." She turned back to look at him as if he were a horse she was on the verge of getting rid of. "The Terrans send me all their unlicked cubs," she said tersely. "The girls—I do not call them women—are still tied to their nursemaid's apron strings. The boys have not been housebroken. I can only imagine that Margala knows I tolerate no nonsense." She turned to face front and kept moving.

The hills were low and rolling, covered scantily with spice-bush and weeds. The weeds were tall, spiky, and equipped with a wide variety of things that stuck to clothes and socks, burrowing into the fabric and coming out again in tender spots. The ground was dusty, irregular, pockmarked with animal burrows and rocks and eroded places. Camilla kept up a steady pace. Bobby, whose basic idea of grass was a layer of green shredded plastic over foam on a concrete base, found it hard going.

There were insects. He had rather hoped the Darkovan insects wouldn't bite a Terran—incompatible metabolisms or something. It was a vain hope.

There was dust in the air, clinging to the inside of Bobby's nostrils, drying his mouth. He had never thought much about drinking water; the fountain had always been just down the hall. He started to drink from his canteen, wondered how much he could spare, watched Camilla, and realized she had not touched her canteen at all. Of course, she might be able to store water like a camel, he thought sourly.

Lawrence of Arabia, he remembered, had made a point of

refusing to drink until his desert tribesmen did. That was on a teledrama he had seen at the Academy. *Come on, Bobby, be a hero.* It was hard when the inside of his mouth was growing drier and drier, and tasting nastier by the hour. That old woman had practiced this for a lifetime, he thought resentfully, plodding along more and more slowly. His back hurt from the unaccustomed weight, for he was no hiker; his feet hurt and there was no relief in sight.

At the top of a hill, Camilla stopped and surveyed the land, shading her eyes with one hand. "Try your finder, Bobby," she said absently, and uncorked her canteen. Bobby turned it on and wondered if he shouldn't try to hold out a little longer. It was embarrassing to be outdone by an old woman!

"Drink, *chiyu*," she said harshly. "I'm not going to pack three bodies out of here because of Earthman's *kihar*." He uncorked his canteen and started to drink; she stopped him, one hand on his canteen. "Slowly, or you'll be sick."

Bitter at the fact that he needed a babysitter, he drank slowly, as she suggested, corked the canteen and moved on when she did.

By the time the crimson sun was halfway down in a violet sky, Bobby was ready to face the fact that he was not going to make it to sunset. Every step was agony, and his breath was coming short. His legs ached and his pack gouged into him, resting against bone or the wrong muscle, an agony of discomfort. He was plodding, one foot in front of the other by a conscious act of will. He had exhausted the inspiration of heroes long ago; either they were made of different stuff than Bobby Ffoulkes or it was this damned alien planet where the gravity felt wrong, the air was too thin, and even the texture of the dirt and weeds were wrong.

He had also exhausted the necessity to be a man; Camilla, by that standard, was much more of a man than he was. In a wheezing voice he acknowledged it.

Camilla turned around, her eyes cold fire in a weather-beaten face. "Call me that again, and I'll leave you where you stand. Think I consider it an honor, to be called a man? I am a woman; learn that well, *chiyu*, and remember it."

Bobby gaped resentfully and decided Camilla had decided—just like a woman—that his comment was a slur on her ugliness rather than a tribute to her better qualities. *You*

can't please them, he thought sourly, *whatever you do or say.*
You just can't win!

Camilla looked at him and said nothing, but dropped back
beside him. It was impossible to think nasty things at her
back that way, and carefully he suppressed most of his
brooding. Manhood still demanded that he not quit, at least
not before she did, but he was glad to slow down.

"Where were you bred, *chiyu*?" she demanded abruptly.

"Alpha Colony, ma'am."

She sorted through her memory. "Where there is no out-
doors, but one great building, for the land is so barren nobody crosses it on foot but fools and suicides. Where all
things weigh three-quarters of what they do here, though how
they do this—no, don't explain, Margala has tried." She
turned to face him, looking like a fierce old hawk. "Arrogance is a failing of your kind; physical weakness is not,
unless there is a reason. It is the Amazon wisdom to, always,
seek the reason. But it is a great folly of men to feel they
must do more than they can, for *kihar*; and women to slow
down and walk beside them. Sit down."

He sat; she made him remove his boots and scowled at his
feet. "Did anybody tell you what sort of footgear to wear for
this? Next time, *chiyu*, wear two pair of heavy woollen socks,
or sheepskin boot liners." She fished a vial of salve from her
pack. "Put it on and put your feet up." She looked at the
pack, lying against the nearest rock. "Tomorrow I will help
you fit that to your back; accept the help or not, as you
choose. Now let me make camp tonight and tomorrow; you
cook."

He opened his mouth, then realized he could not get up on
his blistered feet again if he wanted to. While she moved
around and did all the work of setting up camp, he put some
freeze-dried rations in a tin of boiling water and watched until they were done.

She ate as heartily as she had worked, and urged him to
eat, saying acidly, "I will not haul you over the mountains on
my back because you will not refuel your body." After supper, she brought out a small mouth harp from her pocket and
began to play one of the wild, meterless songs of the
Darkovan hills.

The crimson sun set over the horizon and the fire flickered
low. Bobby, suddenly very sleepy, surprised himself by asking,
"How did you become an Amazon, or were you born one?"

"No. Some are, but I was the daughter of a landowner, and I supposed as spoiled and protected as most. It's a long story, *chiyu*, and one I have told to only two people, one of whom is dead." Bobby gulped, imagining the cause of death; Camilla went on, "She was my oath-mother, and more dear to me than mother or sister or any living being. The other is my oath-sister, and almost as dear." Then she said, "I wonder how Alicia Crowley fares tonight?"

Alicia Crowley yawned, counted the rations again, and tried to ignore the nagging pain in her leg. It was beginning to itch, a good sign, but was driving her mad. Her face felt grubby, and her hair itched.

She tried to interest herself in the novel she had brought with her, but she now had it memorized. She stretched and pushed her shoulderblades together to ease the ache in her back, and made the hourly entry in the log.

Stay with the plane. It was pounded into them at flight school that the most foolish thing a pilot could do was abandon the plane, except under extraordinary circumstances. Planes were easier to locate from the air than people. Alicia Crowley sighed and yawned. It was an everpresent temptation to pack up and leave, just to be doing something. Any form of action felt better than none to her. She picked up the advertisements in the back of Roger's *Fortuneseeker* magazine and pored over the queer little ventures in daydreams of instant wealth.

Maybe this was Roger's form of doing something.

Camilla and Bobby were up at dawn. By unspoken consent, Bobby made breakfast while Camilla packed. He had never cared for freeze-dried rations and was surprised at how satisfying they were. Camilla ate with a hearty appetite; he found that satisfying, too, almost a tribute to his cooking. A mild breeze blew through the underbrush, bringing with it the faint, sharp smells of the scrub vegetation. Somewhere an insect or a harsh-voiced bird called.

Camilla packed her half of the load and came over to the campfire, where Bobby was frowning down at what was left. "Scrub them with sand," she said neutrally, "and bury the leavings. The trash goes at the bottom of your pack. How are your feet?"

He tried to judge whether he could walk another day on

them without admitting he needed help; Camilla snorted. "*Kihar* is a luxury I don't carry on the trail. Take off your boots, salve them with this, and wear these." She tossed him two rolled-up pair of native, hand-knit socks. When he had his boots back on, she directed him in the packing of his backpack, and settled it for him on his back. They covered all traces of their campsite and walked on, guided by the sun and the compass and Bobby's beacon-finder.

He was sore; there was a vast difference between working out in the gym and actual outdoor action. But the soreness was working itself out as he walked, and he had not expected that. Something flew past out of a bush, startling him. The Black Hills loomed up ahead, craggy and barren, making the hills they were now in seem green and inviting, almost homey. A bird ran across their path as if in a road race. Camilla, silent until now, pointed out the flowers and leaf patterns on some of the bushes, their use, their names, and some of the geological formations of the rocks. Bobby began to realize that this was an entire world, and listened with some interest.

They climbed higher and higher, and even though the sun grew warmer as the day wore on, the wind developed a thin, chill edge. Bobby's feet were beginning to hurt again before he realized he had been enjoying the walk. Despite Camilla's instructions, he suffered the aching feet in silence a long time for pride's sake, and began making a game of it. *How long can I hold out?* But his step slowed and became plodding. *It's only pain,* he told himself.

Camilla fell back beside him. "So we lose another day to your foolishness," she rasped harshly. "Take off your boots." She scowled at what she saw, and not just because his feet smelled. "Blisters. Of course. More blisters than common sense." Her hand lashed out and caught his cheek. He yelped and hit back; her hand caught his wrist and held it hard. "I should send you back alone to the Terrans and let the *kyorebni* eat you on the way back," she said coldly, her eyes hard. "You, a little boy who cannot resist playing his little games when there are lives at stake, have been far more trouble than you're worth, so far. Now dress those feet and walk beside me the best that you can and follow either my lead or my orders or go back home to Mama. Is that understood?"

Bobby swallowed hard, and then, swallowing his pride, said, "I don't understand. I know I've made some sort of mistake, but I don't understand why it seems to be such a big one. I got blisters, but we've been walking a long way, and I'm no hiker. I'm trying my best, but it's not my world and I'm a raw beginner in this."

"The beginning of wisdom," Camilla said much more gently. "Some blisters are inevitable, yes. But if you cripple yourself, we cannot go on, and any delay may mean the lives of Alicia Crowley and her partner. We have a saying, 'There are none so old they cannot learn, and none so young they cannot teach.' But to my sorrow I must remind so many of you, 'There are none so *young* they cannot learn!' "

Roger was raving. Alicia Crowley felt his face and found it hot. She tried to give him another fever pill; he looked at her with dull brown eyes and muttered, "Bitch."

"Sit down, shut up, and take it," she snapped, her patience worn thin by four days of boredom, pain, and worry.

"Poor Roger," he said nastily. "Great big Lish has to look after Poor Roger, doesn't she? What is it, Lish? Feeling bad because you've gone places and I haven't? All those parties I get into on your skirt-tails. All the nice missions we get because Lish Crowley is running things. Ever since we were classmates at the Academy, Lish Crowley has been the big shot and Poor Roger has trailed after her."

Her face white, Lish made a fist. "Take this damn pill, Roger, before I deck you and stuff it down you. You're sick and wounded and raving. If you want out I'll be glad to oblige you—that little caper of yours that got us into this has already taken care of that—look me up when you're out of Rehabilitation and we'll talk about it."

Roger's answer was an obscene invitation.

Lish took the pressure points of his jaw and forced his mouth open, dumped pill and water down it, and forcibly closed his mouth, stroking his throat exactly as if he had been a recalcitrant animal. Her eyes went to the beacon. Damn that rescue party, would they ever arrive?

As Roger slept again, she paced the floor of the wreck, biting her lip. She should have known—there had been inklings all along—of Roger's resentment of her success, his jealousy. She had dismissed the inklings as nonsense. If she had been one of the flashy, brilliant types to whom success came easily, the sort Roger so desperately envied and wanted to be like, she could see it. But Lish was a plodder; her success came through hard work, and Roger knew it. He had tried to drag her away from it often enough.

They had been classmates, and friends; by their senior year nobody had thought about Lish without Roger, or Roger without Lish. They were friends, and nobody sensed the curdled hatred under the friendship. The friendship, irretrievably broken by Lish's discovery of Roger's *kireseth* smuggling, died, leaving only an empty ache.

When would that rescue team show up? It was going to be a long night.

The little moon Kyrddis was rising over the crest of the hills when two shabby, shadowy figures approached the wrecked Terran aircraft. Lish Crowley, sleeping lightly in her restless anxiety, woke instantly and froze in the pilot's seat, unmoving and almost not breathing. One hand went to the gun she now carried at all times. In the dim multiple moonlight she could make out the robes and headcloths of the desert tribes, so unlike the tailored outlines of a Terran party. There were only two of them, and they were on foot.

There was one of her, and she was armed. Her leg was badly inflamed by now, but she could still see to shoot straight. She had the gun nearly triggered when the smaller figure called softly, "Alicia Crowley?" The accent was that of the Domains.

She said nothing. A second voice added to the first. "Captain Crowley? We're from Headquarters in Carthon. Lieutenant Ffoulkes and Camilla n'ha. . . ." His voice trailed off as if he had forgotten and was embarrassed. Lish Crowley laughed.

"Come on aboard, friends. I hope you brought some help. We have one down and one wounded and no way of getting this bird out of here."

Camilla undid her pack and opened two collapsible aluminum poles. She arranged a hammock sling between them and fastened two crossbars for rigidity. "I was prepared to pack both of you out if need be," she said.

Bobby's mouth dropped. "On foot? Just the two of us?"

"And this is the first time you asked how we would do this?" Camilla snapped. She pulled a bottle of highly compressed gas out of her pack. "Your half, *chiyu*," she said in an impersonal tone. Bobby opened his pack and set up a second stretcher and gas bottle. Camilla lashed them together and, to the amazement of her younger companion, attached what seemed to be a balloon to each corner. Carefully she inflated the balloons. She and Bobby carried the unconscious, drugged Roger to the first stretcher; Lish Crowley gratefully sat down on the second. Bobby took the back; Camilla the front; they set back out over the hills.

"Balloons like this have been used by the Terrans to fly with, have they not?" she asked. "That we dare not do in hills like these, but if they will fly, they will surely relieve our backs of half the weight. I thought of this while I pondered how the weight of things can vary from place to place in the Terran Empire. Margala gladly let me use the markings, and I think will use the idea. We will see if it works."

"I hope it does," Bobby said fervently.

Lish laughed. "Good old Camilla. She tore several strips off my hide when I was just out of training. Told me if I was a sample of what Terrans bred in women, we should all be sold to the Drytowners for pets. Weak sister was the least of what she said."

That was a novel idea to Bobby. "You, too?" he demanded.

Lish, light-headed, kept on talking. "You got the—what I mentioned on the radio. Didn't you? I don't want that stuff loose on Earth! Look, Roger didn't mean any harm. . . ."

"Relief," Camilla growled. "Sister, I am not concerned with what he meant or did not mean to do. I am concerned that the kireseth is not sold as a pleasure-drug among the Terrans. Paah. If I were you and could not control someone under me any better than that, I would return and beg the Mothers to teach me the simplest of girl-lessons."

Lish, abashed, stopped talking while Bobby gaped at hearing another laced into in harsher terms that she had ever used on him.

"You won't be too hard on Roger, will you?" Lish asked again, and then was silent.

Bobby's aircraft was waiting for them at the edge of the Black Hills, and so was his six-pack. As soon as passengers and cargo were loaded aboard, and Roger restrained by the crash web, and everyone had used the facilities to clean up and had eaten, he opened the beer and passed it around. The downcheck that was awaiting him for careless piloting—that had better be awaiting him, or the A.C. didn't know her business—no longer bothered him. He had earned it. It seemed to him there was quite a bit else he had earned, too.

He flew them into Carthon, helped unload Lish to the hospital, Roger to a prison hospital, and Camilla to bachelor womens' quarters, all for a night's sleep. In the morning, the A.C. called him in to report.

"So, you think you did well," she asked.

Bobby stood his ground. "No, ma'am. I made mistake after mistake," he admitted. "Some of it was just plain stupid; I was cocksure, and wouldn't listen. But we got the job done."

"You did." The woman the natives called Margala thought a minute, and looked into space. "What do you think of Camilla as a partner?"

Bobby swallowed. "Ma'am, I think she's competent, very competent. Her only fault is that she can't work with people."

A slight smile played around Margala's mouth, as if she were remembering. "She can't, eh? You mean, she is not pleasing. She is abrupt, blunt-spoken. . . ."

"Abrasive, belligerent, yes, ma'am." Bobby frowned, as if he detected something going imperceptibly wrong here.

"You wouldn't work with her to train native pilots, then? That was the price she demanded for taking on this mission."

Bobby thought it over rapidly, and to do him justice, the damage he would do his career for refusing only entered his head for a moment, in passing. "I think I could, yes, ma'am."

His superior officer grinned openly. "Abrasive, belligerent, abrupt, intolerant of nonsense, a woman who has never bothered to cultivate a pleasing personality—no, she would not be a diplomat. But has it ever occurred to you that this is the perfect description of a basic training officer?" Margala's grin became laughter. "And as far as she's concerned, you've won your wings. Congratulations, Lieutenant Ffoulkes; you've graduated."

After a few minutes, Bobby laughed too. Then he said, "When do we start?"

WHERE THE HEART IS

by Millea Kenin

The sky was a light, luminous gray, and the sun shone like a pale pearl behind the thin, permanent cloud cover. On the islands, silver-green foliage and purplish rocks were reflected in the quiet sea. The slender, red-haired girl called Marja turned the tiller fractionally and let out sail, catching every bit of the slight breeze with practiced skill. She wondered if the damp warm air, the muted colors would ever stop seeming wrong to her.

Her little brother and sister noticed nothing amiss. "Look, there's a Sirene!" Dori cried.

"Where?" Ken asked. "No, that was just a slicewater's fin."

The younger children had known no other world. Wherever they would come to live, on any of scores of planets, no doubt pale-gray skies and warm seas filled with little islands would be the measure of home for them. For Marja, home was very different—a great red sun in a violet sky, mountains, cold clear air full of scents that she could remember clearly, even though she could not remember any of the details of her early childhood.

Darkover! There were pain and fear blotting out the details of her first memories, and warmth and love in her present life, but she knew that one day she would return.

The dim purples and grays here on Sirenia never seemed to be quite in focus for Marja, though her eyesight had been checked thoroughly and proved normal. But it was worse today. She felt dizzy, almost nauseated. Could it be threshold sickness? Dio, Marja's foster mother, had warned her of this danger that could come with the changes now beginning to take place within her body. If the sickness did not pass quickly, she would tell her parents tonight.

"It is *so* a Sirene!" Dori bounced, and was caught roughly by her brother.

"Sit down and stop rocking the boat!" Ken growled in a voice that was deep for a little boy.

"Marja," Dori cried. "Ken hurted my arm!"

"I was just trying to keep her from falling out of the boat."

"I was not going to fall out!"

"Stop fighting, both of you." Marja gave them only a little of her attention. She could see by the shape of the narrow triangular wakes that cut the quiet water that three Sirenes were swimming toward their boat, and she took in sail and waited to see what they wanted.

Soon they came up to the sailboat and took an upright position like humans treading water. They were sleek, streamlined beings a little larger than humans, with rubbery grayish-lavender hides. They wore necklaces and bracelets of twisted golden wires with shells strung on them. They had smooth, inscrutable faces, with flat dark eyes; their ears and nostrils were slits that could close tight. They spoke in frequencies no human could hear.

Greetings, little sister.

Their telepathic message was, as usual, clear to Marja. She did not know why neither Dio nor Lew, her father, could communicate with the Sirenes. It might have been a function of her own particular kind of *laran*, or it might have been the Sirenes themselves who chose to speak with her alone. They had asked her to promise not to reveal that she could understand them until they were ready—whatever that meant—and she had reluctantly agreed. Reluctantly, because her parents were involved in a project to try to communicate with the Sirenes, so far in vain; it was painful for Marja to conceal something so important from fellow telepaths whom she loved.

Greetings, she replied. These three were Marja's friends, and she sent a sense of glad recognition; they had no names that she could call them by.

You must go back. All of them were agitated. *It is time to tell your father about us.*

Why now? What's the hurry?

The cage-makers have taken an elder of the Sisterhood, and they are trying to make your father—

Now communication broke down; she could not grasp the concept the Sirenes were trying to convey, though each of them attempted, in obvious desperation, to express it in a different way.

Never mind why, sent the largest and eldest Sirene. *Your father will be in danger if you don't tell him to link with us through you.*

All right. Marja prepared to come about.

"What are you doing?" Ken asked.

"Going home."

"But we just got started!" Dori protested.

"The Sirenes say Father is in danger. We've got to go home and help."

"The Sirenes talk to you? I thought nobody could understand them."

"What kind of danger?"

Both children spoke at once, and Marja answered, "Yes, they tell me things in my mind, just the same as human beings do, except I can't always understand them. I don't understand what kind of danger, though they've been trying to tell me. But they say to hurry."

Vance Tellerin's fist crashed down on Lew's desk. "Dammit, Lanart, the only reason you got hired for this project is your so-called wild talent. There's not a thing you're doing now that any college kid couldn't do better for half your salary. Now we've tried just about every damn thing else and you're going to have to produce."

The other man's scarred face stiffened. "Even if I could guarantee the ability to force rapport with a member of a nonhuman species—"

"You're trying to tell me you don't think you *can* do it?"

"I don't know if I can." He kept his voice carefully level. "I'm trying to point out that it could be very dangerous if I succeed."

"I can understand your being scared, but—"

"Listen to me, Van." Lew did not raise his voice, but something in his eyes made his supervisor step back a pace. "You can't understand. I've been through things I'd much rather not talk about. When I say danger, I don't mean just to me. To begin with, it would be more likely than not to kill the Sirene involved."

"That's a risk I'll take responsibility for."

Did Vance think of himself as a military commander: *go out, kill or get killed, on my head be it?* On Darkover, even in armed conflict one never so surrendered one's own responsibility. Lew could never make Vance understand this; he gave him another, more urgent reason.

"As we have mentioned in our reports, from the little Dio and I have been able to get from the Sirenes, we have come to the conclusion that they are telepaths in communication with one another, but blocking us—whether deliberately or because their minds simply work differently from ours we do not yet know. If we kill one of them, it is likely that others will know, and we don't know what their reaction will be."

"We have no evidence that they have any weapons or even any capacity for violence."

"We don't know what they have!" Lew found he was raising his voice, despite all his efforts to remain calm. "Isn't that the whole point?"

"We know they have a technology based on principles we can't guess. They produce pure gold without the use of fire. Terra needs that information."

"You've been getting pressure from higher up, is that it, Tellerin?"

Perhaps it had been rash to goad the man. Vance Tellerin's chest swelled and his face flushed. Then he relaxed, and his lips twitched in a brief ironic smile. "Well, yes. That's it in a nutshell. That's why we can't wait for Ordaz's number-theory experiments or Project Orphan to pan out, not unless we can prove we've tried everything else. If you don't try your psychic whammy—"

Lew winced. Well, he could hardly resent Tellerin's contempt; the feeling was mutual.

Tellerin went on, "Or if it doesn't work, I'll have no option but to let Karajan go ahead with his stress-tolerance tests and autopsies of the subjects. We've got to have something to show for our efforts by the time the next ship from Terra arrives."

Lew thought of the elderly female Sirene now penned in a tiny pool the size of a solitary cell. The worst that could happen to her as a result of anything he might do was sudden death. Even that was preferable to the slow torture Karajan's experiment would inflict on her.

"All right." He rose to his feet and stood towering over the other man, knowing, as always, that Tellerin resented this. "We can go ahead as soon as Dio can leave her orphans."

"Why do you need her?"

"Because she is the only person on this whole planet who is

trained as a psi monitor. Believe me, if I could keep her out
of it, I would." The sensitivity that was part of his wife's em-
pathic gift would make it difficult for her to remain outside
the rapport, and would leave her vulnerable to all the pain
both he and the Sirene might experience. But she would have
to be there, to keep track of his pulse, his breathing, his
muscles; he would be unaware of his body.

Lew and Tellerin went to the pool where Dio and Anji
Wong from Samarra worked with their charges—two Sirenes
found as infants washed ashore on a rocky cove after a
storm, slightly injured, no adults in sight. They were about
three standard years old now, and much like human children
of that age. It might be many years, if ever, before they developed the telepathic powers that would enable them to be a
bridge between their native species and their adopted one.
Lew's children and the other human children on Sirenia often
came to play with them, but they were not there now. Lew
remembered that Marja had taken Ken and Dori for a sail
and a picnic on the next island.

The two orphans came swimming up to the side of the
pool, deliberately splashing with their broad flippers. Their
voices sounded like tiny squeaks until they held their commu-
nicators—encased in waterproof plastic—to their lips. "Come
in the water with us, Anji." "Come play ball." The sounds
were transformed into human auditory range. The young
woman with short black hair joined the two in the pool, while
Lew explained to Dio what was going to happen. She was as
distressed as he about it, but could not see any alternative.
There was no point delaying the inevitable.

Within a few minutes Lew was lying on a cot set up next to
the small pool where the old Sirene swam listlessly in circles,
while Dio sat next to him, not actually touching him, fingertips near a pulse spot in his wrist. He stared into his matrix,
the blue starstone that he always carried but rarely removed
from its leather pouch.

Gradually he began to perceive the surface thought patterns of the person in the pool. For herself there was defeat,
despair—but not resignation. There was power, though not a
power that could be used to save herself. Not her own power,
exactly—a power that she was in touch with and trusted in,
in some ultimate way, despite her belief that she was beyond
help.

He dimly perceived in that mind a discipline, foreign to his experience, that reminded him nonetheless of a Keeper. He sent a telepathic message and knew it was received, though not how much was understood. He warned her of what he was going to do. *If you can relax, not resist, let me in, it should not hurt. If you must block, I must try to break through.*

He put forth the focused-psychic force that was his hereditary gift, and came up against the solid wall that was there with all Sirenes. Like a ray of light focused by a ruby to a laser, his thought went through the matrix, sharpened, narrowed, intensified, irresistible—

It was like an explosion. He had planned all along to cut the connection at the last minute if it was the only alternative to destruction, but it happened too fast. He learned a million things at once, jumbled together. (The Sirenes used a kind of *laran* to work inert metals without fire. Much good would that do the Terrans!) He perceived the nature of the Sisterhood and what it was to be an elder, though he could not have explained it, and realized that to force rapport on such a one was like raping a virgin Keeper.

Pain and self-disgust threatened to tear him apart; yet he did not know what else he could have done. He let the wave wash over him (was that his image? no, the Sirene's) and found himself in the cool gray peace of the Overworld.

Urged on by the three Sirenes, Marja had sailed back to the dock as fast as the erratic breezes would allow. Ken, pleased at his skill, had made the boat fast to the mooring. The Sirenes swam under the dock, where they would be hidden in the shadows. *Hurry!* they urged the children.

"Come on, quick!" called Marja and started running toward the lab building without a glance behind. She could sense telepathically that Ken and Dori were keeping up, though they were startled and confused. She almost always could sense the location of everyone she cared for as well as their surface feelings.

What her father was feeling right now terrified her. She could not keep from getting pulled in, as to a whirlpool: her father's loathing of what he was being forced to do, the Sirene's despair and pain, pain, pain!

In her own body she was overwhelmed by nausea and vertigo. It felt as if she and everything around her were dissolving into formless turbulence. She fell, or the path rose up to meet her, and she did not know whether she hit hard ground or melted into an eddying stream.

Then she was standing in a quiet gray place. Others were there too, far away in different directions. One was a tall young man whom she knew—though he had two hands and his face was unscarred—to be her father, Lew. Another was a very beautiful Sirene, whose face wore a calm and radiant smile, and who seemed to float above the gray surface where Marja stood, upright, as Sirenes did when holding a position in the water. A third was a young man whom she had never seen before. He looked slender but strong, and so strange were the colors in that place that she did not know whether his hair was red or white.

Although they were in different places, Marja found that she could approach them all at the same time, and all of them seemed to be approaching her. She was not walking step by step, but gliding over the ground as she had sometimes done in dreams. Yet she knew that she was not dreaming this; she was not locked in her own mind, but in a place where many minds could meet. This, she was sure, must be the Overworld.

Gradually they neared one another and began to converse telepathically. The Sirene explained that her people had been blocking communication with the humans, except for Marja, until they had learned enough from the girl to feel safer about dealing with these strange beings who had invaded their planet. Yet they had been aware of a great deal that was going on in the minds of the participants in the Project, and had gotten enough of a sense of what forced rapport was to know that Lew's attempt could kill both her and him, if Marja was not part of the link.

Maria did not yet understand why her presence was necessary. The Sirenes classified *laran*, studied, developed and used it in a very different way from Darkovans, and they seemed to think that, of the developed telepaths on Sirenia (herself, Lew and Dio, that was) she alone had the right kind.

Nonetheless, something had gone wrong. This was not what was supposed to have happened. The three of them were stuck in the Overworld, unable to return to their bodies, and if they did not soon do so, they would die.

The strange man replied. No, not a stranger. *Regis!* Lew sent a glad thought, as if he were greeting an old friend he had expected never to see again. *Where are you?*

Here, and on Darkover. He smiled. Marja now learned
that he was Regis Hastur of Project Telepath on Darkover,
head of the new Telepaths' Council that had replaced the old
Comyn Council.

I could go back! Lew thought, and his joy was shadowed
with grief: this new development, where all Darkovan telepaths regardless of ancestry might meet as equals, had happened too late for his brother Marius.

*Yes, but you don't have to. You are a link, right where
you are. This event—painful though it is on your end—has
opened a channel for communication between Darkover and
Sirenia. It can be reopened forever. You can start a circle
there; we'll help.*

But what has gone wrong now, and how can it be mended?
Marja wondered, and Regis heard and answered. This had
happened when she was beginning to get threshold sickness,
and had brought on a near-fatal attack. Lew had more or less
assumed that threshold sickness would not be a problem for
Marja, since her *laran* had been well established long before
puberty.

Regis explained that, as part of Project Telepath, there had
been an attempt to find whatever records had survived of information lost during the Ages of Chaos. Histories of particular families had enabled them to reconstruct some of the
stages in the breeding program that had fixed certain *laran*
gifts in the Comyn families and made them somewhat rare
among other Darkovans. Early onset of *laran* had nearly
died out, precisely because it was associated genetically with
really terrible threshold sickness.

So what Lew would have to do would be to draw on the
strength of Regis's circle to return to his own body, and then
to get into rapport with Dio and get her help with Marja.
Here in the Overworld, where there was no such thing as
weather, Marja found herself shuddering as if with cold at
the thought of the pain that awaited her once her consciousness was reunited with her body, though she could not feel it
now.

She awoke to find herself lying on a cot beside the pool.
Dori and Ken must have run for help and had her carried
here. She felt bruised all over, and from the sick taste in her
mouth and raw feeling in her throat, she knew she must have

vomited, but she had been washed and wrapped in a blanket. Dio's face bent over her, worry relaxing as their eyes met.

Her slim, fair foster-mother sighed and hugged her. "How are you feeling, dear?"

"Awful!"

"Any blurring of vision? Any sense that things are not quite solid?"

"No! Things are awfully solid!" She grimaced.

"Let me know *immediately* if you start feeling dizzy, or if things start to dissolve. You'll have to get up and walk, no matter how sick you feel."

Marja raised herself on one elbow. There was a brief moment of dizziness, but it passed before she could mention it. Lew lay on the next cot, with the two younger children curled up with him, and the Sirene leaned on her elbows on the rim of the pool. All of them wore exhausted grins.

Lew's boss, Vance Tellerin, was standing some paces off, looking baffled and annoyed, but no one was paying the least attention to him.

Marja lay back and relaxed. More poignantly even than before, a memory of the hills and bloody sun of Darkover came to her, and she vowed that one day she would return. But now she knew there was no hurry. Home, according to an old Terran saying, was where the heart is. And now she understood—with a little giggle—what that meant. Hers was beating steadily inside her chest, and while she lived she would have to carry it with her wherever she went.

SKEPTIC

by Lynn Mims

"It had to happen sometime," Jason Allison said grimly, "and it's happening now."

David Hamilton looked up from his sheaf of reports. Project Telepath was running smoothly; the newest batch of telepaths were completing their tests and entering the orientation classes. Jason's disquiet was disturbing.

"What's the problem, Jason?"

Allison threw down a dispatch "flimsy" in answer. David read: "Caleb Hargraves and aide arriving Thendara Spaceport on liner *Palladium*. Hargraves to conduct investigation of Project Telepath under authority of Senator Mark Velosin. Project Telepath officers Allison and Hamilton advised to co-operate with Hargraves in every way. Casterbridge, Alien Anthropology."

"So? We've had other guests."

"Not like this. Hargraves is a professional skeptic." Jason smiled at his friend's surprise. "He makes his living—a good one, it seems—exposing charlatans and psi-quacks. Between witchhunts he works the university lecture circuits."

"If he's coming here to find charlatans he's going to be disappointed," David said. He tried to lighten Jason's mood, adding, "We were bound to get someone like Hargraves sometime. Since the Council began training off-world telepaths there's been no way to keep the news from spreading.

"Besides, we're in good shape with Medical and Anthropology, Jason. *They* know what we're doing; and they control the money. We'll manage."

"Maybe. Only—well, I did a little checking. Hargraves is a legend among debunkers. To him, everything is either faked or misinterpreted data. He claims he's never seen conclusive evidence that telepathy exists and he's always after new targets. I'm afraid that this time we're it."

"Also, we're not fakes." David put the reports aside.

"Come and sit down. We'll start planning how to cope with Hargraves."

"I hope we can," Jason said. He abandoned his worry with an effort. "All right. Who can we use to demonstrate basic telepathy—?"

David paused at the edge of the hospital plaza and drank in the beauty of a late spring morning. The clouds hadn't lasted through dawn, so the Bloody Sun burned garnet in an aquamarine sky. The wind lapped at his fur-lined jacket; after the winter storms it felt almost friendly. Through the oil-and-plastic tang of the spaceport it carried a hint of green things and cool stone. David drew it in contentedly. It was the smell of home.

—*Hargraves won't know that.* He shook himself and walked toward the spaceport HQ, where Hargraves and his assistant were quartered. The *Palladium* had touched down the day before; David had missed it. He was curious to see what Jason's "professional skeptic" was like.

Jason met him in the HQ lobby. "We're a few minutes early."

"How was the first meeting?"

"Cool. Hargraves is surprising, but his assistant—I want to get her away from him long enough to run some tests."

David smiled. "Redheaded?"

"If anyone ever fit the pattern, Sasha Hargraves does."

"His wife?" David felt the familiar prickle of intuition tap his spine. Jason shook his head.

"Sister. I'm glad you're here; you're a lot more sensitive than I am, and—here they come."

Daivd turned in time to see Hargarves and his sister separate from a group of Terran civil servants and come toward them. He studied them carefully.

Hargraves was younger than he'd expected; somewhere in his thirties. Dark hair, silvering prematurely at the temples, made him look older. He had the impressive dignity of an experienced politician, with the hard accusing eyes of an inquisitor. His smile was a purely temporary decoration.

David felt vaguely uncomfortable as the man approached. He set it down to apprehension and turned to the sister. Jason was right: if anyone had ever fit the pattern—

Sasha Hargraves was tall, nearly as tall as David. Maybe ten years younger than her brother, and not much resemblance between them. Her auburn hair, gray eyes and fair complexion set her apart from every other Terran in the lobby. In the right clothes she could pass as one of the Comyn. Or could she?

There was something missing, and David identified it as a sense of presence. A non-telepath, with those looks? She met his eyes, her own glinting with humor and something more. Curiosity? And when had he ever had to wonder? —Damn, Hargraves can't be rattling *me* already!—

Hargraves had shaken Jason's hand and was now reaching for David's. His faint smile vanished when the other didn't respond. "Dr. Hamilton?"

"Welcome to Darkover," David said. "We hope we can make your visit worthwhile."

"I'm sure it will be," Hargraves agreed. He let Jason point the way out, kept on speaking as they emerged into the morning. "First—are you a telepath, Doctor? I understand they have a taboo against touch."

"Against casual touching, particularly with strangers." David wished for a second that he'd broken the habit. Something about Hargraves was making him damned uncomfortable and he wanted to know why. "As for being a telepath—not much of one, but somewhat. I pick up emotions more than thoughts. There are much stronger telepaths with the Project."

"I'd like to meet them," Hargraves said. He continued to ask questions about everything he saw—people, buildings, the color of the sky. Abruptly he stopped and pointed. "And that, gentlemen?"

He'd found one of the few places to get a good view of Thendara's biggest landmark. "Comyn Castle," Jason said. "The seat of government here for God knows how many years. It's now the headquarters of the Telepath Council."

"Telepath Council." Hargraves kept watching the massive building—visible now and then through gaps in the spaceport towers as they walked. "Darkover was ruled by a telepathic aristocracy, correct? Until five or six years ago, when the last remnants succumbed to internal troubles. Interesting. They claimed magical abilities—"

"Not magic," David said flatly. "Science. Science of a sort Terra never developed, but just as firmly based on natural law as any of our own disciplines."

"And just as useful. That castle was built using matrix

techniques." Jason added, "It's said the major blocks were fitted into place without the touch of a human hand."

"Indeed," Hargraves murmured. "Legends are always instructive. Nothing else provides so much insight into the ways a culture perceives its universe."

David cast a quick look at his friend. Jason's hands clenched, then relaxed as he got control of himself. "These— legends—are pretty definite, Doctor."

"Certainly. Certainly. Always truth at the bottom of a legend, however warped by tradition and how many centuries—twenty, is it? Or longer?"

"Not longer, Caleb," Sasha said. She had a low, well-trained voice. "No one is sure how the time rates match: the old M-AM drives did strange things to subjective time, but it's been no more than 2100 years since the Lost Ship that founded Darkover left Terra. Plenty of time for cultures to grow and die several times over. Darkovan history is documented only since the Empire's arrival and the century or so preceding. However, those documents record interviews with Darkovans whose immediate ancestors *did* witness the Castle's completion—using the matrix techniques." She smiled apologetically. "It's in the tapes, Caleb."

A note of mockery echoed in Hargraves's voice. "I rely on your memory, Sasha, as always." The mocking tone remained as he added, "Gentlemen, I hope it's not much farther to your offices. I'm quite ready to begin my studies."

"We're almost there," Jason said neutrally. David's spirits rose. *Let's see what he says when he's seen Kathie and the others!* he thought.

The hospital doors swallowed them a few moments later.

The afternoon was a disaster. It started well enough: the two physicians carefully led the Hargraveses through the test results Project Telepath had gathered in its two years of existence. At first Caleb seemed indifferent; then he started asking detailed and mostly intelligent questions. Sasha said little, but she followed the discussion with almost desperate intensity.

Talk of telepaths' physical characteristics led naturally to talk of their various abilities. Jason emphasized the earliest project findings, including David and his freemate Keral's rescue of Regis Hastur's lover and infant son. Sasha interrupted her brother's dry questioning.

"So you and Keral—a native? You and Keral anticipated

the assassin's attack, even though you were in another wing
of the hospital?"

"That's right."

"How? What did it feel like?"

"It's not easy to describe," David said slowly. "I knew they
were in danger, but there wasn't any verbal cue. I just knew."

Hargraves shot an annoyed look at his sister. "Strange. I
would have thought that room would have been under constant electronic surveillance, considering the importance of
the young woman's family and the diplomatic situation."

"It was," Jason said shortly. "The killer knew his business
and disabled the system."

"Oh." Hargraves made a pothook in his old-fashioned
black notebook. David fought down anger. *I wonder why he
bothered to come. His mind is obviously made up. The sister
. . . we'll see.*

He decided it was time to offer Hargraves a demonstration.
Kathie should have her "exhibit" set up; that should give
Hargraves headaches if he tried to explain it away.

Jason described the exhibit's origin. "We wanted something
we could use to test for telekinesis; until the Project began,
large-scale telekinesis without a matrix was almost unheard
of. Several Project members are telekinetics—one of them
gave us a lot of trouble." Jason spared an instant to think of
Missy.

David was thinking how much trouble it had been to refine
the "exhibit" to pass Hargraves's scrutiny. Waste of time. The
newly arrived telepaths didn't have the training to produce
really spectacular tricks—and the Comyn and older members
of the Project had better things to do with their talents than
providing a skeptic like Caleb with entertainment.

Luckily, they had a born performer in Kathie Marshall, the
daughter of the Terran Legate on Samarra. Kathie had visited Darkover years before; she had returned in the second
batch of Terran telepaths. Her skills with a matrix were excellent, and she liked to show them off. *We'll show him Kathie
first, then the newcomers' practice session and after that—
well, let's hope this does the trick. Because there isn't much
more we can do!*

Sasha was watching the hospital personnel. The Project offices were all outside the major departments, deliberately isolated, but there was a scattering of technicians in the halls.
David nearly missed greeting a favourite nurse and swore to

himself. *Usually I can spot Forrest anywhere in the wing. What's wrong with me, anyway?*

They turned down another corridor and stopped at the first door. "Here we are," Jason said. "This isn't our usual lab, but we wanted a little extra room." He touched the door tab. "As you can see—what the—"

David had a split second glimpse as he looked over Sasha's shoulder. Kathie's setup was simple: a network of tubing in a supporting framework, filled with colored liquids. Kathie used her *laran* to keep the fluids moving in defiance of gravity— and then, to conduct separate drops and globules into the open air. It was a breathtaking (if useless) sight and Kathie was proud of it. The scarlet and cobalt liquids were flowing as the door opened; the first free-floating drops were forming. And then, with no more warning than Kathie's protesting cry, the entire framework shivered into pieces. The "exhibit" landed in the center of the lab table with a highly anticlimactic crash.

Kathie was heartbroken. "I don't understand, David, it always worked before." She turned to Hargraves. "You've got to believe that, sir."

Hargraves nodded gravely and made more notes. "Psi powers are notoriously erratic," he said. Kathie stared at him in sudden anger.

"But that's the point. The whole reason for the Project is to show they don't have to be—" she saw Hargraves wasn't listening to her and fell silent. David saw her bite her lip, trying to keep her disappointment where Hargraves wouldn't see it.

He saw that hurt, defensive look again and again, as the "kids" of Project Telepath greeted Hargraves and failed his silent challenge. Twin girls whose rapport was so total they'd developed a private language stood mute before him; a red-haired teenaged boy's clairvoyance deserted him, but he was too proud to admit it. "Wait," he called desperately as Hargraves turned away. "Just once more, I know I can do it if you'll just—" His thin shoulders sagged. "Just give me another chance," he finished.

David touched his shoulder in comfort. "I know what you can do, Peter, and you know. That's what's important." He wished he had more to say but that was all he could offer. Peter tried to smile. "Sure, Dave."

He found the others waiting for him in the hallway. Hargraves looked bored; David thought of Peter's woebegone face and decided it would be easy to hate Caleb Hargraves.

"I think we've seen enough for one day," Hargraves announced. "If you'll excuse us, we'll be returning to our quarters."

David and Jason shrugged. *Now what?* David thought. There wasn't any obvious answer.

David felt a deep sense of relief as he and his friend relaxed in his rooms. He could almost feel his soul uncurl and stretch itself now that it was free to do so. Jason let go in another way: a series of searing oaths he'd never picked up from Terrans. "Where does Hargraves come off anyway? We didn't ask him here. We didn't have to be so cooperative. So what does he do? Treats us like cheap fakers from some red district pleasure house!"

He cooled down even more, to bitter quietness. "While you were with Peter I tried to get some reaction from Hargraves. *Any* reaction—just a little human feeling. It was like making conversation with a mannequin."

David had picked up a wooden carving—*chieri* work, a love-gift from Keral—and was stroking it. Now his hold on it tightened in excitement. "Yes. That's a good way to put it. No human response and no human emotions—"

"You didn't pick up anything from him?" Jason whistled. "I remember Regis said that might apply to him. He said people with minimal *laran* often have incredible barriers—and need them, to keep their sanity. Do you suppose Hargraves is one of them?"

"It makes sense," David said. "Something is driving him besides greed or ambition. There are easier ways to satisfy both than the life he's chosen."

"But why should everyone else fall apart around him—I don't know." Jason dismissed the thought. "I'd like to test Hargraves, but I can't see him going along with it."

"Neither can I. We talk to Sasha."

"Sasha? Yeah, that's an idea." Jason smiled for the first time in hours. "I'll keep Hargraves busy tomorrow morning and you can talk to her. If anyone knows what makes him work, she should."

"I think so." David spoke with unexpected force. "She could be the key to this whole problem."

"I hope so. Because we need one."

Getting Sasha Hargraves free from her brother was easier than David had anticipated: she called him early the next morning. The comm screen lit as he was reaching for the controls.

"Dr. Hamilton? I'd like to speak with you—now? At the Project office? All right. I'll be over in a few minutes. And thanks!"

He rehearsed his opening words as he waited for her in the lounge where the first members of the project had met. When she entered he forgot them. The empathy that was his greatest gift came shockingly awake as she closed the door behind her. *I didn't notice this yesterday? How did I miss it?*

For today he caught a rich stream of emotional imagery. Curiosity was there and wariness, strong humor . . . and below that hints of frustration and old pain. A complex, compelling personality had generated those feelings.

She accepted a seat and settled into it before speaking. "I have to apologize for Caleb's behavior yesterday," she said. "He's brilliant, but he has all the subtlety of a—what is it, your desert beast—yes. All the subtlety of an *oudrakhi.*" She grinned. "And he's not bothering to use it!"

He had to grin back. "I thought it was his usual behavior. How long have you worked with him, Sasha?"

Too long, she thought, but answered, "Part time, for four years. Full time, a year, since I got my degree. I'm a historian. So I do Caleb's initial research, then come along for the ride— and to act as oil-spreader."

"I can see where he needs a peacemaker." *And is that what she's doing now?*

Her grin faded. "Dr. Hamilton, your project's in danger."

"From your brother?"

"Yes." She looked at her hands a moment, gathering her nerve. David could feel her reluctance, the sense of betrayal. *I never really thought I'd have to move against him . . . and I did love him, once.* She sighed deeply and straightened.

"I don't know the whole situation, but I do know that Senator Velosin wants Caleb to bring him a negative report. He seemed almost to have a grudge against Darkover—as though he'd lost money here. Does that mean something to you, Doctor?"

"Call me David. And I think it might." *We never learned who was behind the worldwreckers.* "Go on."

"Caleb didn't want to accept the job at first. But he

agreed to do the initial research." Sasha had handled that, as usual. What she had found had made her eager to come to Darkover; and had turned Caleb's indifference to passion.

"You have to understand, Caleb's an honest man, but he really believes that anything he can't touch or see doesn't exist. He dismissed the Darkovan records as propaganda for the Comyn; the Terran records were another matter." She shrugged. "Only a fool—or my brother—could read the accounts of the Sharra Rebellion and *not* believe in matrix sciences. Those records, plus the medical data from your project, have him closer to admitting psi talents exist than he's ever been—and that's why he's dangerous. He's afraid."

"Of what? That we might be real, or that we might *not* be?"

"I don't know. I doubt he knows."

David paused. The most important question was still unasked, though he thought he knew the answer. "Why are you telling me this?"

Guilt and reluctance built a tangible wall around her, choking off her reply. She struggled against it fiercely. "After Caleb and I left here yesterday, I slipped back and spoke with some of your people." She forced the words out. "I—I can usually tell when someone lies to me, when Caleb isn't around to laugh at my 'intuition.' Your people believed they could do what they claimed, and I believe them. I can't let Caleb make laughingstocks or worse out of them—or let him perjure himself with a false report. I can't. And I won't."

She hung on the edge of tears. David thought it was a good thing her "intuition" was valid; otherwise she'd be terribly vulnerable. She startled him by laughing hoarsely.

You don't think I open up like this to just anyone, do you? I've been searching for telepaths for years: that's why I teamed up with Caleb. I've been so much alone.

Not now, nor ever again. Rapport hummed between them, delicate as the tone of a crystal bell. Not as deep or sweet as David's tie with Keral (how could anything match that?), but echoing a hunger he understood too well. Until he'd come to Darkover it had been a part of him.

The rapport ebbed, leaving a legacy of warmth and half-sated hunger. Sasha's face was subtly different; relaxed, as she began loosening her long-held mental armor. "It feels strange to know I was right to keep looking," she said. "Now, if we can only convince Caleb."

"Maybe we can. You said he was impressed by the project's medical records?"

"The brainwave patterns. The fact that you'd given psi talents a physiological basis—oh, I see." She rose and stretched, letting more tension fall away. David nodded.

"We show him *your* EEG. We'll see what he says about having a telepathic sister."

"All right. Jason's bringing him now." David finished placing the electrodes. On impulse, he flipped the EEG's activating switch. "Nervous?"

He hadn't really had to ask; the remnants of rapport practically shouted it. Sasha's smile was unsteady.

"Yes. I can't help it. This could backfire, you know. If he—oh!"

The last threads of rapport snapped painfully apart. Sasha winced; David swore softly. Something was going wrong *again*.

Hargraves didn't throw the door open, but he gave that impression. He strode directly to Sasha's side, across the exam table from David and the EEG tape. Jason appeared at the door and stopped just inside.

Hargraves looked down at his sister briefly. "So," he said, "I expected something like this. What did they tell you? Or should I ask what you've told them?"

She stiffened. Jason came a few steps closer. "I tried to explain this on the way here, Hargraves. This was partly your sister's idea. We don't coerce anyone into—"

"I've heard enough, Dr. Allison," Hargraves said flatly. "I didn't think it would take long for two psychologically-trained men like yourselves to make use of my sister's naïveté. I've suspected you'd lost your objectivity for some time," he added, "though until now you've managed to conceal it."

"Good God, man, do you hear what you're saying?" Jason's outrage hardly seemed real to David. The whole scene was remote, not a living confrontation at all. That impression remained even when Sasha pulled the electrodes free and sat up.

"After three years with you, brother, one thing I'm not is naïve." Her voice quivered with barely suppressed rage. "If you want a family fight, I'll give you one. But let's take it where we won't be interrupted."

"Fine." Hargraves stepped back to let her stand. She preceded him to the door, halted there. "I'll be back," she promised flatly. Then she and her brother were gone.

Jason stared unbelievingly after them. "That man is insane. He's stark, raving mad!"

When he got no reply he looked back at his friend. David was studying the incomplete EEG tape, with a face as white as his tunic. "So that's it," he breathed.

"What?"

"The reason Hargraves has never seen a psi talent work. The reason no one could show him one yesterday—or today." David removed the tape from the EEG, seemed to come back to life. "I need to talk to Kathie and the others," he decided. "I know I'm right, but I'd like to check with them anyway before I spring this on you—or Sasha. Lord knows, she deserves an explanation."

"Just what have you come up with?" Jason demanded.

"Something unique. Even for Darkover. Something unique."

It was evening before David was ready to share his discovery. By then, he was fairly trembling with excitement. The evidence was spread out on the work table in his room; he only had to wait for the others to arrive.

Jason came first, bringing Regis Hastur with him. "Jason has been telling me about Hargraves. Is his blindness really that important to us?"

"Sasha—his sister—thinks it is." David sketched out what Sasha had told him about the senator's desire for a negative report, and his own suspicions. Regis's expression hardened in distaste and anger. "There's no way to prove any of this?"

"Not right away," David said. "But now that we know where to look—"

"We can try to *find* proof," Jason finished. "But that doesn't solve our current problem. What do we do about Hargraves?"

"That's something we've got to work out." David glanced at the chron. "I hope Sasha will come; she's the key to the problem. But until she does, let me tell you more about what went on yesterday—"

The door buzzer sounded a few minutes later. Sasha moved hesitantly, as though she might break; her gray eyes hid behind puffy, reddened lids. They widened as she saw

Regis's white-haired elegance. She managed a polite greeting and accepted a chair next to David.

"Caleb's in his room," she said. "If he wasn't my elder I'd say he was sulking. But he's still speaking to me—I think." She rested her head on her hands for a moment. "Did you get your record, David?"

"I did indeed. Look." Everyone moved closer as he pulled the EEG tapes to him. "Here's the printout from today's run—yours. The one above it is a nontelepath's pattern and the one below is a telepath's—mine, as a matter of fact." Sasha smiled.

They all bent over the three strips of tape. "I see," Sasha murmured. Her fingers traced over the middle line, following its jagged dips. "Your line has a certain pattern, and so does mine. This other one doesn't—though it really isn't that great a difference." Doubt echoed in her thoughts, revealed inadvertently by fatigue and emotional turmoil. *Such a little thing. And Caleb—God help me, I was so sure this afternoon, but he was, too. The Comyn*

The Comyn do not lie.

Her head jerked up. She met Regis's quiet gaze, then turned away. Her face burned redder than her hair.

"It's all right," David said gently. "It takes time, getting used to other telepaths. It was hard for me, too. You'll learn."

"I'd better." She looked back at Regis. "I'm sorry. Forgive me?"

"There's nothing to forgive. As David says, when you've been among us awhile you'll pick up our customs easily. You will stay?"

"No way Caleb can stop me." She made a hiccoughing sound that David realized was meant to be a chuckle. It had been a rough day for Sasha—and tomorrow wasn't likely to be any easier—but she still had some humor to draw on. "I've been wanting to tell him off for months."

"That's the spirit," Jason told her. He bent down again to the EEGs, frowning. "What the—?"

"That's what I spotted this afternoon. See, Regis? Sasha?"

Regis caught it first. "The telepath pattern diminishes until it's hardly visible. Does the decrease coincide with Caleb Hargraves's arrival?"

"Exactly. And if we'd had Kathie, or Peter, or the twins

hooked up to the EEG, their patterns would show the same changes."

"Are you saying Hargraves is a walking, talking telepathic damper?" Jason asked.

"Yes."

Sasha shook her head. "Poor Caleb. Searching all these years for psi talents and never finding any."

"I feel sorrier for the people he's investigated," Jason said grimly. "A lot of them probably were fakes—but how many weren't?"

Regis sighed. "Such a gift—gift? A curse! Perhaps Desideria has heard of such. Or perhaps—perhaps he is a telepath, whose *laran* turned inward, blocked as a defense against some unendurable pain." Regis sighed again, his metallic eyes distant with memories.

"Either way we've got a problem," David said. "He probably has the usual sort of barriers as well; even with the damping effect we should have been able to pick *something up* from him. But if we could break those barriers—and I don't know how we'd manage that—we might break his mind as well."

"Then what can we do?" Sasha asked.

David could hardly bear the sight of her drawn, miserable face. *What can we do? Besides let him go? At least Sasha'd be out of his range*. The thought jumped at him. *Out of range?*

"We gamble," he said, and reached out to brush Sasha's hand. "Are you willing to risk your brother's anger? Or worse, if it'll help him admit that we—and you—aren't lying to him?"

Her eyes glimmered silver as she nodded. "All right."

"Good. Then go get some rest. You'll need to be strong tomorrow." She began to protest, but cut it off. David waited until she had gone to speak. "Here's my idea—"

Hargraves showed all the signs of a sleepless night when David saw him the next morning. Had resentment and anger kept him up, David wondered, or had the argument with Sasha borne positive fruit?

In any case, he didn't object to David's joining him at breakfast. "I want to apologize," David said. "If our—"

"The apology isn't necessary, Doctor," Hargraves interrupted. "Sasha made it plain she willingly cooperated with your—testing program."

"I also reminded him I was a legal adult and didn't need his permission to do anything," Sasha put in from behind David. She set her tray down next to his and sat.

"I'm glad it's settled, then," David said politely. "Hargraves—would you let us make a record of *your* EEG?"

Hargraves seemed unsurprised by the request. "I'll go along with it," he said, while mopping the last bit of egg from his plate with a piece of bread. "Just what do you want it for? You think *I* might qualify for membership in your project?"

He was laying the sarcasm on a little too thickly, David thought. Now that he knew what to expect he could feel the damping effect too, a pressure along his nerves. He didn't let it affect his professional facade.

"Who knows? I want your EEG for the same reason I wanted Sasha's—for comparison and statistical research. And speaking of Sasha's EEG, when we've taken yours I'd like you to see hers. You'll find it interesting."

"I'm sure I will. Especially since she hasn't told me about the results—Sasha, is something wrong?"

A note of genuine concern entered his voice. Sasha's breakfast lay half-eaten; she's propped her elbows on the table and her head on her hands. For the first time, David saw traces of something besides pride and mockery in Hargraves and warmed to him a little.

Sasha raised her head. "I'm all right. I just had a rough night is all."

"You're sure?"

"I'm sure! Just—" She looked away, swung back to face them squarely. "Be careful, brother. Watch your head, will you? I had some really ghastly nightmares about you."

Hargraves had begun to reach for her; he pulled back as though burned. "Sasha—"

"Don't start again, Caleb." She sounded weary rather than angered. "I don't want to hear it." She slipped out of her seat, leaving the tray. "I'll meet you at the hospital."

Her brother's eyes followed her out of the cafeteria. He frowned, forgetting David's presence: his face reflected honest worry and apprehension. Then he recovered. "I suppose we ought to follow her, Doctor."

The streets were crowded and noisy, as the night workers

headed for their quarters and morning shifts reported to their offices and construction sites. They hurried along in the thin reddish light, coats drawn tight against the early chill. Comyn Castle glistened with a light coat of snow; ice glittered from spaceport roofs. Hargraves shivered. "Is this average spring weather?"

"Actually, it's pretty mild. The snow'll melt by noon." He grinned at Hargraves's discomfiture. "Now you know why the Darkovans' hell is a cold one."

"Y-yes." Hargraves walked a little faster.

There was one major square between the transients' quarters and the hospital. Foot traffic was slacking off, motorized haulers becoming more common. A line of them entered the square from the right, their snarling roar drowning the other street noises. David pointed.

"Convoy. Let's get across before it blocks the street."

Hargraves nodded. They scurried across, out of the long line's path. Then Hargarves stopped and swore. "Dropped my stylus. Wait for me."

He hurried back toward the convoy, his eyes fixed on the concrete. The haulers—used to cart building supplies from the port warehouses to construction sites—were uncovered platforms. About half were fully loaded, the rest carrying bulky or awkward materials. Their noise rattled David's teeth from this distance; he wondered how Hargraves could stand so near so calmly. He nearly missed the quick swing of Hargraves's dark head as the man sneaked a look at the haulers. He was taking a long time to hunt for a cheap stylus. . . .

David swore and went after him. He understood Hargraves's purpose well enough: he was deliberately disregarding Sasha's warning, daring Fate. A predictable reaction, but it annoyed David even though he should have expected it.

The convoy was almost past. Hargraves quit hunting his stylus, straightened to watch the last haulers go by. He saw David's face and started to say something.

A crack like a monstrous branch breaking drowned his words. That, and Sasha's soundless scream: *David! Caleb! Get down!*

David lunged with the first word, caught Hargraves solidly. They landed sprawled on the frigid concrete.

Something went *spoing* lazily above them. David risked a look up. The steel strip that held the haulers' cargo in place had broken and was swinging free about three meters overhead. David watched it move and started to laugh.

Hargraves got to his feet. Wordlessly, he offered the younger man a hand. Sasha came pounding up, and threw her arms around her brother's neck. "I'm sorry, Caleb. I took a side street and got lost, so when I saw you I thought I'd join you and that sound—" she paused to catch her breath. "From where I was it looked like that thing might hit you," she finished.

"I see." Hargraves disentangled himself very gently, stepped back. His eyes moved from her to David, and there was reluctant acceptance in them. "What made you react as you did, Doctor Hamilton?"

"Sasha's yell."

"I didn't hear a thing. And you were looking at me, not the cargo hauler—" For an instant David thought he was going to reject what he had seen. But he sagged, and spoke.

"I believe you have some brain-wave recordings to show me, Doctor?"

And as quickly as that, it was over.

Three people came to see Caleb Hargraves off: David and Jason and his sister Sasha. Sasha was still recovering from the shocks and strains of her first days on Darkover. "When you said I'd risk Caleb's anger, 'or worse,' I didn't think you meant I'd be risking his life! Or yours, David."

"We didn't. We gambled on a pretty sure thing—you."

"I don't understand."

"You were outside Caleb's effective range. His damping effect is severely limited by distance. We gambled that your *laran*—augmented by your love for your brother and fear—would be able to reach me even though I *was* within his range. It did."

She nodded doubtfully, then grinned. "He spent his last two days examining that binder and trying to learn if you had sabotaged it to give him a 'demonstration.' Of course the hauler crew didn't like that, but they gave him the binder for analysis. Structural weakness; as though the steel just crumbled."

"Yeah," Jason said. "A matrix can do that—and Kathie wanted to prove she still had her touch."

"And you weren't in any danger because it broke high,

where it couldn't reach you. So much for my prophetic dreams."

"As upset as you were, it would have been surprising if you hadn't dreamed about Caleb."

"So you set us both up, guiding me to where I could see it happen, and gambling . . . well, it turned out well enough this time. But let's not do it again!" Her voice softened as Caleb drew near. "Caleb?"

He didn't try to touch her. "You're sure you want to stay?"

"I'm sure. Take care of yourself, brother. And come back now and then. Who knows?" Her voice broke. "We might work together again."

He smiled sadly. "I don't know. But we'll see." Now he did reach out; she hugged him, let him go. "I hear the loading chimes," he said. "Take care, Sasha. I hope you're happy here." A little of his former manner resurfaced. "I'll send word on how the senator reacts to my report. You'll probably enjoy it."

He exchanged polite farewells with David and Jason, turned and merged into the crowds. As they walked away, David heard Sasha crying.

"I was thinking," she said unsteadily. "For the rest of his life Caleb will either believe I tricked him—or he'll spend his life knowing there's a universe around him he can never reach."

"At least now he knows it's there," David said. A second later they stepped out of the spaceport—going home.

A RECIPE FOR FAILURE

by Millea Kenin

Darkovan Proverb: "It is ill done to chain a dragon to roast your meat."

Soon after it became clear that Darkover would never join the Empire, the Empire gave in and joined Darkover. This was the beginning of a new Copper Age for sapient beings, but not all the results were fortunate. For instance, there was Black Angus, the Thendara restaurateur, who imported, from a newly rediscovered world in a distant part of the Galaxy, a dragon and a dragonrider. Dragons having long been extinct on Darkover, the great bronze-colored creature provided a unique spectacle for customers at Angus's restaurant, The Standing Rib. They flocked there—once—to watch the dragon roasting their chervine and rabbithorn to order. Few of them returned, however; the food did not equal the show.

The dragon, whose name was Broth, and his rider T'spoon had a special sort of *laran* different from the kinds known on Darkover. Broth could communicate only with T'spoon, although the dragon apparently learned Cahuenga as rapidly as the man and seemed to understand everything anyone said. Broth was capable of teleporting while in flight, and enjoyed exploring Darkover, but returned to the restaurant too late to cook dinner so often that Angus finally kept him chained during working hours, despite T'spoon's warning that a depressed dragon won't produce much fire.

A still worse problem—from the restaurant owner's point of view—was that Darkover is lacking in firestone, which dragons must chew in order to belch fire. Angus provided Broth with plenty of good, rich charcoal, but on this fuel Broth produced flames that rose and died quickly, searing the outsides of the roasts till they were black while the insides were still practically raw.

It was impossible to correct this situation, so eventually

239

Angus closed the restaurant, and T'spoon and Broth returned to their home planet. Once again it was proved that, while it may be rare to chain a dragon to roast your meat, it is still far from well done.